THE DEVIL SHE KNEW

RENA KOONTZ

THE DEVIL SHE KNEW

Copyright © 2018 RENA KOONTZ

Cover Art © 123RF

Book Design by J R Burns Consultancy

ISBN:978-1-7322709-1-6

ISBN: 1-7322709-1-0

www.renakoontz.com

First published in 2013 by Crimson Romance

Other Heels & Handcuffs Novels

Love's Secret Fire
Thief Of The Heart

More From This Author

Crystal Clear Love
Broken Justice, Blind Love
Off The Grid For Love

For Ron,
Always my twin

ACKNOWLEDGMENTS

As always I thank —

My husband, Jed, for keeping the romance alive;
My friend, Shirley, who keeps my stories on track;
My family and friends for their support;
Police, fire, and law enforcement personnel everywhere.

Black rivulets swirled in the white porcelain sink, gurgling in the drain as it swallowed her old identity. Her head under the faucet, Cassidy Hoake watched the waves of dark liquid fade while she continued to massage her scalp under the warm water. The box said to rinse until the water ran clear. Just a few more minutes.

She grabbed a towel, draped her head, and stood, rubbing vigorously with her eyes closed. Ready or not, she looked at her reflection in the mirror behind the sink.

The new look surprised even her. Gone was the thick, auburn mane her mother had often bragged about. She'd replaced the shoulder-length locks she'd worn since high school with a lustrous black, short haircut that she planned to spike up and out and fringe to frame her face. She stared wide-eyed at herself, then walked barefoot into the bedroom and retrieved a pair of burgundy-framed eyeglasses from the bureau. Thank goodness she'd discovered that year-round costume store. Buying items for a disguise was easy.

Standing in front of the mirror again, she took a deep breath and carefully edged the eyeglasses up her nose. Her eyebrows raised in surprise at the result. She barely recognized herself. Surely, he wouldn't.

Clay Cestra gently laid his nephew in the crib and switched on the overhead mobile. Four stuffed bears in football jerseys and helmets began to circle slowly around a plush football in the center. Softly, the Ohio State fight song played, making him smile. He checked to make sure the baby monitor was switched on, then quietly walked out of the nursery, leaving the door halfway open. Carrying his sister's cell phone, he walked to the bathroom.

He knocked on the open bathroom door. "I'm going in to work early, Sis, and relieve Dan. Are you sure you're okay? Do you want Dan to bring you anything?"

Maggie Armstrong sat beside the toilet, her back against the wall and a white washcloth molded to her forehead. She opened her eyes and inhaled tentatively. "I think it's stopped. Remind me to never order bleu cheese dressing again. Just ask Dan to come straight home. I'll be fine, go." A weak hand wave punctuated her words.

Clay stepped into the bathroom and leaned over to kiss his younger sister on the forehead. "Jack's asleep." He handed her the phone. "I'll call and check on you when I get to the station."

He retrieved his gun from the top of the china hutch and tucked it into its holster as he walked to the car. Opening the car door, Clay smiled. Who would've ever thought when he intro- duced his partner to his sister they would end up together? Maggie said the minute she looked into Dan's eyes, her heart lit up with stars. He turned his gaze to the sky. It glowed tonight with a thousand different lights. That must be how she felt.

He drove to the Stakron police station, the full moon casting everything below in a hazy shadow. The midnight shift was his favorite. The city looked softer in the dark and usually, by mid-shift, would be quiet except for the stray drunk, burglar, or speed demon.

Hopefully, tonight would be no exception.

Cassidy loved the chimes on her mantel clock, one of the few treasures she had left of her mother. It chimed in the other room and she counted twelve bells. Midnight and she was wide awake. Tomorrow, she started her new life, or at least would try again to forget her old one. The gold clock under its glass dome stuck out in the dowdy room like a rose in the desert. She had no furniture in there except for a folding card table and two chairs she bought at a garage sale. The room was a combination kitchen and living area squished into one square space. Her bedroom was just as sparse, with only a recycled full-size mattress and box spring on the floor in the corner and a scratched and worn nightstand and lamp. She'd cleaned the two rooms as best she could, but the carpet still looked filthy and the windows seemed permanently stained.

A dozen second-hand throw rugs she'd laundered twice protected her bare feet from the dirt-packed carpet and marked a path through the apartment, like the yellow brick road leading the way for Dorothy. She tiptoed along the rugs to the apartment door, knowing it was latched, but needing reassurance. She checked the deadbolt, patted the door chain, and then made sure the two windows in the front room and the one in the bedroom were locked. She'd rented here for two weeks now and still the noises of the other tenants unnerved her. How long would it take to get used to that?

Fully clothed, Cassidy pulled the blankets back and slipped into her make-shift bed, longing for the soft cotton comforter on the four-poster she used to own. That was another thing she would have to get past, sleeping with her clothes on. Always ready to run.

She dozed fitfully, ready to wake the second the radio alarm filled the room with soft jazz. She bathed, applied her makeup, fussed with her new hairstyle until it was just right and stepped into The Packing Place's uniform—black pants and a brown pullover shirt. Yesterday, she rode a test run on the bus to familiarize herself with the route. The seven-ten bus would get her to the store about twenty minutes early. A good way to start her first day on the job.

Cassidy walked in the front door of the store with her shoulders straight and her head high. She remembered an old commercial slogan that suggested "never let them see you sweat" and decided it would be her new mantra. She could do this. She had no other choice. Her funds were low and she'd been on the run long enough to be tired, really tired. She needed to fly under the radar for a while.

The first handshake with her new boss felt wrong. Warm, slightly clammy, yet forceful, almost clutching, sending a sensation up her arm like a band of tiny ants in a convoy. Wayne Keaseling released her hand and she raised it to the back of her neck, thinking to smooth her hair and shake away the uneasiness. His lopsided smile didn't help.

"You observed what we do here yesterday afternoon, so you know a little of what to expect. I wanted Rosie to train you. She's my assistant manager. But she's not back from vacation yet, so we'll start you with someone else. Any questions you have, any concerns, you come to me." He placed his hand over his heart. "I want you to be happy here."

He turned toward the front of the store and called out to his other employee. "Amber?"

Amber Malone appeared in the doorway flashing a bright white, even-teethed smile that said at one time she wore braces. She inspected Cassidy from her sneakered feet to her oversized glasses.

Cassidy likewise eyed her new co-worker. Amber had a pierced right eyebrow, a pierced tongue, and a microdot in the left side of her nose. A two-inch wide magenta streak highlighted her shoulder-length midnight black hair. Straight cut bangs hung into her eyes, which were outlined in heavy black, as if she used a charcoal briquette to make herself up.

Amber raised the pierced eyebrow and a tiny shudder jolted Cassidy's spine under the intense scrutiny, the second time in her first ten minutes on the job. It was as if Amber saw right through her disguise. Had Cassidy been more like the thug she was running from, she could have changed her name along with her looks and paid for forged documents to authenticate her new persona. But who knew how to do that? Besides, she'd had to show identification to rent her dingy apartment, so a fake name was out of the question. Did Amber recognize her? It was unlikely.

Standing with a hand on one hip, Amber shifted the wad of pink bubble gum in her mouth, cracking it three times in the process. "Sure, Boss, I'll train her."

"Get rid of the nose doo-dad and the gum first. I'm going to the bank and then to the other store. I'll be back later."

He walked out the rear employees' door and Amber stuck out her tongue at his back, giggled, and offered Cassidy a conspiratorial grin. "Welcome." She extended her hand and widened her smile until it reached her eyes, immediately easing Cassidy's anxiety. Unlike the boss' handshake, Amber's was warm and firm, but not dominating.

"I heard you just moved into town. Where'd you come from? No ring on your finger. Have a boyfriend? If you don't, make one up or he'll be all over you. Come over here. I'll show you how to clock in."

Cassidy stood dumbfounded. "What? Who?"

Amber strolled to the computer keyboard and began punching keys. "Don't worry. It will take a while. He'll be on his good behavior at first. Use your name to sign in and you'll need a password. What do you want to use?"

The entry bell chimed and both women looked toward the front door at the day's first customer. Amber smiled and leaned forward onto the counter, using her arms to squeeze her breasts into the opening of her collared shirt.

"Good morning, Officer Good Body. I was a very bad girl last night." She swiveled her hips. "Don't you think you should hand-cuff me and take me away?"

Mouth agape, Cassidy watched her ball her fists, lock her wrists together, and extend her arms to the police officer standing at the counter.

He chuckled, the movement crinkling his eyes. "Good morning, Amber. You're in rare form this morning."

Amber winked, straightened, and began typing on the computer screen. Cassidy stepped up behind her in time to see a shipping label appear on the screen.

"This is the new girl, Cassidy." Turning to Cassidy, she raised her hand toward the cop. "We have a lot of regular customers. You'll get to know them pretty quick. C.C. is my favorite."

Cassidy turned to the police officer. His dark blue uniform fit snugly, stretching over a broad chest and trim waist. He blushed at Amber's words and extended his hand.

"Clay Cestra. Nice to meet you."

Handshake number three. This one strong, confident and quick. Almost enticing. Much nicer than the boss's.

Amber stepped to the counter with a printed label and handed Clay a pen. Cassidy watched him scrawl his initials on the bottom line and slide a small shipping bag to Amber.

"See?" She showed Cassidy the label. "C.C. That's the way he always signs."

"Good luck with the new job." He spoke over his shoulder as he strode to the door. "I'll see you tomorrow, Amber."

The door chimed again when he exited.

"The police drop off these packages every morning to go to the lab. Some poor drunk got busted last night. These are the swabs. All we have to do is generate this label," she pointed to the button on the computer screen, "and have them initial it. It's usually C.C. coming off the midnight shift or on daylight and he knows the drill. It's only when he's off or on the afternoon shift that someone else comes in."

Amber pointed her forefinger at Cassidy. "Make sure you get this label initialed or it fucks up their chain of evidence. Your initials will show up in this corner. I'll show you where this goes."

Through the course of the morning, Amber explained how to work the computers, how to pack and ship items, and how to operate most of the office equipment designed to provide printing and copying services for customers. She had an easy way with the regulars, calling most of them by their first names and openly flirting with the men.

Cassidy gasped when Amber offered to cook spaghetti for an elderly man and promised a special dessert. He left the store chuckling.

"You wouldn't really go out with him, would you?"

"Nah, he knows I don't mean it. But it makes him feel good to think I might give him a tumble. And I love men. Who knows? If I were drunk enough I might."

The look on Cassidy's face made her laugh.

"You might as well know right up front. I drink. I smoke weed. I like to party. and have a good time. Life is too short not to. Most of the girls who work here call me a slut behind my back. I don't give a damn what they think."

"How long have you worked here?"

"Four years. The boss keeps threatening to fire me, but he won't. I always get to work on time and I'm good at my job. I do what he asks me to do. Everything he asks."

The day passed quickly. By the end of her shift, Cassidy felt comfortable processing the basic shipments, called drop-offs because they had preprinted labels on them. Under Amber's guidance she also managed ground, air, and high value shipments and performed multiple copying tasks. Amber proved to be a good teacher, letting Cassidy think through the process and correct her own mistakes while sweet-talking the customers, since the task took a little longer than usual. Everyone was patient. They clocked out together. Amber waved cheerfully and said she'd see Cassidy the next morning.

Cassidy flopped into the back seat of the bus for the ride home. Her feet hurt, her back ached, and she'd broken two fingernails. Each time she bent to pick up a heavy package Amber reminded her to use her legs, but the throb in her lower back screamed she'd have to do a better job tomorrow.

2

C lay clocked out the next morning and called his sister on the way to ship the night's saliva samples to the crime lab. He wanted to make sure she'd fully recovered from her suspected food poisoning episode, and if she was still dragging, he'd offer to babysit for the day. He could sleep when Jack napped.

Since his sister had gotten married, the department separated him and Dan Armstrong, giving each man a new partner and, most of the time, keeping them on different shifts. Maggie said she liked it that way. She only had to worry about one man at a time.

Clay often wished he still partnered with Dan. This month, Clay was on the midnight shift and Dan worked the four to midnight slot. Their shifts overlapped, giving them time for "police talk" outside of Maggie's earshot. Last night, he'd come close to mentioning the new girl at The Packing Place, but he wasn't sure why. What was there to say except she was a new face at the counter?

As partners, they were already close, but Maggie had strengthened that bond. Dan was more of a brother than an in-law. They both loved Maggie more than their own lives and the instinct to watch each other's back had intensified.

Maggie assured Clay she was fully recovered from her episode of intestinal distress and urged him to sleep for a few hours. That afternoon, she had a list of minor repairs that needed completed in several tenants' apartments.

Clay and Maggie had inherited two five-story apartment buildings from their parents, who were enjoying their retirement years in Florida. That their parents were still together was like the eighth wonder of the world in his mind. He remembered the day they sat at the kitchen table, each with a pen in hand, poised over divorce papers. He and Maggie had huddled in the hallway, terrified. Their parents hadn't known they were there.

Maggie had buried her face in his chest, muffling her tears, and whispering "Please God. Don't do this to us." He'd merely watched horrified. The nightly arguments had escalated, and through the thin walls of the three-bedroom ranch Clay had listened to months of arguing and cursing until finally, the discussion about divorce. He was to live with his father, wherever that was going to be. Maggie would stay with their mom.

He and his sister stood clinging to each other, spying on their parents. Clay heard his father say, "I don't want to do this. Not really."

"Me neither," his mother whispered.

"We have two kids in the other room. If for no other reason, we should stay together for them."

His mother nodded and tears spilled down her cheeks. Clay gulped when his father reached across the table and shook hands with his mother.

In one swift movement, his dad took the divorce papers, ripped them in half, and tossed them in the trash.

Maggie was jubilant. He was doubtful. He remained doubtful for years, watching them interact with each other, waiting to see something more than obligation. He supposed it happened sometime during his teen years when he was obsessed with cars, girls, and sports. One day he saw them kiss. It was brief but tender.

And as everyone grew older, they grew closer. Seeing them now, in their golden years, outsiders would never know they were once a signature away from splitting up. But he knew. He still had the papers to remind him.

Ironically, he thought his own marital woes would resolve the same way. He'd believed that right up to the second she signed the divorce documents.

When his parents decided to relocate to the retirement community, they turned their apartment buildings over to their kids. Together, Clay and Maggie managed Cestra Chalets I and II, which were actually luxury apartments in an upscale part of the city.

Clay lived in Chalet II, which sat directly behind Chalet I, where Maggie, Dan, and six-month-old Jack lived. They each had taken over a major portion of the first floor of their buildings, demolished walls and gutted the insides, and converted the new, enlarged space to their own sprawling apartments with two bedrooms, two baths, an office, formal dining room, and eat-in kitchen. Maggie transformed a portion of her office into a nursery after Jack was born. Clay swore he'd never have to do that. One divorce was enough for him.

He threw himself into being a cop. There had been several fascinating women in his life, but nothing serious. Unlike Maggie, who wore her heart on her sleeve and embraced passion, love, and commitment, he applied the brakes whenever a woman's expectations rose too high. Funny. He always broke up with them at their kitchen table.

Happiness now centered on his role in a uniform helping people when on duty, and the electrical, plumbing, painting, and other maintenance chores that came with operating two large apartment buildings. All service oriented, he often said. He enjoyed working with his hands, fixing things, and thought after several years of learning on the job he was pretty good at it. Dan also helped with building maintenance. The two of them swore there was no repair or maintenance problem they couldn't solve with a six-pack of beer and their combined talents.

"Call Mrs. B and tell her I'll be over this afternoon to change her faucet," he told his sister. "I've got one more midnight shift and then I have a day off. I'll clean the Osborne apartment then. We weren't planning to show it before that were we?"

"No. That's fine. But wouldn't you like to do something fun on your day off?"

He laughed. "Fun? Ah, I think I had some of that in tenth grade."

"I keep telling you there's more to life than work, big brother."

"Log it on my to-do list one of these days. I'm just arriving at The Packing Place to drop off some samples. I'll talk to you later. Love you."

He gathered the two evidence packets on the front seat and stepped out of his truck. As he approached the store, he saw Amber and the new girl through the storefront windows. He liked Amber, despite her over-the-top attempts to flirt with him and her criminal record. She made him laugh and there was nothing phony about her. She laid it all out there for anyone to see, like it or not.

The new girl had seemed a little edgy yesterday. He chalked it up to first-day jitters. "Good morning, ladies."

Cassidy stood beside Amber watching her process a shipment. Amber smiled and winked at Clay, then turned to Cassidy.

"You should be able to handle that. Remember to make sure he initials the label."

Cassidy moved uncertainly to the first shipping register and punched the keyboard. She looked at Clay and swallowed hard. He tried to ease her nervousness.

"Don't worry. By next week you'll be able to do this blindfolded." He pointed to a shelf on the back wall. "Take a form from that second slot, punch in the codes on these samples, and then process it. I'll initial it after your label prints."

He smiled but watched her hand shake when she reached for the shipment form. He snagged a pen from the pen cup. "Do all customers make you this nervous or just the cops?"

That generated a reaction that surprised him. Her head jerked up, her hand flew to her throat, and the color drained from her face just as Amber walked over.

"You got it, Cass?"

"You better process it," she whispered. "Excuse me." She turned and scurried to the back office.

Clay cocked his head and raised a questioning eyebrow. His cop's instinct had jumped to high alert. "Is she like that with all the customers?"

Amber punched numbers on the touch screen as she answered. "No. She's doing really well."

"She talk much?"

"Hardly at all. Plays it real close to the vest. We were busy yesterday, so there wasn't much chance, really." Amber slid the computer-generated receipt toward him. "Don't get too interested. I might get jealous."

Clay smiled as he folded the receipt and tucked it in his back pocket. He winked at Amber. "You know you're the only woman in my heart. I'll see you tomorrow."

Amber laughed as he walked toward the door. "I wish you meant that."

A good cop has a sixth sense, always on low, spinning silently in the back of his brain. Even when Clay tried not to notice, he picked up signals from people. Body language. Facial expressions. Eye movements.

Cassidy appeared more nervous than she should. The Packing Place had a high employee turnover. It was hard work for minimum wage and, if Amber's stories were true, the owner liked to get a little too familiar with his female hires. Clay had seen a lot of workers come and go in the three years he'd been shipping evidence to the state crime lab. Cassidy's nervousness appeared to be on a different level, more intense than the average new kid on the job.

He shrugged off his thoughts as he turned the ignition and headed home. Whatever was the matter, it wasn't his problem.

Lunch offered the first break of the day. Amber jumped up on the packing table, crossed her legs Indian style, and slid a hoagie from a takeout bag. She took a big bite from the heel and eyed Cassidy as she gingerly removed a peanut butter and jelly sandwich from a plastic sandwich bag.

"That all you gonna eat?"

Cassidy smiled at the dressing smeared on Amber's chin. "Yes. I don't eat much."

"Not me. I love to eat."

That made her chuckle. "You seem to love everything, Amber."

Amber grinned, her mouth too full to respond. Cassidy nibbled at the edge of her sandwich.

"I saw you walking from the bus stop this morning. Where you living?" She wiped her mouth with a napkin.

"I rented an apartment on Fortieth Street."

Amber crinkled her nose. "Fortieth Street? That's not exactly a nice neighborhood. Lot of drive-by shootings around there. It doesn't seem like a place you'd want to live."

"It's all I can afford right now."

"How'd you end up there? I don't peg you for a druggie. And that area is a hangout for dealers. Probably why so many shootings."

Cassidy examined a corner of her sandwich bag. "I've heard

gunfire. It's pretty scary. It's only temporary. Until I can save money for something better."

"Yeah, better. 'Cause you sure don't look like you belong there."

That scared Cassidy. She worked so hard on this disguise. "Why do you say that?"

Amber waved her hand in the air. "Look at you. You're cleaned and pressed. Your nails are done, your hair is fashionable. The glasses are over the top, but you can't help your eyesight, I guess. But you reek of class, not someone who came from the poor side of town. Not someone who lives on Fortieth Street."

Cassidy hadn't considered the need for a back story, a history she could easily recount if someone asked about her past. Amber wasn't prying, she was simply being friendly. Still, if she asked too many questions, Cassidy didn't have ready answers.

Amber eyed her curiously. "You got furniture and stuff?"

Cassidy looked up and edged the glasses up her nose with her forefinger. "No. But I read an ad in the paper that was here yesterday that someone was selling a couch and a chair. I called and can go look at it tomorrow. I work a half-day."

"You ride the bus. How you gonna buy furniture from someone and haul it to your place?"

The entry bell chimed and Cassidy stood. "I haven't figured that part out yet."

Domestics. Clay hated responding to a domestic disturbance call. A lot of them hit too close to home. The shouting. The fighting. The fear that it would escalate to something so much worse. It was bad for the cop responding to the call and bad for the poor schmucks fighting. He'd had a year of that in his own home. One long marital year of picking and bickering and that final slap.

Only one hour left in his shift when this call came over the radio. His luck. He mentally reviewed his anger management training. Ralph Waldo Emerson said, "For every minute you remain angry, you give up sixty seconds of peace of mind."

Clay strived for peace of mind, rarely losing his temper any more. He'd pretty well mastered the respond-instead-of-react technique. When he felt his temper rise, he consciously opened his hand and splayed his fingers. The exact opposite of making a fist. It served to keep him on balance. But it had taken a hard year of marriage to Lauren to get him where he was today. And that slap.

He stopped the patrol car in front of the address dispatch had given. His police sergeant stood on the front porch with a heavyset balding man wearing a Cleveland Browns sweatshirt. A can of beer lay on the top porch step, and the man pointed toward the front door, showed the sergeant a red spot on his head, then motioned toward the can.

Getting out of the car, Clay chuckled. Beer this early? It served him right.

Day three on the job and the assistant manager, Rosie, was on the schedule with Amber and Cassidy. Rosie made it clear she didn't favor Amber and that she would assume Cassidy's training.

Rosie had the most seniority of all the store employees and she did her job efficiently. But she acted like a jail warden watching Cassidy's every move.

Unlike Amber, who let Cassidy think through the steps so she could learn the process, Rosie immediately stepped in if Cassidy paused, shoving her hands from the keyboard and correcting Cassidy in front of the customers. In the first twenty minutes of her shift, she shredded the small bit of confidence Cassidy had acquired in two days.

Amber smiled and winked reassuringly when Rosie answered a phone call and walked into the back office to check a customer's account. "Don't let her scare you," Amber whispered. "You're doing fine. And you're outta here in a couple hours. I'm stuck with her all day."

"She makes me so nervous."

"Don't let her. She knows she can't boss me around because I know this job better than her. So she has to boss you around to feel important."

She nodded toward the two copy machines at the front of the store.

"When you hear her hang up, go check the paper supply in the drawers. She's a stickler for that. It will impress her."

Amber reached under the counter where the pens were stored and grabbed a handful to fill the customer pen cup. "You still gonna go look at furniture this afternoon?"

Cassidy nodded.

"You figure out what to do if you buy it?"

"Not yet."

"Well, if it's not giant pieces maybe we can tie it into the back of my trunk or something. If you decide to buy it, I'll help you move it."

Amber drove a ten-year old faded green Ford Escort with a dented rear bumper, a stone-chipped windshield, and oversized pink fuzzy dice hanging from the rearview mirror. It didn't look like it could make it until tomorrow, let alone serve as a U-Haul. And Cassidy couldn't afford to become friendly with anyone.

"Thanks, Amber, but I don't want to put you out."

The entry bell chimed. Amber turned and broke out into a wide grin.

"Hey C.C. You have a truck, don't you?"

Clay nodded.

"Cassidy needs to borrow a truck. Will you rent her yours?

She needs a driver, too," Amber added, laughing. "She's gotta go pick up some furniture."

Cassidy fought her panic. "Ah, no. Really. Amber's kidding. I'm fine." She raised her hands in front of her and signaled no, like a hockey referee signaling no goal.

Amber turned and arched her eyebrow, causing the tiny star on the eyebrow ring to twinkle. "He's a police officer. It's his job to help the public. And you just said you don't know how you'd transport the furniture to your apartment. I'm sure C.C. won't mind helping, will you C.C.?"

Cassidy stood shaking her head. "I haven't even seen the furniture yet, Amber. I'm not certain I'm going to buy it." She turned to Clay. "Thanks, but I'm fine."

The corners of his mouth edged upward. "I do have a pickup. If you need some help, I'm off tomorrow. I could help for a couple hours."

"No, really. That's very kind, but I don't think so."

"She's scared of her own shadow, C.C. She needs the help. Don't take no for an answer."

"Amber! Stop! I don't need any help." Amber raised both eyebrows but tightened her lips and used her thumb and forefinger to motion that she'd zipped them closed. Cassidy turned to Clay again.

"Really, I'm fine. I planned to look at it today, anyway so, thanks."

"Well, if you can delay that until tomorrow I'll help. What time do you get off work? I'll pick you up here at the store. Where is the furniture?"

Amber chimed in. "You have to go in the morning. She's on the schedule to come in at two and work until close."

Cassidy glared at her and Amber re-zipped her lips.

"That works better for me actually. Do you want me to pick you up here or at your place?"

Suddenly, her stomach knotted and her body temperature

soared to a thousand degrees. "You really don't have to." The last thing she wanted was a cop asking her questions. Damn Amber.

Clay waved his hand. "It's not a big deal. Call them and say you'll be there tomorrow. What time?"

After he left the store, Cassidy turned on Amber, her nostrils flaring. "Why did you do that? I don't even know him. I don't want him knowing where I live or taking me anywhere."

Amber shot back at her. "He's a cop. You can trust him. And he won't care where you live. C.C.'s a good man, he doesn't judge people, even someone he busts. I'm sure he's seen worse places than Fortieth Street. If he's willing to help, you should let him. I don't know what it is with you. Somethin' funny. But you need to trust somebody. And besides, he's hot."

"I don't care how hot he is. You have no right to butt into my life."

"Well sorry. When he shows up tomorrow ready to offer his assistance you just look a gift horse in the mouth and tell him to go home."

3

Clay topped off Dan's cup, took a final sip of his coffee, and rinsed his mug in the breakroom sink.

"So how'd you get stuck helping her move?"

"Not helping her move. Picking up some furniture. I don't know. Amber ambushed me. I walked in when they were talking about the new girl buying furniture and she pretty much railroaded me into helping. The more the girl said no thank you, like she hated the idea of me helping, the more I wanted to."

"Amber? The same Amber we arrested?"

"Same Amber."

"So this is one of Amber's friends?"

That was laughable. "Not hardly. This girl is the exact opposite of Amber's friends. Skittish like a rabbit."

"Shy?"

"No." He paused, searching for the correct word. "More like on edge. Scared."

"Of what?"

Clay laughed. "Of cops, for one thing. At least she seems anxious around a badge. Maybe she'll react differently today when she sees me in street clothes."

His brother-in-law grinned. "Maybe it's that Cestra charm that unnerves her. It sure as hell did me in."

Clay nodded, playing along. "I haven't tried charming her yet, but I'm sure my magnetism is so overwhelming, I don't recognize when it's luring someone under my spell. Seriously, though, something feels off about her, like she's not comfortable in her own skin."

"Maybe she's just uncomfortable going furniture shopping with a strange man." Dan grinned, "You have to admit, you can be pretty strange."

Clay laughed and agreed.

"You only saw her on her first couple of days, right? She probably was nervous about the new job. Working there isn't easy. She makes a mistake and someone's valuables are lost. And you waltz in with court evidence that she has to initial. That's a lot for a first day."

"Could be, but that's not what I'm sensing. She's afraid of something." He shrugged. "We'll see what this little furniture adventure brings."

Cassidy stared out the bus window, watching the rundown two-story homes lining Fortieth Street roll by. Most of them had been converted to apartment buildings with wooden fire escape steps climbing up the brick sides, allowing access to the second floor through a window widened to serve as a door. She doubted the structures complied with building code standards.

Paint peeled from the fiberglass siding on most of the buildings and several gutters sagged in awkward configurations. Even the homes that remained single-family units begged for repairs. Trash peppered most of the front yards.

Slowly, the bus rumbled down the potholed street, transporting her from shabby to swank as it rolled into the more affluent neighborhood of Greenbrier and The Packing Place. Dark and dreary morphed into a bright energy.

Lush trees and rolling lawns were dotted with multi-colored flowers exploding from oversized pots, window boxes, and pristine landscape islands. The windows sparkled and reflected the sun, casting the homes in halos of light. Even the children seemed different.

On Fortieth Street, the kids moped on the front porch stoops, propping up their heads with their hands, wearing yesterday's clothes and bored with today. Here in Greenbrier, the little boys and girls playing in their front yards wore coordinated shorts sets and laughed as they chased balls down the sidewalk.

The parallel between the two neighborhoods and her existence struck her as ironic. She'd had a lush, beautiful life once. Now, she lived in the dark.

She picked at the cuticle on her left thumb as the bus approached her stop. She'd reluctantly agreed to meet Officer Cestra at the store, ashamed to let him see where she lived. If only she'd been more forceful in telling him and Amber no.

She jumped off the bus and had walked less than two blocks when a horn beeped and a green pickup eased to the curb. Clay Cestra stretched across the front seat and the passenger door swung open.

"Mornin'. Hop in." He kept his hand extended toward the door to help her step into the pickup. She ignored it and climbed into the passenger's seat.

"You didn't tell me you rode the bus. I could have picked you up."

"That's okay."

"Where to?" She recited the address she'd memorized from the want ad: 22442 Hough Street.

Clay did a double-take. "Are you familiar with that area?"

She shook her head. "I'm new around here. I haven't learned any of the neighborhoods yet."

He shifted into drive and when the electric locks secured the doors she tried not to think of it as being trapped in the front seat with a policeman. "I'm not sure this is going to be what you're looking for." He eased the truck back into traffic. "But we'll take a look."

After a short time of riding in silence, he asked, "How's the job coming? Are you getting the hang of it?"

She stared straight ahead, her hands clutched tightly in her lap. "I think so. There's still so much that I don't know. Amber's a big help though."

Clay smiled. "She's a character, all right. Where did you move from?"

She glanced at him then returned her gaze to the road. They'd driven into a dilapidated area where houses badly needed cleaned and repaired. Battered junk cars lined both sides of the street, despite the no parking signs on the far side. Trash and debris pimpled several front yards. She gulped. "Is this the right neighborhood?"

Clay drove his truck into an open parking space and nodded. "That's the address right up there. Are you sure the ad said there was furniture for sale?"

She reached into the pocket of her hoodie and removed the newspaper page, showing him the "for sale" ad she'd circled in red.

He shrugged, then reached under the driver's seat and retrieved a small gun that he tucked behind his back into the waist of his jeans, causing her breath to catch in her throat.

"Okay. Let's go check it out."

He jumped out of the truck and walked to the front, waiting for her. She stiffened and momentarily froze when he clasped her upper arm and guided her down the street. Ignoring several whistles and catcalls from an open window of a house they passed, they climbed three rickety wooden steps to a slanted front porch and Clay knocked on the door, rattling the glass window panes.

The door swung open and a large woman stood in front of them wearing a dirty cotton dress with buttons that strained to keep her huge, sagging breasts concealed. Large hoop earrings swung at her ears. Her hair was wrapped in neat rows of pink plastic curlers.

"Whatchoo doin' here, Officer Clay? Ain't nobody called for the poleece."

"Good morning, Mary. My friend here is answering an ad for some furniture."

The woman turned round, bloodshot eyes on Cassidy, rolling her gaze over Cassidy's face, her clothes, and her shoes. She smiled, revealing three gaping holes where teeth used to be, threw her head back, and laughed.

"Well, you just come right on in here, Officer Clay, and see if there is anything you like."

She stepped back, opening the door wider into a dimly lit living room. Two young men in blue jeans and undershirts sat in a haze of cigarette smoke, one sprawled on a couch with his belt undone and his pants unbuttoned, and one reclined in an easy chair. Newspapers piled on a long, low table in front of the sofa attempted to conceal overflowing ash trays and several dirty dishes. Despite the early hour, the room was dark.

Cassidy placed one foot on the metal frame to step inside, but Clay held tight to her arm. "Ah, that's okay Mary. I don't think we're interested after all."

Cassidy shot him a surprised look. "What? We haven't . . ."

Clay dragged her backward onto the porch. "Thanks anyway."

Mary propped her hand on her hip and glared at him. As she spoke, her upper lip curled. "Whatsa matter? My stuff ain't good enough for your hoitey toitey girlfriend?"

Cassidy opened her mouth to speak, but Clay tightened his

grip on her arm, causing the veins to pop and her fingertips to tingle. He leaned into her to nudge her toward the steps.

"It doesn't go with our décor." Now he was stepping sideways, moving into her with his full body, advancing her toward the edge of the porch. Her stomach clenched when thick thigh muscles rubbed against her legs.

Mary screeched at them. "You just hold on a minute. I coulda sold that stuff yesterday, but she said she wanted it so I held it." She jabbed her finger in the air toward Cassidy. "She owes me fifty bucks."

Cassidy gasped and began to protest, but Clay shot her a look to silence her. He reached into his pocket, removed a money clip and counted out two twenties and a ten. He tossed it on the seat of a broken, dirty wicker rocker leaning against the house.

He elbowed her down the steps, all the while keeping his eyes on the woman in the front door. "Thanks for your trouble, Mary."

Mary bellowed a string of curses that questioned Clay's manhood. Even though he forced Cassidy forward he walked sideways, keeping his eyes on the house. She attempted to wrench free, but his grip was firm. Her mouth went dry. One minute he was escorting her to the house and now, he was shoving her from it. It was confusing. And she was angry.

When they were about four houses away, Clay stepped up his pace to close the distance between them and his truck. He touched the keypad to unlock the door, opened it, and practically hurled her into the passenger's seat.

She turned on him the minute he closed the driver's door.

"What the hell are you doing? I didn't even have a chance to look at anything."

The truck tires squealed when he sped away from the curb. "I was going to ask you the same thing," he snapped. "What the hell's the matter with you, coming to a neighborhood like this? Are you looking for trouble?"

"No. I'm looking for furniture. And now, thanks to you, I still don't have any."

He laughed in disbelief. "You can't be serious. How long do you think it would take to get the stink out of that sofa, not to mention the semen stains and puke residue? You really want to sit on crap like that?"

"You didn't even see it. How do you know what condition it was in?"

"What I know, Cassidy, is that if you had walked in there alone you would have found yourself flat on your back on that filthy furniture."

Her stomach compressed so tightly she thought she might throw up. "You can't be serious."

He leveled his gaze at her. "And you can't be that naïve."

Tears welled in her eyes as the gravity of his words sunk in. She nudged her glasses up her nose with a trembling hand and bit her lower lip. Staring into her lap she said softly, "I'm sorry. I-I didn't know what this neighborhood was like."

"It's okay. I'm just glad I was here. Listen, if you are that desperate for furniture, I have some in storage I'll loan you."

She glared at him, automatically shaking her head to decline his offer. She was frightened, maybe even stupid, but she was also proud. She sat up straighter. "I have a check in my pocket. I'll make it out to you for the fifty dollars, but you'll have to wait to cash it. I hope that's okay."

When he threw his head back and laughed, she clenched her teeth, restraining herself from berating him for belittling her.

"You planned to pay for that junk with a check, one that you were going to ask them to hold to boot? Who did you think you'd be dealing with? Bankers? I take it back, you are that naïve. Keep your money, I don't want it."

She spit her words back at him. "I don't need your charity, thanks. I'll pay you back, don't worry. And if it makes you happy, I'll give you cash just as soon as I get my first paycheck. And keep your hand-me-downs. I'll find furniture somewhere else. Please stop at the next bus stop and let me out of this truck."

They'd navigated to a safer side of town and Clay slowed his speed. When they slowed for a red light, he turned his full attention to her. She squirmed under his gaze. "I'm sorry. I shouldn't have laughed at you. That was disrespectful. I forgot you're new in town and unfamiliar with the area."

The stoplight turned green and he refocused on the road, allowing her to exhale.

"The offer to borrow some furniture still stands and it's not charity. If you go on future shopping expeditions based on the want ads, I suggest you check with Amber or someone else first. I'll be happy to advise you. Where do you live? I'll run you home."

That was the last thing she wanted. "Please take me back to the store. I have to work today."

"You're not on until two. It's not even ten o'clock. You plan to sit in the back room all morning? I don't mind running you home. Just tell me where it is."

"You can drop me at the bus stop. I'll be fine."

"For Chrissake. Just tell me the damn address."

Cassidy jumped when he yelled and automatically recited her address. Out of the corner of her eye she watched him open and close his hand on the steering wheel, spreading his fingers wide, flexing, and then re-gripping the wheel.

They drove the remainder of the trip in silence, her heart racing. She didn't want anyone to know where she lived, especially not a cop. Clay slowed the truck in front of her building but didn't shift into park, which kept the doors locked.

"You work until close tonight, isn't that what Amber said?"

She nodded. "Thanks for the ride. Please unlock the door."

"Is this the first night you've closed the store?"

She nodded again and wished he'd let her out of the damn truck.

"And you plan to take the bus home after work?"

"I'll be fine." She yanked on the door handle without success.

"Do you have a cell phone?"

She raised her eyes to him. She did, one of those pre-paid ones from a drugstore. It was all she could afford. "Yes, why?"

"Keep it handy. This is a dangerous neighborhood, especially after dark. You're going to need it to call the police."

He shifted the truck into park and the locks sprang up. Without another word she jumped from the truck, slamming the door behind her. She didn't turn around, but she knew he hadn't budged as she moved up the short walk to the building's front door. It was supposed to be a security door, but the handle was missing. She opened it without a glance backward and yet she sensed him watching, his eyes boring holes into her back.

Once inside, with her apartment door dead bolted behind her, she started to sob. This place was wretched, as bad as where she'd just come from. And now he knew where she lived. She'd never felt this lonely, or this alone, in her life. But her life wasn't hers anymore. And this apartment was temporary, she reminded herself.

She'd be here until she had to run again. Or until that monster hunting her was dead.

4

Relief washed over her in one long, deep sigh hours later when she walked into The Packing Place and clocked in. It was a slice of normalcy, a routine she could use to convince herself that she led an ordinary life.

Wayne Keaseling stood behind the counter with Amber, Rosie, and Leslie, another female co-worker. Keaseling only hired women.

He gave her a wide smile and extended his hand to shake hers. The hairs on the back of her neck prickled to attention as she placed her hand in his. He held onto it too long.

"Well? How's it going? Rosie says you're doing well. This is your first time to close the store at the end of the day, right?"

She nodded. Rosie stood beside him, almost at attention, and Amber stood behind them both, making faces to their backs. Off to the side, Leslie smiled, an amused silent observer.

Rosie extended a clipboard. "This is what you need to know to finish the day, how to balance, close out the shipments, everything you'll have to do. You should memorize it, although once you've done it as many times as I have, it becomes second nature."

Cassidy bit her lip, trying not to smile at Amber rolling her head from side to side and mocking Rosie behind them.

"Amber will help you if you encounter a problem, but I want you to do most of it yourself. You'll be closing on your own pretty soon. We'll review everything before I leave."

Rosie regularly worked a daytime shift. Amber said she refused to work nights or weekends and Keaseling pacified her.

"Thank you."

Keaseling stepped forward and ran his hand down Cassidy's back. She stiffened. "Of course, if you have any problems, you only need to call me."

She stepped away from his touch and pretended to read the pages on the clipboard. Leslie and Amber were attending to customers, so she turned to Rosie. Pointing to a line she said, "Will you explain this to me, please?"

Having effectively dismissed Keaseling, he mumbled he was leaving for the other store and departed. Something about that man made her cringe.

Cassidy suffered under Rosie's tutelage until the woman clocked out at four. She'd received encouraging winks from Leslie and Amber whenever Rosie couldn't see. Finally, it was just her and Amber to work the evening shift until they closed at eight thirty.

The tension in the store dissipated and Cassidy relaxed for the first time all day. The dinner hour regularly was slow and they sat in the back room together, grateful for the break. The customers had been nonstop today.

"So how'd it go this morning?" Amber asked.

Cassidy bit her lower lip and blinked when tears welled in eyes. "Not good. It was a dreadful place and your cop friend scared me to death. I think it will be a while before I try to shop for used furniture again."

Amber laughed. "Yeah, I heard. C.C. called me this morning. He says if I can't give you a ride home he'll come and pick you up. I told you Fortieth Street was a bad neighborhood."

Her eyebrows shot up. "What? He called you about me?"

Amber's smile disappeared. "Yeah. He was madder than hell. Says you don't have a brain in your head. What is it with you? You're white as a ghost."

"I don't like people butting into my life. And I don't need a ride home. I'll take the bus."

Amber stared at her for what seemed like forever, her scrutiny causing Cassidy to shift uncomfortably in her chair.

"Something's up with you, Cass. Not sure what it is. A jealous husband, maybe? A sordid past? It doesn't matter to me what you're trying to hide. Or run from. I pretty much just let people do their thing and I'm okay with it.

"You're trying hard to put up walls and keep people at arm's length. That's cool if that's the way you want it." She shrugged. "For some reason, I like you. Not sure why." She stood as the door chimed, announcing a customer.

"Walls or not, I'll give you a ride home tonight."

Clay jumped in the shower the minute he returned home from his trip to the land of squalor, angry with Cassidy for thinking she could venture into that part of town alone. Angry? He barely knew the woman, yet his reaction had been to call Amber to make sure Cassidy had a safe way home. If she didn't, he was ready to play Sir Galahad and escort her safely, even though she'd fight him every minute of the trip. She'd been stupid and reckless to try to buy furniture like that, and it irritated him.

He stood beneath the pulsating hot water analyzing his reactions, confused by them actually. She could have been hurt and that upset him.

He probably should've told Cassidy when she recited the

address that the house was in an undesirable part of town. He doubted she would have listened. She was determined. Or obstinate. Whatever the word, she was something with her big eyes hidden behind those red glasses and that captivating smile.

Reaching for a towel he shook his head, surprised that she was occupying his thoughts. Glimpsing himself in the mirror, his reflection smiled back at him. That was a rare occurrence. Except for Jack, little made him smile. He took a deep breath. His sister had a list of landlord tasks as long as his arm, so he might as well hop to it. His pleasant thoughts about Cassidy Hoake would have to wait.

But he couldn't keep his mind off of her. When he'd called Amber, he inquired about Cassidy's last name. Amber knew how to unlock Keaseling's file cabinet, which for some reason didn't surprise him, and she provided Cassidy's last name and birth date. He'd tried to sound casual, asking what else was in the file and, scanning the employment application, Amber said the emergency contact information section was blank. Previous employment listed a convenience store but didn't specify a name or location.

He'd asked why Keaseling would hire someone without a complete employment application and Amber snorted. "Have you looked at her?"

His heart skipped. Yes, he had. He was unfamiliar with the name Hoake and she'd said she was new in town, but he suspected Cassidy wasn't from the neighboring areas either. The tiniest touch of an accent hinted she wasn't an Ohio native. At least he could check that.

He called Dan and requested a background search if possible. Police couldn't arbitrarily run a check on someone, of course, but it was easy enough to justify a records request as part of another incident, say a traffic stop. It wasn't a practice the brass sanctioned, but most of the guys did it for each other on the sly. Ms.

Hoake would be a passenger in someone's car tonight, whether she knew it or not.

Amber hadn't been much help enlightening him on Cassidy's living situation either. She said Cassidy was really guarded about her personal information and Amber declared her "a lost soul."

Lost or not, she was living in a hellhole. Someone needed to help her. The girl couldn't work the late shift at that store and take the bus home at that hour. Not looking as good as she looked.

Well, he was a man, after all. She'd climbed into his truck in tight blue jeans, a thin T-shirt, and hoodie. He'd have to be blind not to notice.

He wiped his feet, knocked on the glass of his sister's apartment then slid the door open. Gurgling sounds planted a smile on his face and he walked to the blanket on the kitchen floor and scooped up his nephew. Jack had mastered hunching up into the crawl position on his hands and knees but hadn't yet figured out how to move. He spent most of his time rocking back and forth but making little progress.

"Hey buddy. Still going nowhere?" Clay swung him to the ceiling, eliciting squeals of delight from the baby. Cradled in his arms, Jack giggled and reached for Clay's face with his pudgy open palm, his tiny feet pumping with excitement.

Standing at the island chopping cooked potatoes, his sister beamed. "I swear you are his favorite person in the world. He shows more teeth for you than his own father."

Clay smiled and kissed the baby's forehead. "It's not that hard. He only has two."

Maggie laughed. "Are you staying for dinner? Burgers on the grill and potato salad."

"Sure." He settled Jack on his lap.

"As soon as he starts moving you're going to be up to your elbows chasing him and trying to keep up with the apartments." He gently brushed back a wisp of Jack's hair.

"Tell me about it. I've been thinking I might need some part-time help, just with the cleaning when we lose a tenant. And maybe the yard maintenance." Maggie shrugged. "It's good exercise and I love doing it, but it will take me twice as long if I'm chasing after him. But I'm not sure we'd be successful if we wanted to hire someone. It's not as if it's a daily job, it would only be on an as-needed basis for minimum wage, maybe a dollar or two higher. Anyone who truly needs a job won't find that too appealing."

"Care if I make a suggestion?"

"Shoot."

"Suppose, instead of a salary, we offer a place to live. One of the smaller apartments. In lieu of rent, we have her do whatever you need done whenever, whether it's weekends, Sundays, and even holidays. It would include painting the easy stuff, cleaning, running your errands, all of it."

His sister eyed him. "Her? You have someone in mind for this slave labor position?"

"I do. I don't know if she'll be interested. She seems pretty stubborn. She's the new hire at the shipping store where I drop off the drunk-driving samples most days. She lives on Fortieth Street and takes the bus to work. It's not a good situation."

Maggie wrinkled her nose. "Fortieth Street? How'd she end up in that neighborhood? You sure she's not a crack addict or prostitute?"

"She's no prostitute. She's too clean for that. Nails manicured. Nice makeup and modest clothes."

Clay tickled his nephew's belly and his baby giggles filled the kitchen. "I don't know much about her, to be truthful, except that she seems all alone. Dan is going to try to background check her today. I feel if someone doesn't reach out and help her, she'll end up like Amber. We've told you about her, the drinking and drugs. Amber is smart. If someone had cared enough, they could've set her on the right path years ago.

"It's too late for Amber, but there might be a chance with Cassidy. I figured I'd bounce the idea off of you before approaching her. You could meet her first, interview her or something. What do you say?"

"You seem pretty interested in her. Is she young? Attractive?"

He smiled. "She turns twenty-seven in December and she's not bad looking. But I'm not interested in her, more curious. She's as skittish as a chipmunk. Like she's trying to hide something."

Watching her son's feet pump as if running in the air Maggie nodded. "Well, if you and Dan are going to check her out first, it can't hurt to talk to her. Look at him go in your lap. I'm going to need help for sure."

The next day Clay frowned as he entered The Packing Place. No Amber or Cassidy. Rosie stiffened when he inquired about their schedules. "We are not at liberty to divulge that information."

What a witch. "That's fine. I'll call Amber and ask her myself." He had no intention of calling her. He'd wait until she worked again. But he withdrew his phone from his pocket anyway as he exited the store. That ought to set the old biddy's tongue wagging.

5

Amber bounced into the store pumping her fist. "T.G.I.F.," she chanted, grinning at Cassidy and Leslie.

Her energy was contagious and Leslie laughed. "You're in a good mood today."

"It's Friday and as soon as I clock out, I'm going to par-taye. Meetin' a new guy tonight at my friend's house. He is supposed to be hot, hot, hot and I'm ready for a good time."

She turned to Cassidy. "Why so glum chum?"

The rhyme made Cassidy smile, her first of the day. She held out the work schedule for the upcoming week.

"I'm at the other store all next week with Rosie. I'd rather be in this store. I was just starting to feel like I knew where everything was. I'm going to screw up over there, I know it. I get so tense around her."

Amber studied the schedule. "They bounce us back and forth, you know that. You'll be fine. This is Rosie's way to keep you away from me. Probably figures I'm a bad influence on you."

Leslie snickered. "That's not too far off, you know. You are a little rambunctious for poor little Cassidy here."

Amber laughed and took a playful swat at Leslie. 'Rambunctious. As soon as I look that up, I'll have a comeback for you."

She squeezed Cassidy's shoulder. "You'll be fine. You can always call over here and talk to either one of us for moral support." Leslie nodded in agreement.

The door chimed, beginning a steady stream of customers who made the day fly by.

One hour before close, business finally seemed to settle down.

"What are you doing this weekend?" Amber asked, restocking the box shelves. For all the complaints Rosie leveled against her, Amber was the only employee Cassidy had seen who cleaned, restocked, and reordered without being asked.

Cassidy picked up the box cutter and sliced the binding on another bundle. "Not much."

She eyed Cassidy. "Do you have any plans at all?"

How should she answer that? No she didn't have plans. She didn't have a car, she didn't have a life, and she didn't dare leave her apartment beyond going to work for fear of being seen. All she had were the clothes she'd managed to shove in her duffel bag, a couple pieces of jewelry, her mother's clock, and her laptop, thank God. With neither television nor radio, the world would be lost to her without that laptop.

She'd used the store computer to check *The Arizona Republic* online yesterday and he was still missing. Still on the loose, despite a warrant issued by the state authorities for his arrest. Still searching for her, she was sure of it.

"I guess no answer means no, huh? What are you going to do, sit in that rat hole all weekend?"

Cassidy glared at her. "I'll be fine."

Amber jammed the last of the size ten boxes in their compartment and did an impromptu dance around the room. "Come to the party with me tonight. It will be fun. You'll get to meet some people. Maybe even a guy. Whaddaya say?"

"Um, I appreciate the offer, but no thanks."

"C'mon, Cass. What're you going to do all weekend? I promise to return you home safe. Come with."

"Thanks, but I don't have anything to change into and I'm not wearing this uniform to a party."

Amber sashayed her right hip sideways, propping her hand on it. "Is that the only reason you won't go?"

"No, but it's a reason."

"I've got clothes in my car, all clean. I did laundry yesterday. You can wear any shirt you like."

From some of the comments she'd made, Amber seemed to live out of her car. And she had the nerve to poke fun at Cassidy's apartment, even though she was right, it was a rat hole. "I can't, Amber. Thanks anyway."

"C'mon, Cass, it'll be—"

Cassidy snapped. "I can't. Don't you understand? I just can't."

Amber's eyes widened to the size of quarters. She stared at her, again with that analytical glare, peering right through her disguise. She popped her gum, once, twice, three times, and then shrugged.

"I don't understand, but I get it."

As they turned out the lights and locked the back door, Amber touched Cassidy's arm. "I'll drive you home."

"No thanks. You have a party and a new man waiting. I'll be fine."

"The party is just getting started. I have plenty of time. And I promised C.C."

Cassidy gasped.

"Let's go," Amber urged, ignoring her reaction. "It's late, you shouldn't be taking a bus. I'll drive you home and I promise I won't ask why you can't go out. In fact, I promise I won't ask you one of the seventy-two questions I'm desperate to ask. Deal?"

Cassidy hesitated, but a ride home was much more attractive than the bus. She acquiesced and, true to Amber's word, they made the trip in silence. Amber touched her arm as she stepped out of the car.

"Rosie gave you a card with all the employee phone numbers on, didn't she?"

Cassidy nodded. "Mine's on there, too. You need something, you call. Day or night."

Friday night. The weather was unseasonably warm for the end of summer and the kids took full advantage of it to party. The police dispatchers had been kept busy through the evening with complaints about loud music, fistfights, and drunken crowds spilling into the streets.

Clay and his partner drove to their third disturbance call of the night, this time as the second responder for a house party out of control. As they approached the Briarwood Street address, a handful of partygoers ran from the house screaming "Cops!"

Clay watched the runners spilling off the porch and spotted Amber bolt down the steps and run toward a backyard. He jumped out of the passenger seat and chased her.

She didn't get too far, running barefoot. He grabbed her upper arm and spun her around, eliciting a high-pitched squeal.

"What the hell are you doing here?"

She huffed to catch her breath. "Oh C.C. You scared the crap out of me."

He squeezed her arm, causing her to yelp and reach for his fingers to loosen the grip. "Ow. Back off, man."

"You promised me you'd stay out of trouble."

"I did. And I swear to you I wasn't smokin' nothin. I had one beer. Smell my breath. You'll see." Her mouth opened into a wide circle and she exhaled.

The flashing red and blue lights threw eerie highlights across her face as he half dragged, half-walked her toward the police cruiser.

"Aw c'mon, C.C. Give me a break. Please don't bust me. I swear to you, I wasn't doin' drugs."

He opened the rear car door and urged her into the backseat, placing his hand between the door frame and her head as a protective cushion.

"Son of a . . . please C.C., don't do this."

He slammed the door and walked toward the house to find his partner, who had gone inside to help. Minutes later he returned and slid into the driver's seat. Turning the key, he eyed Amber in the rearview mirror. She hung her head, her long, streaked hair covering most of her face.

"Is your car here? How'd you get here tonight?"

"I came with a friend," she mumbled, without looking up. He backed into a nearby driveway to turn around.

"Please, C.C. I'll do anything for you. Anything."

"Look at me." She raised her eyes to the mirror.

"What I want you to do for me is stay out of trouble."

She folded her hands together at her chin. "I will, C.C., I promise. Just don't bust me. I can't do jail again."

"I'm not arresting you, hon. I'm taking you home. But it's the first and last time you get a break like this, understand?"

She gulped in air and blinked back tears. "Yes, sir, I do. Thank you."

"What were you doing here anyway? You know it's a violation of your probation to hang at a party like that. No drugs or alcohol. The judge didn't say one beer is okay."

"I know, I know. I'm really sorry. It won't happen again."

"Who were you here with?"

"My girlfriend. She wanted me to meet someone. And a couple other friends."

"Amber, if they are drinking and smoking, they can't be your friends. They will only get you in trouble. You should think about making new friends."

"I know. I'll try, I promise."

The ride continued in silence. He tried not to let Amber see him watching her wipe tears from her cheeks. Once she regained her composure, she stared out the rear window. Eventually, she spoke.

"I tried to get Cassidy to come tonight. Now, I'm glad she didn't."

His heart jumped to his throat, an unexpected reaction that surprised him. "Didn't she want to come?"

Amber caught his gaze in the mirror. "She never said she didn't want to come. She said she couldn't."

"Maybe she had other plans."

"No, I specifically asked if she had plans. She blew up because I asked her more than once to come with. She raised her voice and snapped, 'I can't come, don't you understand?' I didn't, but I dropped it."

"Can't? Like not allowed?"

"Can't. Like she was afraid to. Something's up with her, C.C. She's smart, too smart to work for minimum wage. She has class, but she treats me like an equal. She doesn't look down her nose at me like most of the others at the store. I like her. But she's so jittery. She eyes everyone who walks in the store like she's going to run out the back door screaming if they yell boo."

Clay smiled. "You've got class too, honey. You just never let it show 'cause you prefer to get a rise out of people."

She smiled and raised her chin in the air, her confidence restored. "I gave her a ride home tonight, like I promised you."

"Thanks."

"There's going to be a problem next week, though. Rosie has her over at the other store all week. I checked the schedule and Cassidy closes on Wednesday and Thursday nights. I'm off

Wednesday because I work Saturday, but I close at the Green-brier store on Thursday."

The other packing store was located on the far side of town. Cassidy would likely have to ride two late buses to her apartment. That idea didn't sit well. The realization that he cared about her safe transport confused him. Well, he was a public servant, after all.

He stopped the patrol car in front of Amber's apartment, which he knew she shared with a roommate. He stepped out of the car and opened the back door to let her out.

Fresh tears filled her eyes.

"Thanks, C.C. Really. I owe you."

"Yes, you do so remember what I said. Behave."

She winked and took several steps toward her building, which he noticed had a security door that actually closed and locked. Better housing than Cassidy's.

"Amber!" She stopped and turned.

He reached into his pocket for his money clip and freed a twenty from its grasp. He held it out to her. "If I pay for your gas, will you pick her up Wednesday night and drive her home?"

Amber tilted her head. "What is it with you and her?"

Another jerk on his heart. He shrugged. "Nothing. But like you said, there's something not quite right with her. She sets all my cop's instincts in motion."

Amber laughed and reached for the money. "You sure that's all she sets in motion?"

Heat crept up his neck to his face and he was grateful for the dark. "I'll drive her home Wednesday, but what're you going to do about Thursday?"

He sucked in a deep, slow breath, already conflicted by his plan. "I'll pick her up."

6

She awakened with a jolt, sweat clinging to her upper lip and soaking the hair on the back of her neck, her breathing rapid. The nightmare was always the same.

The woman standing there, smiling and waving. The pop pop pop from the gun. Then the shocked look on her face and life leaving her eyes. She crumbled to the ground and behind her, he stood, glaring at Cassidy through the store window. Then she was running, running . . .

She woke up screaming, wrestling with the blanket and sheet entrapping her legs. Panting, she reached for her laptop before remembering she couldn't connect to the Internet from these apartments. Damn. She wanted to check the headlines in Arizona. Maybe they'd caught him.

Dark circles outlined her eyes when she reported to work Monday morning. She'd given herself a pep talk on the bus, but her dream and staying holed up in the rat hole most of the weekend had undermined her strength. Her walk to the fast-food restaurant two blocks from her apartment, where access to the Internet was free, had been accomplished with clenched teeth and eyes wide. The young teens loitering around in twisted ball caps and drooping jeans scared her, even in broad daylight. She clung to her laptop so fiercely, her hand ached. On top of all that, there had been nothing in the news about reputed mobster Tony DelMorrie.

Rosie must have had a rotten weekend as well, because she was relentless in her criticism, at one point making Cassidy mad enough to consider quitting. She resolved on Tuesday to kill Rosie with kindness, asking her loads of questions and admiring her knowledge of the business. It seemed to work, although today, Wednesday, Cassidy's nerves as well as her confidence were frayed.

Rosie was General Patton with breasts and she considered this store her store. She'd worked for the company for more than ten years and seemed reluctant to give up the old ways for newer technology. She avoided any of the computer shortcuts Amber taught Cassidy, such as pushing the one-, five-, or ten-dollar bill buttons on the touch-screen cash register, opting instead to plug in the amounts using the individual digits.

"You have to do it this way," Rosie chastised the first time Cassidy touched the five-dollar key.

"Why?"

"Because that's the way it's done."

"But Amber—"

Rosie bristled. "I'm teaching you the correct way to operate in these stores. Don't follow Amber's lead or you'll find yourself making mistakes and getting into trouble."

It didn't make sense and confused Cassidy. Thrust into a different store layout with new customers, she fumbled around looking for items she easily located at the Greenbrier store. Under Rosie's constant eagle eye, she made register mistakes and was slow at packing items.

It was only mid-week and it felt like she'd already logged forty hours, especially since she wasn't sleeping well. She eyed the clock. Less than thirty minutes and Rosie would go home.

Her relief was brief. Through the rear door window she watched Wayne Keaseling parking his van. She braced herself for his inevitable attentions.

"Well hello, Cassidy. Rosie says you're learning fast. How do you like working at this store?" He stepped beside her and ran his hand down her back. She stiffened and stepped away.

"It's fine, sir."

He jerked his head backward. "Sir? How about Wayne?"

Cassidy smiled but remained silent.

"Rosie tells me you've beat her into work every day this week. I'm impressed. No one ever arrives before Rosie."

"I take the bus to work. It drops me off early."

He raised his bushy eyebrows, greeted a familiar customer, then nodded at Rosie to handle the shipment. He placed his hand between Cassidy's shoulder blades.

"Let's go into the office and talk."

Her stomach tightened and she choked back the question on the tip of her tongue. Was she in trouble? Did he know about her?

Keaseling sat down at his desk and waved to a folding chair, the only other place to sit in the room. "You don't have a car?"

"No."

"Where do you come from that you ride the bus?"

"It's actually two buses to get to this store. I'm temporarily staying around Fortieth Street." He didn't react as if he recognized the area.

"Two buses to work all the time? Is that a hardship?"

"Only two buses to this store. I ride one bus to get to Greenbrier. But it's not a problem."

He paused, studying her, eliciting goose bumps on her arms as if it were winter and she was outdoors without a jacket. His eyes traveled down her legs and back up to her face, pausing momentarily on her breasts.

"Getting to work would be easier if the schedule kept you at the Greenbrier store, correct? Would you like me to coordinate that?"

Warning bells sounded in her head. It was the way he looked at her, taking her measurements with his eyes, mentally stripping her of her clothes.

"I don't want to put anyone out. Thank you."

"You would be doing no such thing. I'm sure you and I could make an arrangement that would keep you scheduled at the other store. You know, you scratch my back and I'll scratch yours."

She stopped breathing.

He waited.

She noticed his hands for the first time, long bony fingers with fingernails longer than a man should wear. He slowly tapped his forefinger on the desk, waiting.

A knock and Rosie thrust her head inside the door. "It's pretty busy out here. I could use some help."

Cassidy was never so happy to see Rosie's scowling face. She jumped up and followed Rosie to the front of the store. Faced with a steady stream of customers, Keaseling eventually left without further scheduling discussions. Cassidy breathed a sigh of relief, although she suspected it was temporary.

Business slowed to a crawl after the dinner hour. Cassidy was vacuuming when Amber strolled in wearing a too-tight tank top, cutoff shorts, and flip flops despite the cooler evening temperature. She'd added a neon green streak to her hair.

"Hey!"

In spite of her sour mood, Cassidy smiled. "Nice color."

"Thanks. I'm green, like environmentally safe. Get it? How'd it go today?"

Cassidy shook her head. "I'd much rather be at Greenbrier

with you. She tells me everything I do is wrong. She makes me make mistakes."

Amber laughed. "She's on a power trip. Don't let her bother you."

They walked into the back and Amber hopped onto the packing table, crossing her legs. "What are you doing here?"

"I, um, I was close by when I remembered you worked tonight. I figured I could give you a lift home so you wouldn't have to take two buses."

"Amber, you don't have to go out of your way for me."

"I'm not, don't worry."

"Close by where?"

"Just close is all."

She eyed the schedule hanging on the wall and chuckled. "Rosie works a half-day tomorrow. You'll only have to endure four hours of torture. It will be like a holiday."

Cassidy looked at her and tugged on her right ear lobe. "Yeah. Now if only Mr. Keaseling will stay away."

Amber straightened, more alert. "Why? What happened?"

Cassidy recounted the office conversation regarding the schedule. "I don't think he'll let the subject drop."

Amber jumped off the table and straightened her clothes. "Don't worry about him, I'll take care of it. C'mon, let's lock up and get out of here."

Dan's database search was a dead end. No record found for a Cassidy Hoake, including variations on the spelling of her first and last name. That meant Cassidy had not had a parking ticket nor a misdemeanor of any sort on record throughout the state and didn't possess an Ohio driver's license.

If Clay wanted information run on her nationwide, he'd have to send her name through the FBI's National Crime Information

Center and that would raise too many red flags. It was one thing to check her out as a phantom passenger in a car accident, but messing with NCIC was a no-no.

Clay reviewed his options en route to The Packing Place Thursday night to pick her up. He'd just have enough time to run her home, drive back to his own apartment to change into his uniform, and report to work by eleven thirty for his midnight shift.

But maybe, while she was locked in the front seat with him, he could learn a little more about her. It was crazy, but he couldn't stop thinking about her. He'd even dreamt about her and woke up with a hard-on, something that hadn't happened in a long time. He didn't try to recall the details of the dream, too afraid of what he might remember.

He'd barely had contact with the woman and yet she was consuming his waking thoughts and now invading his sleep. Here he was driving to pick her up when she probably wouldn't show the slightest gratitude for the gesture. Of course, if she did, which would he prefer? A handshake or a kiss? Jesus. Where did that come from? He was only concerned about her safety. After all, he was a public servant and it was his duty to help citizens in trouble.

He pressed the buttons to roll down the windows in the truck. If he was going to help this particular citizen, he needed to get rid of the bulge in his pants first.

Thursday breezed by for Cassidy without a hitch. It was the end of the month and Rosie spent her hours working on ledgers and billing the monthly charge accounts. Keaseling never made an appearance. By eight o'clock that night, feeling certain that the coast was clear, Cassidy exhaled a lungful of air it seemed she'd held all day.

Filing the day's shipments in the office while Leslie balanced the cash registers, they groaned simultaneously when the door chimed. Late customers were the worst. Usually they were in a rush and most times inconsiderate of the hour.

If this was a complicated shipment that kept them at the store late, Cassidy would miss her bus. She plastered on a forced smile, emerged from the back room and gasped.

"What are you doing here at night?"

Clay Cestra smiled. "Nice to see you, too."

"We're about to close. If you have something to ship, it won't go out until tomorrow."

He spread his empty hands wide. "I'm not here to ship anything. I'm here to chauffeur you home."

His words so stunned her she took a step backward. "I-I don't need a ride, but thank you."

He shrugged. "It's not an option you have to exercise, ma'am. Are you ready to leave?"

Leslie emerged from the back office in time to hear his question. "We're balanced and the safe is locked. All we have to do is clock out and turn out the lights."

Clay circled the counter and walked toward the back door, which only the employees used. Cassidy's stomach jumped. Apparently he'd been in the back room before. With Amber? Just the two of them? What made her think that? Why did she care?

The women clocked out, turned off the lights, and locked the door. Clay waited outside with his hands tucked in his jean pockets. When Cassidy turned away from the door, he reached for her elbow and escorted her around to the front of the building, crossing the parking lot to his truck.

"I really don't want to ride home with you. I'm fine taking the bus."

"Get in."

He opened the door and all but hoisted her into the passenger seat. He hopped into the driver's side, turned the key in the ignition, and shifted in gear. She jumped when the automatic locks clicked into place.

They traveled in silence. She'd be damned if she was going to make small talk with him. He had no right to bully her like this, although when two police cars zipped by with sirens blaring, heading in the direction of her building, she couldn't deny a twinge of relief that she wasn't on the bus and wouldn't be forced to walk the two blocks to her apartment.

From beneath half-closed eyelids, she watched his right arm shift gears. A strong hand tensing and releasing muscles that flexed to full biceps. A little farther to the left, she observed his thigh tighten when he engaged the clutch. More muscles.

She swallowed a mouthful of air in an effort to calm the butterflies in her stomach, detecting the slightest hint of soap and woods or musk. Soft but not feminine. He smelled clean. He wasn't unattractive either with his short dark hair and mustache. What color were his eyes? She'd never noticed.

Clay broke her reverie. "Were you busy today?"

"Pretty much nonstop."

"You ever work in retail before?"

A cautionary cramp turned the butterflies into angry hornets buzzing in her stomach. "Not like here."

"Where'd you work before?"

"Um, I worked in a convenience store. It was mostly just cash register work, nothing like what I do now."

"Where?"

She turned to look at him. "Why do you want to know?"

He shrugged. "Just asking. Making polite conversation. You know, like civilized people do?"

She didn't respond and they continued the trip in silence. Up ahead, police cars blocked Fortieth Street. Clay cruised to the officer standing at the roadblock and leaned out the window.

"What's up, Pat?"

"Hey, Clay. What brings you down here? Double murder in

those apartments down there. We're not letting anybody through."

Cassidy gulped. Now what?

Clay gestured with his open hand. "My friend lives there and she'd like to pick up a few things. Will you let us down there? I'll keep an eye on her for surveillance sake and we'll be in and out in ten minutes tops. I'll log a supplemental report and take full responsibility."

"Wait. No." Cassidy grabbed his arm then jerked her hand back quickly as if electrocuted. She hadn't meant to touch him.

He turned to look at her, his eyebrows furrowed. "What?"

Words escaped her. Her hand tingled from the touch and her pulse quickened. From fear? Or something else?

"What apartment number you headed to, Clay?" Pat Tatman asked.

Clay stared at her, waiting for an answer.

She couldn't find her voice. She didn't want him in her apartment. She didn't want to be this close to him even now. If she didn't stay in the rat hole tonight, she had nowhere to go. This couldn't be happening.

"Cassidy. What's the apartment number?"

She blinked. "One-twelve."

Clay spoke again to the officer and he motioned for one of the cruisers to move. They crept slowly through the barricade and down the street. Cop cars were everywhere. In front of her building, a sheet covered a bulky form on the sidewalk. A body?

Clay stopped in the middle of the street, a half block from her building, parking beside another patrol car. He mumbled for her to stay put, jumped out, and walked around the rear of the truck.

She heard him acknowledge someone before he opened her door and extended his hand. "This is a crime scene so stay beside me and don't touch anything. We'll have to be quick. Let's go."

In a daze, she took his hand and a hundred bolts of electricity shot through her arm. He held it as they moved up the sidewalk.

At the door he acknowledged another policeman and explained their mission.

Then they were inside, walking down the short set of steps to the bottom floor and her apartment door. Clay stood expectantly when they halted in front of one-twelve. Her heart stalled in her throat. She didn't want him inside, didn't want him to see what she had sunk to.

"Do you have your key?"

She turned watery eyes to him.

"Can you wait out here?"

"No, ma'am."

This was definitely a low moment in her life. She inhaled a ragged breath, shoved her glasses up her nose with her index finger, removed the key from her purse, and unlocked the door. She regularly left a light on in the kitchen, casting the living area in shadows. But not dark enough to conceal the hideousness of the place.

Clay grasped her upper arm and walked farther into the apartment, glancing first toward the dinette, and then to the floor, no doubt noticing the braided throw rugs as he moved across them to the bedroom. He switched on the overhead light and crinkled his nose at the mattress in the corner.

"Why do you live here? Do you like this?"

Her temper flared. "Of course I don't like it. I'm down on my luck right now. This is all I can afford."

"Pack your things. All your stuff. You can't stay here."

She yanked her arm from his grasp. "I don't have anywhere else to go." She sensed his demeanor soften.

"Don't you have any friends?"

Her breathing was faster than usual, partly from anger and partly from fear. "No."

"Why is someone like you all alone?"

Her head snapped up. "What do you mean someone like me?"

For the first time he smiled. Straight white teeth that gleamed right up into his gray eyes. "Take it easy, Cassie. You always act like you're ready to fight with me. I didn't mean it as an insult. More of a compliment." He raised his chin toward the closet.

"Grab your clothes. I have a place you can stay tonight and as soon as the area is clear we'll come back and move you out of here."

Her eyes widened. "I'm not staying with you." Although after looking at him in tight blue jeans and a polo shirt that clung to his body like skin, the idea didn't seem too repulsive. Maybe under different circumstances, in her former life.

But he was a cop and she was a fugitive.

He chuckled. "I didn't invite you to stay with me. Gather your stuff and be quick about it. I have a business proposition for you. I'll tell you when we're out of here."

She moved uncertainly toward the clothes closet. "I can't afford higher rent."

"Don't worry about it. Hurry up. We should get out of here."

She yanked her duffel bag from the closet shelf and tossed in all of her clothes. She tucked her laptop safely in between the jeans and shirts and moved into the bathroom for her cosmetics and a few linens, keenly aware that Clay watched every move. He looked away momentarily when the mantel clock chimed.

"Would you mind grabbing that, please? I don't want to leave it here."

He shook his head. "I can't let you out of my sight. Crime scene, remember? You'll have to take it."

"But the crime didn't happen here."

"That's a technicality, hon. Sorry." Her heart fluttered. *Hon.*

Within minutes, everything she owned was stashed in the duffel. She gingerly took the clock from the mantel, wrapped it in a bath towel and eased it into a shoulder bag.

"Anything else?"

"No."

"Do you have a pen?"

"In my purse." She reached in and retrieved a pen from The Packing Place. Clay picked up the duffel and slung it over his shoulder. He reached for the keys in her hand and locked the door, then turned and scrawled the time, the date, and his initials on the wall beside the door frame.

Back at his truck, he helped Cassidy inside then spoke to an officer, reviewed a page on a clipboard, and signed. As they drove slowly out of the parking lot, Clay nodded and waved to several different policemen. And then they were on the highway.

"Where are we going?"

He grinned. "You know, if I thought you had a sense of humor I'd say my place. But I don't think you'd appreciate the joke."

She sat up straight. "I have a sense of humor." The retort sounded childish, even to her.

"Really? We're going to my place."

"That's not funny."

He threw his head back and laughed. The sound sent tingles through her. "That's what I thought."

Even as he teased Cassidy about taking her home a pulse in his chest boomed, embracing the idea. What the hell? One restraining order was enough. No need to set himself up for another emotional disaster. When it came to women, he overextended himself, giving and expecting too much. And then he got screwed.

He wasn't going to lose everything again because of an irrational woman. Cassidy certainly fit that description. And he had more to lose this time. He needed to re-establish his distance, resurrect his impartiality. With most everybody, he'd mastered the technique.

He barely knew this woman, yet she had a baffling effect on

him. He'd been unable to stop thinking about her and now, with her next to him on the seat and their destination The Chalets, he did wish they were going back to his apartment. It had been quite some time since he'd wanted to bring a woman home. And this one wasn't the least bit interested in him. Yet he couldn't keep himself from stepping into her life.

She threw off vibes that said "don't touch," and even stronger signals that hinted she'd take off at the drop of a hat. She'd packed her duffel bag and it had practically emptied the apartment. Yet, she had nowhere to go. And he had no idea where she'd come from. Perhaps it was the mystery that intrigued him. Cop curiosity.

It didn't explain the jolt he felt when she grabbed his arm. That was more chemistry than curiosity, and it charged every part of his body, including the manly one. Been a while since a woman had affected him like that, too.

"How long have you lived there?"

She clutched the clock protectively in her lap, her gaze riveted on the windshield. "A little over a month."

"Where were you before this?"

Her head jerked up and she stared at him. "I'm originally from O'Hara Township. It's a suburb of Pittsburgh."

He raised a skeptical eyebrow. A clever answer. Amber was right, she was evasive. "Ah, I thought I detected a tinge of an accent. Are you a Steelers fan?"

She nodded.

"What brought you to Browns' territory?"

"I, ah, I needed a change. Where are you taking me?"

Hmm, change of subject. She was good at this.

"My sister and I own several apartment units, called The Chalets. You can stay in one of the vacant ones tonight. Do you have to work tomorrow?"

"Yes. It's my short day, ten to two. Where's the closest bus stop?"

"I should be home by nine at the latest. I'll run you in."

"Please, Mr. Cestra. I can't repay you for all of this. I still owe you fifty dollars for the furniture fiasco. I don't want any favors and I don't need your help."

"Clay."

"What?"

"Call me Clay. Mr. Cestra is my dad. He's in Florida."

They cruised into a parking lot and stopped in front of a five-story brown brick building decorated with flowering balconies. In the rear, off to the right, an identical building flanked the first one, connected by what appeared to be a lighted park area and a pavilion, from what she could see.

Clay checked his watch. "I'm running late. I'll place you in one of the semi-furnished apartments for tonight."

He wrinkled his forehead. "I'm pretty sure the sofa is a pull-out. Tomorrow, we'll talk to my sister and see about better accommodations."

"I can't stay here."

He raised his voice. "Well, Miss Hoake, where would you like to go? You can't stay at your apartment and you said yourself you have nowhere to go. Amber might take you in if you call her. Or you can sleep in my truck tonight. It will be parked outside a police station, so you'll be safe. You decide. But make it fast. I'm trying to be a nice guy here and it's going to make me late for work. Where would you like to go?"

Without waiting for an answer, he shoved open the driver's door and exited the truck. He walked around the front, yanked open the passenger door, and extended his hand.

She hadn't said a word.

"I thought so. C'mon. If it makes you happy, I'll charge you rent."

Avoiding his hand, she swung her legs from the cab and stepped down to the asphalt. This was a bad idea on so many levels, she told herself as she turned and reached for her clock. Her heart raced. Clay snatched her duffel bag from the truck and placed his hand on the small of her back, guiding her to a darkened sign that said Office.

"Wait here." He fished a key from his pocket, unlocked the door, and stepped inside. Thirty seconds later he was at her side, a ring of keys jingling in his hand. "This way."

Again, he directed her with his hand, moving her toward the rear building. His touch sent a thunderbolt through her body. Despite the cool evening temperature, she dabbed at tiny beads of sweat above her lip and yanked at the collar of her pullover, hoping for a quick shot of cool air. Maybe she had a fever.

They walked along an in-ground swimming pool and passed several picnic tables. She saw a second pavilion and a handful of freestanding charcoal grills. Giant urns of flowers bloomed everywhere, having survived the summer heat, and now thriving in September's temperatures.

A couple sitting beside a fire pit that burned bright waved to Clay and he acknowledged them with a return gesture. "This is the common area for residents," he said.

They arrived at the front door of the second building and he unlocked it, motioning for her to enter. Climbing the stairs to the second floor, he guided her to a door at the end of the hall. Unlocking it, he signaled with his hand for her to precede him inside.

She blinked when he switched on the ceiling light.

"It's been closed up for a couple weeks." He opened the sliding glass door to the balcony. "Some fresh air will help. Remember, it's just for tonight."

He disappeared into a room toward the rear. The apartment was sparsely furnished but nicer than the one she rented. A small oval table sat in front of a long floral sofa and an overstuffed chair. To her left, a three-person kitchenette set snuggled against the wall of a long rectangular kitchen.

Clay emerged from the back room. "I didn't think there was a bed here. Sorry. The bedroom is unfurnished. I can pull out the sofa bed for you."

She lifted her hand to stop him. "No. That's all right. Thank you. Whose apartment is this?"

"Mr. and Mrs. Hayes lived here for two years but he developed health issues so they moved to an assisted-living facility. I plan to repaint it before we lease it again."

He strode into the kitchen and she heard cabinet doors opening and closing. "There are a few dishes and some utensils. But no food in the pantry. I'll bring you coffee in the morning. I'm afraid this is the best I can do for now."

"I'll be fine. All I need is a glass of water. Like you said, it's just one night."

He arched his right eyebrow. "It wouldn't surprise me if you took off the minute I left."

She gasped. She'd been thinking she should.

Clay cleared his throat. "I can't make you stay. But I think you should. You can't live out of that duffel bag forever." He turned and walked to the door. "If you do take off, make sure you shut the balcony door, and please lock this door behind you. I'm gonna be late. See ya."

He closed the door behind him and she stood in the middle of the room, where she had stopped upon entering. A cool breeze wafted in from the balcony and somewhere, a horn honked. She wrapped herself in her arms and slowly made a three hundred-and-sixty degree turn. This place wasn't nearly as frightening as the dump she lived in. In fact, it almost felt safe.

If she left now, she could jump on the bus and go . . . where? She had no idea. She couldn't go home to Pittsburgh. Tony DelMorrie would surely have her brother's neighborhood staked out by now. She was estranged from her brother anyhow. He'd disapproved of her relocating to Arizona, calling it a foolish whim, and they hadn't spoken since.

Likewise, her best friend had not heard from her since before the shooting and Cassidy didn't dare call for fear Tony DelMorrie would somehow find out.

She couldn't go back in the direction she'd come and risk running into him. North? South? Another bus ride to the unknown? Another disguise? Another job?

She sank to the floor and caught her head in her hands. Clay was right. She couldn't run forever. At least here, she could save some money and take a break from running. Temporarily. As long as no one found out who she was and what she knew.

She crawled to the duffel bag beside the entrance and reached inside for her laptop. Her stomach sank as if she'd swallowed a stone when she couldn't access the Internet. Wireless access in The Chalets required a password. She snapped the computer lid closed.

It was like hoping to win the lottery, wishing that the Arizona authorities would catch Tony DelMorrie. But those commercials always advertised that it only takes one ticket to win. Would it only take one slip-up to catch the man who was after her? Please God, let it be so.

7

He wondered how Cassidy had fared as he made his way to her unit the next morning carrying two cups of coffee. He knocked lightly.

"Cassidy?" No answer. Dammit. He knocked harder.

"Cassidy? It's Clay Cestra." He saw her distorted eyeball through the peephole then heard the chain lock slide and she opened the door, dressed in The Packing Place uniform. One corner of his mouth edged upward as he extended a cup toward her. He stepped forward, leaving her no choice but to back up and let him in.

"I didn't know how you liked your coffee. I have sugar and cream packets in my pocket."

She looked at him wide eyed, like a frightened puppy.

Remembering his conversation with Maggie last night when he called to inform his sister of their new guest, he blurted out, "Did you have soap?"

"Excuse me?"

He walked to the coffee table and emptied his pockets to include two stirrers. "My sister read me the riot act for not making sure you had soap."

"Oh. It's okay. I used shampoo."

She selected one sugar and one powdered creamer and dumped them in the steaming cup. "Thank you."

"Did you sleep okay?"

"Fine, thank you."

"So how come you didn't run?"

She gasped and stared at him. Bingo. He'd hit a homerun with that one. The coffee cup jiggled in her hand.

"If you give me an answer, I promise not to ask any more questions, at least not this morning. What made you stay?"

She glanced down at the carpet, looked out toward the balcony, lowered her eyes to her feet then leveled her gaze on him. "I didn't know where to go."

He took a deep breath, releasing it slowly along with the tension that had knotted his neck muscles wondering most of the night if she would bolt. "Okay. That's a start. C'mon, I'll drive you to work."

"What about my stuff?"

"You can leave it here."

"But you can get in here while I'm gone."

"So?" She straightened her spine. "So, I don't want you going through my things."

He smiled. She really was smart.

"That's pretty good. To be honest, I hadn't thought of that." He snapped to attention, held up his hand like he did when he was a Boy Scout, and recited, slowly, "I promise not to come in here while you're at work. Cross my heart." His finger made the sign on his chest. "C'mon, we gotta go."

Cassidy didn't move. He opened the door, turned to her expectantly then shook his head. "You have to trust somebody, Cassidy. It might as well be me. If you don't move your feet, you're going to be late."

Reluctantly, she walked out the door and he locked it behind them. They drove to The Packing Place in silence. "I'll pick you up at two."

She turned to him after jumping out of the truck. "I can take a bus."

Clay swore under his breath, shifted into gear, and drove off.

Rosie stood at the front counter when she entered the store. "I thought you rode the bus."

"Yes, I do."

Rosie's lips bunched together in a pucker. "Wasn't that Amber's boyfriend's truck you just climbed out of?"

Cassidy's heart jumped. "Who?"

"Amber's boyfriend. That city policeman. He was in last week asking for her. He called her on his way out of the store. I've heard Amber talk about him, and some of the girls told me she brags about being in his backseat. He's not even man enough to take her to a motel. If I were you, I wouldn't get mixed up with him."

She avoided looking at Rosie. "I'm not mixed up with him. I met him at the Greenbrier store. He's in most mornings. He was riding by the bus stop when I got off and he picked me up." Did that sound convincing? Rosie wasn't listening anyway.

"Well, you might just want to walk next time. You don't know what kind of man he is."

Those words replayed in her mind the rest of the day. Rosie was right. She didn't know what kind of man Clay Cestra was. What kind of man took in a total stranger? Offered to haul furniture for her? Chanced his own career so she could collect her meager belongings from a crime scene to sleep some place safe?

Indeed, she'd felt safe last night. For the first time in months she'd fallen asleep on the couch and not awakened in the middle of the night perspiring. What kind of a man was Clay Cestra?

"You have to trust somebody, Cassidy. It might as well be me," he'd said. But she didn't know him. And something her mother taught her once always stayed with her: "Better the devil you know than the devil you don't."

She knew her demon. He was wealthy, politically connected, a suspected mobster, a killer. She knew who she was running from. She didn't know Clay Cestra. If she trusted him, who was she running to?

Could she afford to trust him? Did she dare let her guard down, let someone close to her? Would he be willing to help her? Could she hope for more? Would she want more?

Another unanswered question plagued her — was he involved with Amber?

Two months of solitude were taking their toll. She'd relied solely on herself for so long, Clay extending a helping hand baffled her. Should she reach out and take it? Would she thrust him and Amber in danger if she did?

Whatever his relationship with Amber, it didn't seem wise for him to pick her up in front of the store for Rosie's spying eyes to see. As soon as she found the chance, Cassidy dialed the Greenbrier store.

"Amber, I have a favor to ask, but I don't have time now to explain why."

Amber laughed. "If you want me to kill Rosie, I already know why."

"Do you know how to reach Clay Cestra?" Her question was met with silence.

"I can't tell you why right now, but he planned to give me a ride when my shift is over. Except, I don't want him to and I especially don't want Rosie to see him over here. I have to leave a message for him. I'll take the bus. I don't want him to come here this afternoon."

"Well, chickie. I can probably get a message to him, but it's going to cost you."

"Please, Amber. It's important."

"If you didn't sound so serious, I'd make you tell me now. You work at Greenbrier next week and you'll spill all the beans about this. Deal?"

"I'm at Greenbrier next week with you?" At last, a bit of good news.

"Yeah. Didn't you see the new schedule? You're here all month. I gotta hang up, we've got customers lined up to the door. I'll get your message to C.C."

Maybe Rosie was right. If Amber knew how to reach Clay, conceivably they could be involved. That didn't matter right now. She couldn't believe her good fortune. She'd be working the whole month with Amber and not Rosie. Perhaps that explained Rosie's acerbic mood.

With Rosie watching, she clocked out at two o'clock and headed toward the bus stop. Just one block from the store a horn blew and she spotted Clay's emerald green truck parked at the curb. He leaned across the seat and shoved the door open.

"What are you doing here?" She hesitated then climbed into the truck.

"Your message said not to pick you up in front of the store. Did the old biddy give you grief this morning?"

"I didn't . . . yes, she made some sour remarks."

"I'll bet. What'd you tell her?"

"I said I rode the bus and you spotted me at the stop. I don't think she likes you."

"She's not the first. Did you eat lunch?"

Cassidy turned to him. She'd ignored her growling stomach for the last two hours. A stale pack of peanut butter crackers she'd discovered on the shelf by the mini-fridge had not taken the edge off her lack of real food since yesterday. That is if you considered peanut butter and jelly an entrée that counted as real food.

"Um, I had something, yes."

"That's what I thought." He flipped the turn signal on, cruised about fifty feet, and turned into a fast food parking lot. "Are you going to tell me what you'd like for lunch or shall I order for you?"

"Really, I . . ." The glare he leveled at her halted her objection. "I'd like a cheeseburger, small fries, and a diet pop. Thank you."

He extended his right leg while keeping his foot on the brake and slid his hand inside his front pants pocket. Bulging thigh muscles stretched the denim material taut around his leg and held her attention like magnets to steel. Reluctantly redirecting her eyes, she leaned forward toward her purse.

"Don't worry. I'm paying."

She scowled in protest.

"All right, then, I'll put it on your tab."

"When are you going to present me with this phantom tab?"

"Don't worry about it."

He ordered food for both of them, then maneuvered to a vacant parking spot in proximity of several picnic tables. He keyed off the ignition and climbed out of the driver's seat, balancing their take-out order and moving toward the nearest empty table.

Clay turned when Cassidy remained inside the truck and stared at her, finally forcing her to join him. Silently, he pushed her food order to her side of the table and took a bite from his burger.

The aroma from the fries fueled her hunger pangs. She surveyed her surroundings, scrutinizing the cars going through the takeout window, stared across the street at the car dealer's lot, and studied the passing traffic. Throwing one leg over the bench, she sat and unwrapped her meal. After the first glorious bite, she shoved three fries into her mouth. She didn't regularly eat fast food, but this was heaven.

Glancing around a second time, she squared her shoulders and enjoyed a second delicious taste, mindful of Clay's eyes on her.

"Are you married?" The question surprised her.

"No."

Thankfully, he didn't pursue the subject. They finished their lunch in silence, tossed their trash, and returned to his truck. The food calmed her nervous stomach, but she chanced one last look at the cars coming and going. Clay started the engine and shifted into reverse, locking the doors.

"Who were you watching for?"

Her head jerked around. "What?"

He smiled, creating laugh lines around his eyes. "You were all over that parking lot, checking out the cars, looking at the traffic, watching the sidewalks. Watching. Waiting. For who?"

"No one."

He shook his head slowly, eased his foot off the brake, and the truck edged backward. Without another question asked, they drove onto the highway and toward the Cestra Chalets. He parked in front of the first building but didn't shut off the engine, keeping the doors locked.

He twisted his hands and clasped them palm to palm, locking his fingers, and stretched his arms leisurely across the steering wheel toward the windshield.

"Cassidy Hoake. I ran your name in the police database, but I didn't find anything." She stopped breathing, tasting terror on her tongue, her heart beating a tune of panic in her ears.

Returning both hands to the wheel, he riveted his eyes on her. "You're not in trouble in Ohio as near as I can tell. But I suspect you're in some kind of trouble. I will ask you one question and I want an honest yes or no answer because if I find out you lied to me, you'll quickly learn what hell is."

She gulped. She couldn't tear her gaze away from his.

"Did you commit a crime?" Tears rimmed her eyes.

"Tell me the truth, Cassidy." His voice boomed.

She swallowed. "No sir. I did not."

"But you are in trouble?"

She couldn't find her stronger voice, so she whispered, "You said one question."

He smiled again and exhaled. "You're correct. I did." He turned the key and the truck stopped running. The automatic locks shot up.

"Okay, I guess the answer to that one will have to wait. Let's go talk to my sister. We have a job offer for you."

Her jaw dropped.

"Don't get too excited. You can't quit The Packing Place. It's grunt work mostly. But the pay is a place to stay. C'mon."

Once again he waited for her at the front of the truck and placed his hand on the small of her back as they walked. Compared to her five-foot-one frame she guessed he was at least six-foot-two. Well built, like most cops.

Clay knocked and the door swung open. A tall, slender woman with long, dark hair and gray eyes that matched Clay's stood in the doorway with a baby wearing a miniature scarlet and gray football uniform perched on her hip. The baby squealed at the sight of Clay and extended small arms with dimpled elbows.

Cassidy couldn't help but smile when Clay reached for the baby, swung him to the ceiling then cradled him in his arms.

"Mags, this is Cassidy Hoake. This is my sister, Maggie Armstrong." Maggie extended her hand and offered a warm smile.

"Come in, please. Excuse the mess."

They stepped into a two-foot entry that opened into a sprawling living area peppered with baby toys and a bright, multi-colored portable play yard in the center of the room.

Maggie smiled at her. "Come sit at the table. It's the only clean spot." Despite the clutter, Cassidy noticed the home was spotless.

"May I offer you some iced tea?"

"I'm fine, thank you."

"Yeah, Mags. We'll both have some tea, please." Clay dragged a chair out and motioned for Cassidy to sit. "Jesus, Cassidy, it's not going to kill you to take a free glass of freakin' tea."

Stunned, Cassidy dropped into the designated chair and picked at an imaginary thread on the pink daisy placemat. Clay sat to her right, their elbows touching, and plopped the baby on the table, facing him. He seemed so at ease with an infant.

Maggie returned with two tall, ice-filled tea glasses, walked back into the kitchen then joined them with her own glass. She slid a spill-proof cup toward Clay, but he was keeping the baby entertained with belly smooches. The women smiled at the scene.

"How long have you been in town, Cassidy?" Hers was a wide, friendly smile that lit up her entire face. Cassidy had only seen Clay smile a handful of times.

"Um, I've worked at The Packing Place for almost a month now."

"Oh. Do you like it?"

How many times did she nestle someone's valuables safely between bubble wrap and packing peanuts and ship them away to a happier place wishing as she did that she could wrap herself in a protective cocoon and ship Cassidy Hoake to a safe, happy place? The thought occurred to her every day. She glanced at Clay but he was all about the baby.

"I'm getting better at it." She halted her bouncing right knee.

"Oh." Maggie looked at Clay, who ignored her as well, then returned her gaze to Cassidy. "Has Clay told you what we'd like you to do?"

"Um, no, not really." Maggie lifted her glass, eyed Cassidy, and sipped her tea. "Clay, why don't you take Jack for a walk? Leave us girls to talk."

Clay straightened and looked surprised, but Maggie insisted. "Go. You make Cassidy nervous and you're making me nervous. Take my son and go do man things." She waved her hand toward the door.

Unceremoniously dismissed, Clay hoisted the baby in his arms, snatched the sipping cup, and Cassidy watched them walk away. Rosie's words echoed in her ears: You don't know what kind of man he is.

What kind of man exuded that much love for a baby not even his own? The best kind. That much she knew.

Maggie folded her hands and leveled a steady gaze on Cassidy. She smiled that wonderful smile again.

"My brother likes you."

Cassidy jerked her head around.

"It's been some time since he's shown an interest in a woman. I'm glad to see it. But let's talk about you for now. Clay tells me you live on Fortieth Street."

Maggie's words continued to roll around in her brain. *My brother likes you.* She nodded.

"That's a terrible place. I can't imagine what led you to end up there. It must be something horrible."

Cassidy's breath stalled. Was this woman psychic?

Maggie continued. "I'm not going to pry." She winked. "Well, I probably will eventually. But for now, here's the proposition I — rather we — have for you. Clay tells me you work every day, but it's essentially a part-time job and that your schedule changes. That will be easy to work around."

Maggie laid out everything Cassidy would be expected to do —painting, cleaning, gardening, office duties, grocery shopping, errand running, "and, if I really learn to trust you, babysitting. Dan and I could use a night together once in a while without our son. Clay takes the baby sometimes, but I never totally relax when he has him. Women are instinctively better with babies, I think. But that won't be for a while.

"You have to prove yourself before I trust you with Jack. In return, you stay here rent free, all utilities paid, in a two-bedroom furnished apartment. You'll have to buy your groceries, although once I know you, you'll certainly be welcome to eat with us occasionally. Dan is a sergeant at the same police department where Clay works, did you know that? They were partners until I came into the picture."

She held up her left hand and wiggled her ring finger, grinning. "Now, they are brothers-in-law.

"There are a lot of times when it's simply Jack and I at home. It would be nice having another woman around."

Cassidy stared at her, dumbfounded.

Maggie didn't seem to notice. "You should know that I would kill for my son, my husband, or my brother. Without a moment's hesitation. I know how to shoot and I know how to defend myself. That is the sole warning I will give you.

"Here's what I know about you. My brother likes you. That, to me, speaks volumes. You're in some type of trouble. Dan and Clay haven't figured out what kind yet. Oh, don't look so startled. They are damn good cops.

"You need a friend, I think, or in our case, friends. And Clay wants you out of that dump you're in. So, it's time for you to make a choice. Come work for me as my lackey, pretty much, and stay here. The rest will work itself out if you let us help."

Cassidy's eyes brimmed. "You are so kind. But you don't know what you're asking. You don't know what you could be opening yourself up for." Without warning, tears began to stream down her face. She removed her glasses and laid them on the placemat.

Maggie reached across the table and clutched her hands. "Can you talk about it?"

"I, I can't."

"Will you keep danger from my door?"

"If I stay here, I can't promise that. It's best I leave." The tears wouldn't stop.

Maggie studied her, clinging to her hands. She released an audible breath.

"Is it your plan to hide forever?"

Cassidy withdrew her hands from Maggie's grasp and

dropped her head into them. She began to sob. "I don't know. I don't know."

Maggie waited for the flood of emotion to subside. She produced a box of tissues and Cassidy blew her nose. A few more gut-wrenching sobs and she'd regained control. But the weight of her burden aged her, if not visibly on the outside, inside, deep within her bones, weighing her down like a one-hundred-year-old woman too weak to make another move. She raised her head and regarded Maggie through eyes wearied by all that she had seen.

"You probably needed that. Feel better?"

Cassidy nodded.

"Can you tell me, in the most generic terms, what the problem is?" Cassidy remained silent.

"I think Dan and Clay will help, whatever it is." She grinned, trying to keep the moment casual. "But, if it's really bad, I'm rescinding my job offer."

Cassidy sniffled. "It's really bad."

"Tell me."

She hadn't talked about it. Not since that woman's body had collapsed beside fuel pump number four. Not since she'd seen him, recognized him, knew that he knew, and watched, as if in first gear, his left arm rise to shoulder level. She'd looked down the barrel of a gun, with only a window separating her from the bullet. It was frightening as hell.

She ducked just as the service station window exploded and the earsplitting sound of a gunshot deafened her. She'd scrambled on her hands and knees, her nose running, her pulse racing, out the back door. Another shot, shattering the sound barrier in her ears.

Stumbling on all fours, crawling toward a garbage dumpster, her purse dragging along on her arm, she'd prayed, 'Dear God. Dear God."

She hadn't talked about it since that phone call from the

detective informing her that her life was in danger, as calm as if he were giving her the weather prediction for the next day.

"He made bail, ma'am. We've lost track of him."

It hadn't occurred to her at first that she would be his target. She sensed it after that first hang up call. She acknowledged it as a fact hours later when her car exploded in the driveway of her townhouse. And she took off, abandoning her job, her home, and her life. She'd been a certified public accountant in a prominent firm, with eyes on a partnership someday. Maybe that was why she now gravitated toward positions behind a cash register.

She'd had three jobs since she fled the gas station, worn two different disguises through four states, always ready to run, always looking over her shoulder. She was exhausted. Bone tired. Nevertheless, she couldn't stop. She took a ragged breath.

"Thank you, Maggie, but I can't stay here. I thought I could, thought maybe I might take a break from running. But anyone I let close will be in jeopardy. I won't do that to you, your son, or Amber." Her heartbeat quickened. "Or your brother. I'm sorry."

Maggie stood. "Please don't make that decision tonight, Cassidy. Consider staying. You'll be safe here. And when you're ready, Dan and Clay will help you do what you need to do. If you let them, they can give you your life back."

Her stomach jumped at the suggestion. Would she ever have her life back?

"Thanks Maggie, but I can't."

Maggie stiffened and her expression turned stern, like a school principal's. "I see. All right. Do you know where you will go?"

Her heart sank. "No." She hung her head.

"Do you have any money?"

One paycheck cashed for her first two weeks on the job, totaling sixty-three hours at minimum wage. And she still owed Clay fifty dollars out of tomorrow's check. "A little."

"Do you have a plan beyond leaving here and running?"

She lacked the courage to answer.

"So what good is it going to do to take off, Cassidy? At least here you're safe for the time being. If nothing else, you can tuck away a little money. And maybe realize you have friends."

"You don't even know me. How can you offer that?"

Maggie revealed a slow, deliberate smile. "Didn't you ever meet someone and know immediately you liked them? I have. More importantly, I think Clay has."

In another lifetime he'd be the prince of her dreams. She shook her head, denying it. "I can only bring trouble to your home."

"Or, we can bring help to yours. Depends on how you look at things. Consider this, Cassidy. Right now, police could be waiting for you outside. My telling Clay to leave could have been a ploy for him to call them."

Cassidy rushed to the sliding glass door. Clay stood near the front entrance on the sidewalk speaking with two elderly women, the baby obviously the center of attention. She turned when she heard Maggie open the apartment door.

"Make your choice. Trust us or take off. I don't know what mistakes you made before you arrived here. But if you run, you have to blow past that man out there. And I do know that would be a big mistake."

8

S he stayed.

Only temporarily. Only until she could build a nest egg and figure out where to go next. That was the deal she made with Maggie and herself. She neglected to include the caveat that Tony DelMorrie could disrupt her plans and send her dashing into the middle of the night to who knows where. Maggie didn't need to know that part.

Clay returned to the apartment, smiled briefly when Maggie informed him that Cassidy had agreed to the arrangement, and then took control.

He suggested a small, two-bedroom unit, but when she objected, saying two bedrooms was excessive, he opted for the Thompsons' former apartment, one floor above his living quarters.

"We can't get into your old place, yet. Maybe tomorrow. But I can show you where you'll be and you can make a grocery list for whatever you'll need. You might as well start today. Maggie, if you have a shopping list Cassidy can handle it."

Newly hired and already, a loser. "I, um, I don't have a car."

"Oh yeah, I forgot. No license either. Well, I'll run you to the store, show you where it is, point out the hardware store where we have an account for our supplies, things like that." He turned to his sister. "What's on my list for today, anything Cassidy can help me with?"

Her stomach executed a perfect one-and-a-half gainer. Was she supposed to be Maggie's personal assistant or his? It sounded like she would be both. It wasn't the labor she minded. It was the man. Already she grew giddy when she saw him, when he smiled at her, when his hand lay so naturally on her back. His touch was like a hot lava rock. She had to keep reminding herself he was a cop and quite possibly Amber's boyfriend, although Maggie made it sound as if he didn't have a girlfriend. Perhaps, as his sister, she was unaware of Clay's private life.

She gasped when he opened the door to her new home. Gorgeous cherry-stained hardwood floors spilled from a full kitchen into a small dining area, where a round oak table and four oak chairs were stationed beneath a chandelier that twinkled in the afternoon sunlight streaming in from the balcony doors. Where the hardwood halted, plush chocolate carpet spread throughout the room, marked with vacuum tracks in the pile. The carpet stretched from the sand-colored walls of the furnished living room into a bedroom where a double bed with headboard, matching bureau, and chest shined from furniture polish.

A full bath opened off of the bedroom, decorated in bright greens and yellows. She stared at the double sink and jet tub. She hadn't enjoyed a bubble bath in months.

She turned wide eyes to Clay, who stood uncomfortably close behind her, so close she could feel his body heat. "You want me to stay here?"

"Don't you like it?"

"Are you kidding? It's beautiful. Wouldn't you rather lease it and collect rent money? I could never afford this."

"Don't worry. You'll earn it. Let's get your stuff from last night. Then we'll hit the grocery store. Maggie always needs diapers."

For the next three hours they were side by side, walking through the grocery store, stopping in the hardware store, picking up his uniforms at the dry cleaners, and making a bank deposit. Clay explained her job more fully. He wanted her priority to be helping Maggie with whatever she needed, but he also expected her to clean vacant apartments, help him paint and clean carpets, and whatever easier maintenance tasks popped up.

"The more active Jack becomes, the more help she'll need. Maggie will work around your schedule. You'll have time for yourself to socialize. But there is a waiting list for these units, so sometimes the turnaround has to be quick. Occasionally, it might eat up your whole weekend."

She smiled. "That's not going to make a difference."

He regarded her with one eyebrow raised. "Why is that?"

"I really don't have a social life."

"Why?"

She reached for the truck's door handle. "This isn't going to work if you're always interrogating me." Damn. He hadn't turned off the key yet and she was locked in the truck with him. She twisted to reach the lock, but the seatbelt crossing her chest held her tight.

"All right, I'm sorry. I didn't mean it to sound like an interrogation. I'm simply curious about you, that's all. You intrigue me."

She caught her breath. "That's not a good idea."

He shrugged. "Probably not. C'mon."

Maggie had bed linens, paper towels, and soap ready when Cassidy returned. She'd purchased a few items for her own pantry—peanut butter and jelly, wheat bread, milk, butter, and coffee after Clay said the unit had a coffee pot. He'd tossed lettuce, ranch dressing, carrots, tomatoes, a multipack of instant soups, a variety pack of cereals, popcorn, and a container of ice cream in the cart, all which he unloaded in her apartment. He held up his hands when she protested and said it would go on her tab.

"I didn't need ice cream."

He propped his hands on his hips. "Don't tell me you don't like ice cream. That's un-American. How are you going to make a milkshake without ice cream? You like milkshakes, don't you?"

She laughed. "Yes. Chocolate. But we didn't buy syrup."

He winked, causing her heart to skip. "I'll pick some up tomorrow. Keep a list of other things you forgot. We can make another store run tomorrow. What time do you have to be at work?"

"I don't return until Monday morning at eight. I'm at the Greenbrier store with Amber for the next few weeks. I should figure out the closest bus stop to here and check the schedule. And," she tried to sound casual, "I was wondering about Internet access. Is there somewhere close where I can use my laptop?"

He nodded. "We offer that for our tenants. I'll give you the password." He ignored her inquiry about the nearest bus stop. Instead, he walked to a wall and straightened a brightly painted picture of a garden with a white picket gate. He seemed hesitant to leave.

"How'd you get the name Cassidy? I don't think I've ever heard anyone called that before." They stood in the center of her new living room. Outside, daylight had faded to dark. This was surreal, chatting with him as if it were an everyday occurrence. She liked it.

"If I tell you, you'll only laugh at me."

He smiled, crinkling his eyes. She'd seen that smile often today and it warmed her. "Well, I can always use a good laugh. Tell me."

"My dad claimed to be a descendent of Neil Watt McIntyre Cuthbert. He's the man who shot Hopalong Cassidy in the left leg."

His smile broadened into a wide grin. "You're kidding, right?"

"Nope. I was going to be his last child and he was determined to name me Cassidy."

Clay cleared his throat. "Uh, you do know that Hopalong Cassidy was a fictional cowboy, don't you?"

She rolled her eyes. She really should create another reason for having her name. No one ever believed her.

"I know that and you know that. But my dad insisted that Mr. Neil Watt McIntyre Cuthbert was a real person whom the author used for his character in the comic books and movies. And he insisted he was some great-great-great descendent."

Now Clay laughed outright. "You're right, that's funny. Maybe I'll call you Hoppy for short."

She laughed, too, another thing she hadn't done in a long while. "Please don't."

"Where's your dad now? I'd like to hear the longer version of this story."

Her smile disappeared and she dropped her gaze to the floor. "He died when I was little."

"I'm sorry." The silence between them grew awkward. "Well, I better go. See you tomorrow. If you need something that can't wait until then, call me." He handed her a business card with a police badge embossed in the right corner and his contact information printed in royal blue beside it. Flipping it over, she noted his cell number handwritten on the back.

She bolted the door behind him, turned and leaned against it, staring at the card in her hand. What the hell was she doing?

Clay leaned against the wall outside Cassidy's apartment door and squeezed his eyes shut. What the hell was he doing? The last thing he needed was a relationship.

He could tell himself that Cassidy was in some sort of trouble and that he simply wanted to help. A police officer was, after all, a public servant.

He could tell himself that he only thought about her every other hour last night because he was convinced she would bolt and he hoped if she did, she locked the apartment behind her.

He might convince himself that spending the afternoon with her running simple errands hadn't been the most fun he'd had in a year or that, once she relaxed, they weren't extremely compatible. Hell, he'd been as comfortable with her as with Maggie, only he enjoyed being with Cassidy so much more.

She had an arousing effect on him, standing in the middle of the room laughing and talking about chocolate. Jesus, his craving came to attention against his will. Maybe it had been a while since he got laid, but his body reacted as if it were possessed by a teenager with raging hormones. Even as he walked from her floor down to his, an erection throbbed behind his zipper.

Cassidy was so different from his ex-wife. Lauren reeked of self-confidence and assumed control in any situation. Aided by her six-foot frame, which allowed her to tower over most women and face men eye-to-eye, Lauren operated on the assumption that the world was hers and she allowed you to live in it.

Even in bed she'd dictated the action, regularly taking top and pacing the encounter to suit her needs. The act had ceased to be enjoyable for him three months into their marriage. It wasn t long afterward that he'd depreciated to an accessory in her world, someone to escort her to dinners and service her needs, someone to fight and make-up with, someone to swing at.

He flexed his left hand opened, closed, opened wider, closed. The divorce had publicly humiliated her and she'd sworn vengeance. She'd attempted murder.

Cassidy and Lauren were like sun and snow. Thinking about Lauren chilled his heart and his ardor. For now, that was a good thing. He had time to call Maggie and then he had to roll to work.

After tonight's midnight shift, however, he was off until Monday. Just like Cassidy.

9

Cassidy stretched, luxuriating in the smell of the fresh sheets and the support of a firm mattress. She hadn't slept as soundly since she'd left home, her real home, the one where her mother and brother slept right down the hall. Dreamily, she glanced around the room then let her eyelids slide closed again.

She smiled, heard the noise, and bolted upright. A rhythmic tapping, coming from the living room. She blinked the remainder of sleep from her eyes and aimed her ear in that direction. Knocking. Someone was knocking.

She glanced at the digital clock on the nightstand and exclaimed out loud. It was after nine.

Barefoot, she ran to the door to peek out. Clay stood in the hallway. Opening the door a crack she inserted her face into the gap.

"Hey! I don't have your number so I couldn't call. Are you still asleep?"

"Can you give me a minute?"

He smiled. "Sure, let me in. I brought you coffee."

She slid the safety chain and opened the door. Clay strolled into the living room, turned, and furrowed his brow at the sight of her sweatshirt and jeans.

"Did you just wake up? You look like you slept in your clothes."

"Yeah, I, ah, kind of fell asleep in them last night and was too lazy to get up and take them off. Excuse me. I'll be right back."

She hurried to the bathroom, washed her face, brushed her teeth, and slipped into a clean T-shirt. She finger-combed her hair, grabbed her glasses from the sink and returned to the living area. Clay sat at the table sipping his coffee.

He held out her cup as she approached. "Thanks."

"You'll have to give me your cell number. I could have called first. I thought you'd be up. We have a little work to do today."

She ran her hand through her hair. "I don't usually sleep this late. I don't usually sleep well at all. I just kind of died last night."

"It's probably a lot quieter here than your other place."

She nodded.

"I've already had breakfast, but you have time to eat. We're cleaning a vacant one bedroom and I'll show you how to vacuum the pool. It's cool, so I doubt anyone will be using it today, but we don't close it until the end of the month and until then it has to be maintained. While you're doing that, I'll wrestle with a clogged drain. Then we can work on the vacancy."

"I don't need breakfast. I can start now."

"There is a toaster in the kitchen and I saw you buy bread. Have a piece of toast and then we'll start." He stood to leave.

"We can run over to your old apartment tonight and get the rest of your things unless you have plans."

With who, she wanted to ask. She shook her head.

"Good. Then it's a date. I'll meet you at the pool in about a half-hour."

Dutifully, she toasted a piece of bread, but she barely tasted it. "It's a date." He had to have meant it as a figure of speech, but her heart had catapulted to her throat when he said it, making it hard to swallow her breakfast.

She washed the plate and knife and stacked them in the drainer. Grabbing her hoodie, she slipped into her tennis shoes and walked to the pool. Clay was in the outbuilding. He'd donned a sweatshirt as well and wore ass-hugging jeans. Mentally, she shook the image away.

He explained how to assemble the pieces and force the air out of the hose, and then demonstrated how to vacuum the pool floor. The key was not to break the suction. There was something therapeutic about rolling the triangular vacuum head across the bottom, picking up bits of debris and bugs with each swipe.

Ahead of the brush lay a dark, dirty surface but behind it, the plane was wiped clean, like a second chance at a new life. Was that what Clay was, a mechanism to clean up her past? Her second chance?

Yesterday, telling him the origin of her name and laughing with him about it, she'd relaxed and forgotten her fear of his occupation or his motives. He'd simply been a man she was attracted to. She couldn't deny that. She'd been mildly disappointed when she finally closed the door behind him. He hadn't seemed like he wanted to leave and she hadn't wanted him to.

Now, today, they'd be spending hours together. And tonight he'd offered to take her back to Fortieth Street. If he was free on a Saturday night, why wasn't he spending it with Amber?

"Nice job."

She jumped at his words.

"I'll show you where to stow this equipment, then we can hit the vacant." Within minutes, they were walking to the first building and Clay was explaining their tasks.

"It was painted before the former tenants moved in and they were here only for a year. They retired to Marco Island. We don't have to repaint, but the walls need wiped down, the kitchen should be thoroughly scrubbed, everything needs swiped clean, and then we'll shampoo the carpets. How about if you start in the kitchen? Clean all the appliances, swab out the cupboards, and shine the counter. I'll take the two bathrooms then start on the walls."

This was another lushly carpeted two-bedroom, partially furnished unit that already looked clean enough to occupy. But Cassidy bent to the task of spit-polishing the kitchen. More than an hour later, she emerged looking for Clay. The afternoon light highlighted a cobweb swinging from a return air vent high in the ceiling corner over built-in book shelves. She relocated the stepladder Clay used earlier to replace a light bulb and wedged it into the corner.

If she stretched, she could clean the vent with the duster. She climbed the ladder, nearing the top and leaned to reach, but she was too far away. If she stood on the top step, she might reach it, but there was nothing to balance her from there.

"Whoa. Please be careful," Clay said, coming into the room.

"I can almmmooost reee-ach this but . . ."

"Stop before you lose your balance." Clay walked up behind her and grabbed the sides of the ladder. "The wall will keep you from falling forward, but you could tumble backward. I'll brace you from behind but be careful."

The ladder swayed slightly when he stepped on the bottom rung and then two strong hands took a firm grasp of each of her thighs. She stepped on the top of the ladder, braced her hand on the wall, and tried to dismiss the electrical charge shooting up her legs. Through her jeans she could discern all ten of his fingers supporting her and she imagined what it would be like to have them creep north, slowly to her . . .

"You okay up there?"

"Um, yeah. I got it cleaned."

"Thanks. I won't move. Step down one at a time, carefully, please."

She began her descent, cautiously lowering her left foot to the next rung, then easing her right into place, acutely aware of Clay's hands running along her sides as she descended. By the third step, the tops of her legs and her butt skimmed Clay's chest.

"One more step," he uttered in a raspy voice.

She led with her right foot this time, brushing his thigh and sinking into the circle created by his arms when she settled her other foot. Unless he moved, she could go no farther. Heat from his body caressed her back and his breath brushed her left ear.

"Don't do that again, please." He whispered with his nose buried in her hair. "I don't want you to get hurt."

Cassidy tightened her grip on the ladder and closed her eyes. If she leaned back the tiniest smidge, she'd have total contact with him, against his chest, wrapped in his arms.

His mouth remained at her ear. "We both worked hard today. If things were different, I'd suggest we take a shower right now."

Goose bumps pimpled her skin and her stomach somersaulted.

"Maybe another time," he suggested. Then he hauled her backward into his embrace, lifted her feet off the ladder rung, and stepped down to the floor. His grip eased and she stepped out of his arms.

"All we have left is to shampoo the carpet. That won't take me long. What if we get cleaned up and go grab something to eat, then we can swing by Fortieth Street and get the rest of your things."

Her pulse pounded in her ears. Despite his attempt to sound casual, his cheeks were flushed.

She felt the urge to flirt. "Are we cleaning up together or separately?"

Just as she'd hoped, she caught him off guard. His head snapped up, his eyes widened, and his cheeks transformed into red beets.

She raised both hands, laughing. "Just kidding."

He grinned. "Too bad. I wasn't." He folded the ladder as he

spoke. "How about I knock on your door in, let's say two hours, maybe a little longer? Does that work?"

Cassidy narrowed her eyes as she watched him gather the remaining cleaning materials. "It's Saturday night. Why don't you have a date with Amber?"

He stopped and turned. "What?"

"I only have dirty clothes, a handful of linens, and some pantry items at the other apartment. I don't need them tonight. Wouldn't you rather spend time with Amber?"

He squinted, staring at her lips as if she spoke a foreign language and he had to read them for translation. "Why would I do that?"

She swallowed, suddenly uncomfortable, overheated, probably by all the work she'd done and antsy, most likely because she wanted a shower. Clay stared at her, waiting for a response. His love life was none of her business. But her heart pounded and her lips locked, making it difficult to ask a question she didn't really want to know the answer to.

"Cassidy? Why do you ask if I'd rather spend time with Amber?"

"It's just that, um, I know you don't have all your weekends free and I thought, well, you know, you'd want to be with your girlfriend."

His eyes squished into horizontal slits. "My girlfriend?"

She nodded.

"What makes you think Amber is my girlfriend?"

Now she squirmed. If only she hadn't said anything. "Well, um, I've heard talk at work."

This time, his head canted to the left. "What kind of talk?"

"Nothing, really, just, you know."

"No, I don't know. Please tell me."

She sighed, wondering if it would be less painful to throw herself off the balcony. "Well, I just was told that you were seeing her and that she has talked about, um, being in your backseat."

He looked bewildered. "Amber told you this?"

"No. No. I just, um, I heard some stuff."

"The kind of stuff that made you assume we were dating?"

She nodded. "I apologize. It's none of my business. I just thought . . ." What the hell, she didn't know what she thought. She was an idiot for opening up a can of worms when things had been going so nicely.

Clay smiled. "Amber's not my girlfriend. If you want to know about my backseat you'll have to talk to her. I'm not saying anything except that I'm not dating her and I never have. I'm not dating anyone, unless you agree to grab something to eat with me later."

It was her turn to register shock on her face.

"Going out later would be a date?" She was fighting fear again, but this time, it was the fear that she'd allow this man in. As close as he wanted.

He shuffled his feet. "No, not necessarily. It could be two people who worked hard together and deserve a beer and a burger. Or, it could be a date. We won't know until we try."

"Wh—why do you want to date me?"

He bent, picked up the overloaded bucket, mop, and ladder, and walked toward the door. "Damned if know, Cassidy. You make me crazy when I'm with you and I can't stop thinking about you when I'm not. I'll see you in about two hours."

The door slammed behind him and Clay hauled the cleaning paraphernalia to the maintenance closet at the end of the hall. Christ, he felt like a fourteen-year-old asking a girl out for the first time. His hormones were betraying him again. He'd listened to Cassidy's comments with a tiny voice in his head whispering, "Grab her and kiss her. That'll show her Amber's not your girlfriend."

On second thought, the voice was located well below his head and making its presence known. He hoped Cassidy hadn't spotted his bulging frame of mind.

Amber? Those workers at the store thought he and Amber were dating? It had to be the old biddy. That was his fault, removing his phone from his pocket and faking a call to her in front of Rosie. He couldn't imagine Amber telling them about her arrest and being in the backseat of the patrol car. Knowing her, if she'd talked at all, she'd colored the event to suit her reputation.

Oh well. It was probably good for Amber's esteem and it would keep their focus off of Cassidy.

He'd thought all day about asking Cassidy out. Seeing her bent over cleaning the oven, watching her labor over spots on the tile floor, and clutching her thighs to balance her on the ladder had fueled a fire he thought had died with his divorce. That moment on the ladder with her so close had made him heady.

A door closed and he turned to see her walking toward the exit. What was she thinking? Beat feet or give the guy a chance? Maggie had laid it on the line for Cassidy and she'd elected to accept their job arrangement. That was some indication she wouldn't take off. He wished he was more certain. Maybe after a beer tonight she'd open up a little.

It was ten minutes beyond the two-hour mark when Clay knocked on Cassidy's door. She opened it after checking the security hole and smiled.

"I still don't have your number or I'd have called." He handed his cell to her. "Here. Key it in please."

He watched while her fingers lightly bounced on the screen. She'd changed into a clean pair of jeans and a long-sleeved black and gold hockey shirt. Her face was scrubbed clean with barely any makeup, maybe some stuff on her eyes. She wasn't wearing her glasses. She returned the phone and stood waiting.

"Ready to go?"

She nodded.

He gestured toward the door, but as she approached he asked, "Do you need your glasses?"

Her face registered surprise and she turned, ran to the bathroom, and returned wearing the large, red frames.

"Sorry," she said, inching them up her nose.

They walked silently to his truck, parked right outside the front door. Once inside, he turned the key and eased away from the curb.

"Are you a hockey fan?"

"I love hockey more than football, but I'm a fan of both."

"I like that. Not a lot of women are sports fans."

She grinned. "Maybe the ones you know aren't. But anyone I know is."

They were off to a nice start. Too soon to start asking questions that would erect those cautionary walls around her, so he made small talk about sports teams, the weather, and the songs on the radio. They arrived at a brick building with an orange roof and a matching neon sign declaring it as "Curly's."

He offered assistance after opening her door and for once, she took it. Her slender hand slid into his, her fingers wrapping between his like parts of a whole. Mini lightning bolts shot up his arm and shocked his heart. She stepped down from the passenger seat and he held her hand tight as they walked toward the screen door, briefly dismayed that the distance was so short. Country music drifted out from the open inner door.

"This place isn't much inside, but the burgers are the best. You can order whatever you like, though. If you want to eat healthy, they serve good salads."

She eyed him but remained silent. He was babbling like a child. There was no reason to be so nervous. She was just a woman and this was simply burgers and beers. But his palms were sweaty.

They selected a booth in the back and Cassidy surprised him by ordering a microbrew, a burger loaded, and onion rings. She fussed with the table service, refolded her napkin, and sipped her water while her eyes scrutinized the dining area.

"You're on the watch again."

She straightened her shoulders and forced a smile. "Just checking out the ambiance."

Clay laughed. "Good luck with that."

Their beers arrived and Clay raised his glass. Cassidy tipped hers to touch his.

"Thanks for helping me this afternoon. You did good work."

"You're welcome. But it's my job, remember?"

He sipped a second time then placed his mug on the square cocktail napkin.

"So, why did you come with me tonight?"

She captured his gaze. "Why'd you ask?"

"You're very good at answering a question with a question. It's a skilled defense mechanism."

"Am I?"

He grinned. "Touché."

He waited for her to respond, his question left hanging in the air. She lifted her glass, sipped, then whispered, "Maybe I was hungry."

The electric charge started in the arch of his foot, bolted up his legs, surged through his spine, and settled in his chest, causing his heart to race. Did she intend the double entendre? His body temperature spiked. "For burgers?"

Cassidy hadn't released his gaze. "Wasn't that the offer?"

The waitress arrived with a full tray of food and the spell was broken. His heart pounded so fiercely, he glanced down to assure himself it wasn't apparent beneath his shirt. He watched Cassidy squirt ketchup beside the onion rings and squeeze mustard on the burger. She avoided looking at him, seemingly absorbed in her food.

Halfway through their meal, he was mesmerized. She understood sports, she recognized music, she quoted poetry, and she licked her fingers in a disturbingly suggestive way. He couldn't stand up if his life depended on it, not without it looking like his jeans were a size too small.

He ordered another round of drinks, stretching his legs out beneath the table and propping his arm on the back of the booth. "There are about a hundred questions I'd like to ask you."

She toyed with the wet, tattered cocktail napkin, but he detected a slight smile. "I'm not answering serious questions tonight. Only frivolous ones."

"Oh, I see. Well, then, what's your favorite color?"

She challenged his gaze. "Red. It's a sign of love and passion."

"And do you have those or are you looking for them?"

She blinked and shrugged. "Still looking. Get back to frivolous."

"Uh, what's your favorite holiday?"

"My birthday."

That made him laugh. "I'm not sure the calendar makers are aware of that date, but I'll check. Any brothers or sisters? You must have brothers to know so much about sports."

She shook her head, indulging in a sip of fresh beer. "One brother but we don't get along. More like lots of athletic friends. And a crush on my best friend's brother ever since I was six, so I learned the games to try to impress him."

"Did it work?"

She giggled. "No, he turned out to be gay. So then I had two best friends."

"Where are they now?"

Just like that, the mood changed. Her eyes clouded over and she looked away. "You're interrogating me again. You said you wouldn't."

He sat up straight. "I didn't mean it to sound like that. You can't blame me for wanting to learn about you, Cassidy. It's what two people do when they are out together and getting to know each other. I'm intrigued by you. I . . ."

His words choked to a stop. In the rear of the room, where the staff restocked the napkins, straws, and silverware, he spotted Lauren standing by a tray table, glaring at him, ice javelins shooting from her eyes.

"What's the matter?" Cassidy looked frightened, her eyes wide, an onion ring suspended in mid-air. "Clay? What's the matter?"

"Don't turn around, please."

The onion ring fell to the plate. "What? Please. Is it a man?"

Clay tore his eyes from Lauren to look at her. "What? No, it's not a man. What would make you ask that? It's my ex-."

Oh thank God. For a minute, she feared Tony DelMorrie had found her. She'd let her guard down these last few days, presuming safety in Clay's company. Clay's face paled when he focused on something behind her and she immediately assumed it was him. Anyone who knew about the mob would recognize Tony DelMorrie. Certainly a cop would.

The mood at the table shifted. He was obviously uncomfortable with her there. "Do you want me to walk to the ladies room so you can speak to her?"

That brought Clay's attention back to her. "No. The last thing I want to do is speak to her."

"You seem rattled."

"I'm sorry. I thought she'd left town. I'm surprised to see her, that's all. I think she's gone. Let's not let her ruin our evening."

He bit into the remaining half of his burger.

"How long did you go with her?"

Clay blinked and shook his head, wiping his mouth with a napkin. "I didn't go with her. I married her."

"Oh. I didn't know you meant ex-wife. I didn't think you were married."

Clay pointed his index finger at her. "I'm not."

She chewed another onion ring before curiosity got the best of her. "So what happened?"

Clay grinned. "Well, Miss Hoake, the shoe is on the other foot now and you're the one with inquiries. I'll be glad to answer that if you answer a question for me. For every question you ask, I'll ask one."

Cassidy gulped. "Never mind. I'll ask Amber."

Back in the truck, they drove silently to Fortieth Street. He'd been overly talkative on the ride to the restaurant and now, he'd retreated into a shell. Reluctantly, she admitted she'd enjoyed their banter, and disappointment now that he'd stopped trying to entertain her made her want to pout.

The street looked more dismal than she remembered. Remnants of yellow police tape hanging from the front door of her building and on a nearby shrub flapped in the breeze. Three men stood a few feet from the entrance smoking, their hoods concealing their identities. She recognized the gun Clay retrieved from under the front seat as the same one he reached for on their furniture excursion.

After tucking it in his back waistband, he walked toward the rear of the truck and removed an empty box from the bed, then came to her door. "Stay close," he whispered, reaching for her hand.

They moved quickly up the sidewalk and into the unsecured front door. Cassidy cringed when she entered the apartment.

Having come from the deluxe quarters at Chalet II, this place looked like a landfill.

"There are only a few things in the kitchen, if you wouldn't mind grabbing them," she whispered. She felt like a trespasser. "I'll grab my laundry bag from the bedroom."

"Do you want these throw rugs?"

She crinkled her nose. "God, no."

The hair on her arms rose when she switched on the overhead bedroom light. Someone had overturned the mattress, opened the closet doors, turned over the lone lamp in the room, and dumped her laundry bag of dirty clothes on the floor. There was nothing to find, but someone had searched anyway.

She stood paralyzed, her mind racing. The police? The men milling around outside? It didn't feel like that.

It was him. He'd found her. This wasn't a search for valuables. One look at the room and it was apparent there was nothing to steal. This was a search for clues to her whereabouts. For all she knew, he was watching her now. Her eyes darted to the window, but it was too dark to discern anything outside. She began to shake uncontrollably. Hearing Clay's footsteps coming toward the room she turned, tears stinging her eyes.

"You really should learn . . . hey. Are you okay?" He placed the box on the floor and walked toward her, taking her in his arms. "What the hell, Cassidy? You're trembling."

She melted into his embrace, burying her face in his chest and wrapping her arms around his waist, absorbing his warmth and his strength. Her glasses pressed into the bridge of her nose.

He tightened his embrace, running one hand the length of her back. "Cass, it's okay. I'm here."

She spoke, her words muffled in his shirt. "I have to go. I can't stay any longer." Beneath her cheek she felt his heart leap.

"That's why we're getting you out of here. This is a bad neighborhood."

He didn't know. He didn't understand. He suspected the local thugs.

"No," she whispered. "I have to leave."

He stiffened. Then he stepped back and cupped her chin in his hand, raising her face to meet his gaze. "Please don't," he whispered. He bent his head and she watched his lips open slightly, then capture hers.

His hand slid into her hair and the tentative kiss turned passionate, his tongue plunging into her mouth. He ran his other hand down to her bottom, pressing her against his erection.

"Running isn't the answer." He spoke with his lips against her. "And it's not what I want you to do." He pressed his mouth into hers, wrapping his arms around her, creating a sensual cocoon of safety.

He was total heat, from his thighs to his hands to his tongue, working her emotions into a sizzling frenzy like oil dropping into a scorching cast iron skillet. This man was solid, strong and yet tender. And oh so hot. She leaned into him, returning his kiss, feeling her pulse rate increase and her desire arc. She'd never truly had a man to lean on. Did she dare rely on this one?

Somewhere upstairs a door slammed and Clay released her. "Let's get out of here and we can talk."

Cassidy wiped tears from her cheeks, knelt, and scooped the dumped clothes into the laundry bag. Clay reached for the bag when she stood. "Anything else?"

She shook her head.

"C'mon." He eased his hand between her shoulder blades and nudged her toward the door, picking up the box and balancing the dirty clothes bag on top of it. After locking the door behind them, they made their way to the truck.

Once locked safely inside, Cassidy relaxed her stiffened back muscles.

"Did you have a lease here?"

"Monthly."

"Good. I'll notify the landlord that you won't be renewing." He reached over and squeezed her knee. "Relax, hon. It will be all right. You're out of there now."

They drove home in silence. A thousand conflicting thoughts bombarded her brain. Tony DelMorrie had found her. She sensed it. How close was he? Did he know where she worked? She hadn't spoken to anyone, so he couldn't know about her relocation to the Cestra Chalets.

But if he was watching her now, he'd surely follow them. She swiveled her head slowly in a half circle, her chin moving from one shoulder to the other, looking for a car that moved as they did, or a suspicious onlooker. Nothing. No movement. No vehicle following.

Did he know about Clay? And what about him? Butterflies danced in her stomach when she recalled his kiss and acknowledged his desire. There was no mistaking what he had in mind and she suppressed a smile conceding that she was certainly interested. But what would it lead to? What did she have to offer him? She was a fugitive. And he was the law.

Turning her head she blinked back tears as she looked out the window. Who was the devil now?

10

Arriving at Chalet II, Clay parked in his reserved spot and retrieved her items from the truck bed. She jumped from the passenger seat, waited, and they walked silently toward the entrance.

Since his hands were full, Cassidy opened and held the front door for him. At her unit, she again unlocked the entry for him and stepped back, allowing Clay inside first. He deposited the box on the round table, dropped the laundry bag on the floor, then walked deliberately toward her.

Startled, she backed up until her shoulders were against the door. Clay advanced on her, positioning his arms on either side of her, pinning her in place. His mouth swooped down to capture hers so fiercely, their teeth clicked. He leaned his body fully against hers, thighs against thighs, belly to belly, breasts pushed into rock hard pecs. Heat engulfed her.

She wrapped her arms around his neck and pressed into him. Yes, yes. This was the real hiding place she sought, inside his arms, inside him.

He eased her eyeglasses to the top of her head and cradled her face in his hands, his gray eyes clouded with desire. "Jesus, how I want you. Ask me to stay." He whispered his request, capturing her lips before she could answer.

She came up for air. "Wh-what?"

He gently sucked her bottom lip into his mouth while his hand moved from the side of her face to the base of her neck. "I don't want to leave." His tongue caressed the lip before releasing it. "But I can't stay unless you ask me to."

She returned his kiss, forcing her tongue between his lips. He groaned softly. She released his mouth and whispered, "Please Stay."

Clay kissed her harder, bruising her lips and burning his way into her heart. She lowered her hands to his sides and yanked his shirt from his pants. Sliding her hands beneath, she caressed his back, appreciating the sinewy, hard muscles under her fingertips.

Clay caught his breath, drew back, and gazed into her eyes. "Jesus, Cassie. You drive me crazy." He dropped his hands to the hem of her jersey and slowly eased it up. Lifting her arms to help, in seconds the shirt lay in a heap on the floor. Clay gazed at her breasts, partially concealed by a white demi-bra, and then cupped them in his hands. "You're beautiful."

Squeezing them together he ran his tongue along the cleft, sending delicious chills down to her toes. His thumbs massaged her nipples through the material while he spread tiny kisses across every inch of her chest. She grabbed his biceps, registering somewhere in her brain they were too thick for her fingers to meet, and gently nudged him backward.

"Can I take you to my bedroom?"

He smiled, dropping his hands to grasp hers. "I thought you'd never take the hint."

She stepped out of her shoes and he followed, then she led him through the dark to the bedroom and drew him to the bed. A pole lamp directly outside the window cast them in shadows. Stepping up with one knee she crawled on top of the bedspread, turned on her knees, and faced him. Urging him close to the bedside she reached for the edge of his pullover.

"Let's keep this fair," she whispered, starting an ascent to remove the garment. Clay reached between his shoulder blades, grabbed the shirt, and yanked it over his head.

The first glimpse of his sculpted chest, muscular arms, and lean waist caused her mouth to go dry. Grooved obliques framed washboard abs that begged to be kissed. A tribal armband tattoo wrapped around his left bicep, positioned just above where his shirt sleeve would end. She licked her lips and swallowed hard. "Wow."

He forehead wrinkled. "What?"

She ran her eyes over every spot of tightly stretched skin, noting a sprinkling of crisp chest hair branching downward toward his rippled stomach muscles. "You're spectacular to look at."

He wrapped his arms around her waist and engulfed her in a kiss, easing up onto the bed on his knees, then gently drawing her down with him to the pillows. Facing each other on their sides, he ran his hand from her waist down her hip to her thigh. His eyes gleamed.

He caressed her thigh through the denim and whispered, "Cassie, I've thought about you in my arms almost since the first time I saw you. You hardly know me. Are you sure you're okay with this?"

She reached for his cheek, feeling soft stubble beneath her fingertips. "I could ask you the same thing."

He rolled on top of her, urging her legs apart with his knee. "I've never wanted anything more." He covered her mouth with his, hungry, forceful, taking possession. Then slowly, he began to spread kisses along her neck and shoulders, traveling to her breasts. Adeptly, he reached beneath her back and unhooked her bra. He'd barely slid the cotton fabric away when his mouth enclosed her breast, his tongue tantalizing her nipple.

Her toes curled at the sensation and she dug her fingers into his back. He rose on his elbows and stole her mouth again, kissing her more passionately. He began another journey along her neck, over her breasts, down her belly, and to the waistband of her jeans. Each kiss ignited a spark within her hot enough to fire up a kiln. Indeed, she was on fire for this man.

He nimbly unclasped the snap on her jeans and used his tongue to forge a path to the elastic edge of her panties. Clasping her hips with both hands he whispered, "Lift up," and she obliged, feeling jeans and undies slide down her legs in one fluid movement, dragging her socks off her feet as well.

He placed his first kiss on the underside of her left knee, using his tongue to make tiny swirls. A vision of chocolate and vanilla ice cream swirling together, mixing and melting under the heat of his lips popped into her head. He slowly advanced up the inside of her thigh, causing her to arch her back and lock her jaw with each inch of progress. When he settled his mouth between her legs, she whimpered.

"I knew you'd be sweet," Clay murmured, moving his hands beneath her bottom and squeezing her cheeks.

Surrender. It was the only word she could think of to describe her plummet into this man's control. Sweet surrender.

He kissed, he licked, he probed with his fingers, bringing her to the edge of ecstasy. She reached down and laced her fingers into his hair.

"Clay, please. I want you inside me."

He rose on his knees, smiling, still clad in his jeans. She watched as he unsnapped his pants and slid jeans, boxer briefs, and sweat socks off in one smooth maneuver. Before dropping the clothes, he reached into his back pocket, removed his billfold and extracted a condom. Ripping the foil packet with his teeth, he slid the condom over his erection then leaned forward to gaze into her eyes, supporting himself on his hands.

"Are you sure?"

She raised her legs, wrapping them around his hips like a wrestler capturing his opponent in a body scissors grip, and applied pressure with her feet against his butt to urge him closer. When he filled her she cried out and tilted her head back, inviting his kisses along her throat.

Their bodies conspired to play a love concerto, moving rhythmically with each other, slowly building to a crescendo of ecstasy, finishing in a powerful finale. Cassidy gasped his name as spasms of release overcame her, while Clay whispered hers with his face buried in her neck. Her breath came in tiny puffs, like a skilled marathon runner pacing herself, and with her eyes closed, she eased her way down from glory.

She threw her arm across her face as Clay gently rolled off of her and onto his back.

"I didn't expect that to happen," she whispered.

"Me neither."

"I think you should leave." She heard his head move on the pillow, felt his eyes on her, but he remained silent.

"This isn't a good idea, you and me. I can't . . . it just won't work." She rolled onto her side, away from him, and brought her knees up to her chest.

In seconds, he snuggled behind her, bending his legs to fit her form and dropping his arm across her stomach to press her against his chest. He nuzzled the back of her hair with his nose and placed his mouth against her ear.

"I'm not leaving and you can't shove me away. You're running again, this time from me. But I won't let you go just because you're scared of something." He jutted his hips forward, pressing his erection against her bottom, and slid his hand down between her legs. "You don't want me to leave either, not feeling like this."

When he inserted his fingers inside her she moaned softly and opened her legs. How could she have let this happen? Suddenly, every fiber of her being belonged to him.

"I can't get enough of you. I want to make love to you

again," he whispered and she turned, throwing her leg over his hip and hungrily searching for his mouth, like a baby bird reaching for food from its mother. He was nourishment for her soul.

They lay silent, still connected, dampness clinging to their skin, their heart rates simultaneously slowing. Clay raised his head, bracing himself on his elbows, and kissed her tenderly.

He hadn't withdrawn from her yet and wished he never would. He was like a blind man suddenly gifted with vision who wanted to see everything all at once. In the other room, Cassidy's mantel clock chimed and the corners of her mouth tipped upward.

"That clock is important to you, isn't it?"

Her smile widened and she traced a vein on his bicep as she spoke. "It was my mother's. Once, when I was little, my parents left me with a babysitter and there was this big thunderstorm that absolutely terrified me. I was inconsolable until they came home and I remember my mother rocking me in her arms and telling me how foolish I was. That clock chimed and she told me that it had magical powers. She whispered that whenever she wasn't around and the clock sang, it meant that she was right there with me and I shouldn't be afraid. Now that she's gone, it's really a comfort for me."

He remained silent. Her eyes said she had more to offer.

"Sometimes, I don't even hear it. Other times, like now, I think it's her way of reaching out to me."

Clay brushed her cheek with his knuckle. "I hope she approves of me." Cassidy's smile returned.

Clay moved his finger to her hairline, brushing tiny wisps off her forehead. "So, no parents and a brother you don't get along with."

She spoke softly, her words laced with sadness. "That's me. All alone."

A surge of desire coursed through him, heating him from toenails to fingernails. He kissed her gently and whispered, "Not anymore, honey."

She stared at him in the dim light from the window, those big brown eyes questioning. "This isn't something frivolous, Cassidy. It's not just a fling, because I'm not a fling kind of guy. It's deeper. It's something important, something solid. I know it and I think you feel it. Everything changes now." He stared into her eyes. "We have a lot to talk about."

She ran her finger around his ear to his jaw line. "What if you don't like what you hear?"

His eyes widened to round circles. "I could ask you the same question. I come with baggage."

She smiled and traced his lips with her finger, sending a message to every nerve cell in his body. "Do you have some deep, dark, hidden secret I should know about?"

Memories of that night when his colleagues needed a battering ram to break down the door, when his police brothers were forced to restrain him and ultimately file charges in connection with the stabbing flashed through his mind. That was a dark period of his life. Would she be appalled if he told her about that murderous rage? Would the angel he'd just found take flight, fearing what he was capable of? He couldn't bear it if she did. He kissed the fingers against his lips. "Do you?"

Even as Cassidy stared at him, once again looking like a cornered animal, he knew the answer. First and foremost, he was a cop and he knew a ransacked room when he saw one. He'd been about to chide her about her housekeeping habits just hours ago in her apartment after he'd walked into the kitchen and discovered every cabinet door and drawer open. But he'd swallowed his questions when she dissolved in his arms, trembling in terror.

Someone had searched every corner of that apartment. He knew it and she knew it. The question was, did she know who? He recognized fear. He'd seen it in Cassidy's eyes standing in her bedroom, felt it when he comforted her quivering body. She fought it now when she spoke so softly he barely heard her say, "Yes."

How could he convince her that he would protect her, support her, defend her, kill for her if need be? He hardened inside her, needing to show her strength. And love.

He kissed her hungrily, murmuring against her lips. "Cassie, I think I'm falling in love with you. That scares the hell out of me. But you're scared of something else, something that I'm not going to let come between us."

Staring, she remained silent as he leaned backward to see her face. "I want two things from you. I want you to feel for me what I feel for you. And I want you to trust me. Can you do that?"

She caressed his cheek, her fingers telegraphing heat to his core. Smiling ever so slightly, she whispered, "If we could stay here, if I could stay in your arms forever, those would be easy requests. But there's more involved than just us. And I'm afraid of what could happen if I let myself love you, Clay. I don't want to hurt you. I can't stay."

"Do you trust me?"

They were naked, he was inside her, how could she not trust him? She searched his face with her eyes, nodding ever so slightly.

Rubbing the tip of his nose across the tip of hers he whispered, "Good. That's a start. I want to hold you close all night and make love to you again. When we wake up tomorrow, we'll dig up our skeletons and deal with them. Okay?"

She wrapped her arms around his neck and coaxed his mouth to hers. He took that as a yes.

The high-pitched wail of a police siren jolted them awake. "Jesus Christ," Clay swore, scrambling to crawl over Cassidy and snatch his jeans off the floor.

She tugged the sheet up over her breasts and covered her ears against the continual noise. The digital alarm clock read four nineteen. "What is it?"

Clay frantically dug through the pockets until he located his cell phone and tapped the screen to mute the sound.

"I'm sorry, honey. That scared the crap out of me. Are you okay?"

"What is it?" she repeated.

He read the group message on the screen. "It's an all-out alert. They're calling everyone in. A little girl has gone missing."

He ran his fingers through his hair then crawled from her feet to her face and planted a kiss on her lips. "I'm sorry. I have to leave. Go back to sleep. It's still night time."

Climbing over her legs he stood and began collecting his clothes. "Do me a favor and call Maggie later. I don't think we have any chores that need done in the buildings but check with her."

He sat on the edge of the bed to slide on his socks. Then he leaned over her legs, bracing himself with one hand and reaching toward her face with the other. He caressed her cheek with his fingertips, her skin as smooth as satin. "I don't know when I'll be back. Did you have plans today?"

She shook her head.

"I want to see you when I come home. Please be here."

Her eyes darted over his face, contemplating his request. She tugged her lips between her teeth as if trying to control her mouth. He ran his thumb along the thin line it created.

"Promise you won't disappear on me." He leaned in and kissed her tenderly, resisting the urge to ravish her mouth. He spoke against her lips. "Promise."

"I promise."

Once she heard the door close Cassidy sank beneath the covers and closed her eyes, but she couldn't fall back to sleep. The sheets smelled like sex and Clay, an intoxicating aroma that made her smile. Last night had been like a wonderful dream, the kind little girls imagine when they meet their Prince Charming.

Her reaction to Clay's touch was overpowering. She'd melted like an ice cube on a hot sidewalk when she tasted his mouth. Wrapped in his arms, nothing frightened her. Maybe it was time to talk to him, to ask for help. Time to take down the walls.

She showered and dressed by eight o'clock. She walked to Maggie's apartment and knocked lightly. The door swung open and she and Jack greeted her with wide smiles. Jack extended a slobber-covered finger with a Cheerio on the tip toward her.

Maggie opened the door wider and invited her in. "I didn't have your number. Clay asked me to make sure there weren't any projects that had to be done or anything you needed."

Maggie propped up Jack in his high chair and poured more cereal onto the tray table. "Do you want some coffee?"

"Yes, please."

Maggie reheated hers and handed Cassidy a steaming mug. She nodded to the kitchen counter and a bowl of sugar packets. "Cream is in the fridge."

Cassidy fixed her coffee, passed behind the high chair, reaching out to smooth Jack's hair, and sat at the table.

"When did you talk to Clay?"

Her eyebrows shot up before she could stop them. "Um, a little earlier."

Maggie grinned. "My brother is a private person. When he's home in the evening, he draws the shades on his balcony so no one looks in. I noticed those shades never closed last night. How'd you like Curly's? Did you try the burgers? I assume you had a good night last night? That all-out call scared the hell out of me. You?"

Cassidy lowered her head and studied an imaginary spot on the table, unsuccessfully suppressing a grade-school grin.

Maggie clapped her hands. "Well, now that we have that settled, let's move on. There are no apartment tasks today. I had planned to run to the grocery store but, as you know, Dan is working along with Clay and the other members of the city police department."

She grinned while Jack banged his hands on the tray table, sending cereal flying. "He's teething again and he's a little fussy. I wanted to pick up a few items, but it's a challenge taking him out when he's in this mood."

"I can run to the store for you."

"I thought you didn't have a license."

She shrugged. "Clay didn't have it quite right. I don't have an Ohio license, but I do have a valid driver's license."

Cassidy drove Maggie's white SUV downtown. She glanced at herself in the rearview mirror and smiled at the red and blue ball cap with a scripted "I" she borrowed from Maggie's hall tree and wore low over her eyes. Just in case. This was a calculated risk, going out and about on her own.

But Fortieth Street was on the other side of town and Tony DelMorrie would have no way of knowing where she was staying, or with whom. No one knew. She sat up straighter in the driver's seat, proud of herself for having the courage to earn her keep and run this errand for Maggie. And a little surprised. Spending the night with Clay seemed to have fortified her.

She returned an hour later to find Maggie standing in front of the television, gently rocking a fussy Jack on her shoulder, her attention glued to the broadcast. The local station had its helicopter in the air circling a wooded area where search dogs had led police.

Cassidy stowed the milk and perishables in the refrigerator

and stacked the pantry items on the counter, then joined Maggie. She had dark circles under her eyes and cereal in her hair. Cassidy reached to pick it out.

"It's so scary, so awful." Maggie swayed, rubbing tiny circles on Jack's back. "How could anyone hurt a child?"

Cassidy shook her head slowly, equally as horrified as she watched the story unfold. "Have you been up since four-thirty?" Maggie nodded.

"Did you have the chance to shower?"

Maggie smiled. "No. When he's fussy like this, I usually can't put him down so sometimes, that has to wait until Dan comes home."

Cassidy cleared her throat. "I'll hold him for you if you want to take one now."

Maggie stared at her, assessing the risk. Seeing her hesitation, Cassidy raised her hand. "It's fine if you aren't comfortable doing that. You look beat and I thought perhaps a hot shower would help. If you don't need me to do anything else, I'll go back to my place. I still need to figure out the bus schedule for work tomorrow."

She turned toward the door, but Maggie stopped her.

"Cassidy, wait." She stared at Cassidy as if choosing her words carefully. "You're running from something. Why didn't you keep my car and take off?"

"What?"

"You had a golden opportunity to disappear on a full tank of gas. What made you come back?"

She hadn't even considered running. Yes, she'd worn a cap to conceal her identity but the thought of leaving hadn't occurred to her. Because of last night? Because she didn't want to run anymore? Because she wanted Maggie's life with a baby and a husband who came home to her every night? Tears pricked her eyes. Yes, she wanted all that and more.

"Tell me what you're running from, honey, please let me help."

The words tumbled from her mouth before she could stop them. "I saw a woman killed."

Maggie eyed her carefully. "In an accident?"

Cassidy shook her head.

"Did you tell the police?"

"Yes. They can't help me. Please don't ask me any more questions, Maggie."

The corners of her mouth lifted slightly. "You didn't answer my first question. How come you didn't take off when you had the chance?"

"I, um, I promised Clay I'd be here when he came home."

A smile erupted on Maggie's face. "That was a good promise to keep. You're welcome to use my computer in the office to search the bus schedule."

She eased Jack away from her. "Here, see if he'll go to you. He's pretty tired. You'd be surprised how fast I can shower."

Cassidy took the child in her arms and he whimpered once then settled his head on her shoulder, his lips puckered in a baby pout. Warmth spread through her like honey pouring from a jar as she cuddled him, inhaling the sweet fragrance of baby shampoo and that wonderful scent babies possess of love and trust and dependence.

Instinctively, she caressed his back with tiny circles. Maggie nodded her approval.

Standing in the living room cradling Jack, Cassidy wondered if she'd ever have her own child to nurture, her own man to tend. Someday maybe, a tiny voice in her heart whispered. *But first, you have to tend to Tony DelMorrie.*

11

A search team found the missing girl's body in the brush along the highway shortly before midnight. Dan called Maggie to say he and Clay were stopping for breakfast and then would be home. Knowing she'd wait up for her husband, Clay stopped in before heading to his own apartment.

Maggie and Cassidy had spent most of the day together, she told them, happy to report that she'd slept while Cassidy minded Jack without issue. She repeated the brief details Cassidy revealed about her situation.

Hearing that she'd used the computer to learn the bus route, Clay and Dan sat down to check the search history. She had navigated to the public transit site all right but, low and behold, she'd also searched an Arizona newspaper. Despite reviewing a week's worth of papers, though, nothing they read hinted at why she read it. She told Clay she was originally from Pittsburgh. So what was the connection to Arizona? Did it have something to do with the way she was always on the lookout, always scanning her surroundings?

The three of them agreed to sit with Cassidy at dinner for an impromptu intervention. Except Clay didn't want to wait until dinner. It was time to stop playing games.

He didn't take time to change out of his uniform, didn't call first, and didn't concern himself about waking her up. Never mind that it was after two in the morning.

He pounded with a closed fist on Cassidy's door. "Cassidy? Wake up. Let me in."

He knocked harder a second time. "Cassidy!"

She looked through the security peep, undid the chain lock and opened the door. Her eyes widened when she saw him in full uniform, and her hand clutched her heart. "What's wrong?"

He stormed past her, pointed to the sofa, and ordered, "Sit."

Cassidy closed the door but stood with her hand on the knob. "Are you here to arrest me?"

He exhaled. The entrance might have been a bit forceful. "No."

"Then why the uniform, Officer Cestra? And a gun?"

She was on the defensive again, her chin raised, her eyes alert. He regarded her for a moment, conceded she might be right, and strolled to the round oak dining table. Unbuckling his gun belt he placed it on top of the table with a clunk, dropped his hat on top of the pile, turned and spread his hands palms up. "Better?"

She hadn't moved. Why was she dressed? He eyed her bare feet. She wouldn't take off without shoes, would she? Not likely. That at least bought a little time.

"I'm sorry. I came home a short while ago and I couldn't wait to talk to you. I didn't take the time to change my clothes."

"Or to look at the clock, obviously." Her voice held an icy edge.

"I apologize if I woke you up. I know it's late, but it's important."

"Did you find the little girl?"

"We located her body."

Her eyes widened, but she remained still.

"I spoke to Maggie. You saw a woman killed and you don't tell anybody? Do you realize there could be a warrant out for you as a witness to a crime? What's going on?"

Her fingers tightened on the knob and his chest constricted with the movement. *Oh, honey, please trust me.* Her chest rose as she inhaled and lifted her chin.

"That's what's so important that you barge in here in the middle of the night?"

"Don't change the subject, Cassidy. Tell me what you saw. Tell my why you're running away instead of cooperating with the authorities."

Almost imperceptibly, her shoulders straightened. "You don't know what you're talking about and your information is not entirely accurate."

She tested his patience and he spoke more harshly than he meant to. "Well, then correct my facts. Please."

She stared at him, not moving.

"I'm not the enemy, Cassidy. When are you going to realize that?"

"What are you then?"

It was a fair question, one he wasn't sure he could answer. Might as well be honest.

"As far as you're concerned, I, uh, I . . ." he started to laugh. "At the moment I'm a bumbling idiot."

Well, at least that garnered a smile.

He opened his arms wide and took a step toward her. "Meet me halfway?"

She hesitated for one long, heart stopping minute and then she took a tentative step toward him. In seconds, she was wrapped in his arms and all thoughts of chastising her evaporated. He was exhausted after working twenty straight hours, but his desire sprang to life beneath his fly. He was an addict and she was his fix.

He pressed his lips to hers, dipping his tongue into her mouth hesitantly at first. When she responded, enclosing him in a hug, leaning her hips into his, and opening her mouth for him, he turned to putty in her hands. Sweet Jesus.

"Were you asleep?" he whispered against her lips.

"Not really."

"Why are you dressed?"

She withdrew from his embrace and grinned. "Why don't you take care of that, officer?"

Heated blood coursed through him. Moving his hands to her sides he lifted her T-shirt over her head and marveled at the soft feel of her skin. Drawing her close he unhooked her bra and moved his right hand beneath the elastic to cup her breast, his words snagging in his throat.

"I could hardly concentrate tonight. I wanted to be here."

He slid his left hand down her bare back and wedged his hand between her skin and her waistband, clutching her bottom. She sighed, heightening his already flaming passion.

He spoke between kisses. "I need a shower. Will you wash my back?"

Without waiting for an answer, he took her hand and guided her to the bathroom. While he leaned in to turn on and adjust the water, Cassidy removed two bath towels from the linen closet. He began unbuttoning his shirt, but she moved his hands aside and while she worked the buttons he opened her jeans and sank his hand down the front of her pants to discover her desire matched his.

Minutes later, they were kissing under the beating water, their hands traveling every inch of each other's soapy bodies, touching, tasting, exploring. He turned off the water, handed Cassidy a towel, and dried himself, embarrassed by his obvious intentions. Once in bed, he devoured her until they both were at the point of exhaustion.

Rolling off of her, he disposed of the condom and wrapped her in his arms. He was dead tired. Maybe he was dead.

That had to be it. He'd died and gone to heaven.

Cassidy blinked awake, momentarily stunned by the sound of breathing behind her. Thirty seconds elapsed before her fluttering heart slowed to match the tempo of the soft snores on the pillow beneath his head and a slow smile crept across her face. Clay.

Her eyes adjusted to the dark and focused on the shining alarm clock digits. Less than thirty minutes before she had to crawl out of the cocoon his arms safely encompassed her in. His body heat seeped beneath her skin like healing balm for achy muscles, warming its way to her soul. How she wished it could be like this always.

The events of the last hours played to her mind's eye as if she watched a favorite romance movie. Clay's tender caresses, his fervent kisses, his whispered endearments. In his arms she was beautiful, soft as kitten fur and as bewitching as a temptress. Locked in a mutual embrace they whispered their dreams in between making love, two strangers coming together under the blankets with a physical as well as emotional need for one another.

She hoped to be the mother of two kids someday, he wanted three. She fantasized about a bungalow with a small front yard and a white picket fence. He favored an old farmhouse in the middle of five wooded acres. He wasn't sure about happily-ever-after but regarded Maggie and Dan as examples of what could happen. She remained non-committal, the nightmare that was her life shadowing her future.

She would likely pay for the lack of sleep as the day wore on, but right now, she was invigorated by the hours of intimacy. The sheet lay spread over his right thigh, barely concealing him, and she took advantage of his mostly naked state to admire him in the light peeking through the window blind. Even in sleep he was well endowed, magnificent to look at. He exuded power, like a sleeping lion one knew better than to awaken. And just hours ago, she'd had all of him beneath her fingertips, which somehow empowered her.

Today felt like a new day.

Easing out of his embrace, she envied the deep sleep Clay enjoyed. She hummed in the shower and tiptoed around the bedroom, quietly dressing so as not to disturb him. He slept like a rock in spite of her opening and closing drawers and searching unsuccessfully under the bed and through the dirty clothes hamper for her name tag for The Packing Place. Where the hell was it?

One gentle kiss on his cheek and she was out the door, closing it softly behind her. The hike to the bus stop two streets away was easy. Hell, she could run a marathon this morning. The thirty-minute ride gave her time for introspection.

As long as she kept hiding, Tony DelMorrie controlled her life, just as if he held his gun to her head. It was that simple. Her fear of him sucked the joy out of everyday things like going to work, shopping, or a simple burger and onion rings. Tony DelMorrie was a dark cloud hovering over her.

Clay was the light. He infused her with strength, purpose, and, dare she entertain the thought? Love. Sleeping with him had been more than a physical act, it had been an escape from the darkness. She wanted to remain in his light, but to do that, she'd have to risk her life and stand up to Tony DelMorrie. Again.

Jill Diamond had tried standing up to him and she was dead. It was funny how the women seemed to be on the same schedule most mornings, stopping in the convenience station grab-n-go market on the way to their respective jobs. Cassidy hadn't even known where Jill worked until she read it in the newspaper after her murder, didn't know her last name. But their faces became familiar to each other and the casual greetings turned into brief comments and then mini conversations if there was a check-out line.

Jill standing with her cigarettes and a diet soda and Cassidy balancing hot coffee and an energy bar. They had chatted about manicures and jewelry, laughed at the covers of the scandal magazines, delighted in girl topics. Jill Diamond always had a smile for Cassidy.

She smiled at Cassidy the day she died. She and Tony DelMorrie had argued, the police discovered, and Jill threw a shoe at DelMorrie, smashing it into his foul mouth. The impact chipped his tooth and his anger erupted. He'd followed her as she drove into the fuel station on the way to her receptionist's job. And when she'd relinquished the protection of her car to head inside, he'd strolled up as casually as if he were walking a dog and gunned her down at the front door.

Cassidy watched the nightmare unfold as if in slow motion, spotting the gun in his hand as soon as he moved within eyesight. She'd opened her mouth to scream, but her vocal chords were paralyzed with fear. She turned to look at the clerk, with his back to the window, reaching for something from the shelves below, and the other customers in line, all of them caught up in their own lives, texting, talking on their phones or otherwise distracted. And so she watched in stunned silence as Jill spotted her through the glass, waved and smiled while Tony DelMorrie shot the life out of her.

If the others saw anything, they denied it. Only she stepped forward, recounting the horrific details and accusing DelMorrie of murder. Without Cassidy's testimony, there would be no justice for Jill Diamond.

And Cassidy would remain in the dark. She had to face him

from the witness stand and end this life of disguise if she intended to start a new life, one that included Clay. The bus rolled to a stop and the folding doors opened, allowing a cool, fresh wave of air inside the vehicle. The time had come to confront the devil.

She arrived at The Packing Place at ten minutes to eight with her thoughts weighing heavy on her heart. The store lights were on and Amber's car was parked in the rear beside Keaseling's van. Inwardly, she cringed. She didn't relish a groping match with him first thing this morning.

Stashing her purse in the cabinet and hanging her hoodie on the back of the bathroom door, she looked around the store for her name tag, but didn't find it anywhere. Muffled sounds came through the closed office door, but she opted to stay at the front of the store and not interrupt. Maybe Keaseling wouldn't notice the name tag wasn't pinned to her shirt. That was one of his store rules along with no cell phones during working hours and the ten-second greeting rule when a customer entered.

At precisely eight o'clock, she unlocked the front door and waited for the day's first customer. Within ten minutes Amber rounded the corner, her cheeks flushed.

"Hey, Chickie. Good morning. You look whipped. Have a bad weekend?"

"Um, not really. I'm just short of sleep. I wasn't sure anyone was here. What was going on in there?"

Amber shrugged. "Don't worry about him. He's pissed because Leslie didn't lock the safe when we closed Saturday afternoon."

"So why is he taking it out on you?"

"Because he thinks I did it. I wasn't going to say differently and throw her under the bus."

"Was he yelling at you?"

Amber laughed and tossed her hair over her shoulder. "Yeah, I guess you could say he was yelling."

Cassidy screwed up her face to look at her. "I don't understand."

"Don't fret, Chet. It's handled."

Keaseling appeared behind her, tucking in his shirt. He nodded to Cassidy, then leaned against the far counter with his arms folded across his chest.

"Amber," he barked, "the hair?"

She flashed him a wide smile, reached for a rubber band and fashioned her hair back into a ponytail. She turned to Cassidy and wrinkled her nose, moving to stand beside her at the counter.

Only the low tones of the radio providing background music cut the cumbersome silence.

"How was your weekend?" Cassidy finally asked.

"Believe it or not, I stayed home. No wild parties for me."

Customers trickled in throughout the morning keeping the women moderately busy. Keaseling remained leaning against the counter, manifesting a dazzling smile when a patron walked in but scowling when the store was empty.

"Name tag, Miss Hoake?"

"Um, I'm sorry, sir. I must have left it pinned to my other shirt."

He glared at her. "That's a rules violation, you know. I could send you home for it and dock you for the hours you miss. Fortunately for you, it's busy enough today that we need the two of you here. Make sure you wear it tomorrow."

"Yes, sir."

Finally, at noon, he said goodbye and the women released a collective sigh.

Amber yanked her hair free. "Damn, I thought he'd never leave."

Cassidy rushed into the office to search the floor, the desk, and any little cranny in which her name tag might be. Nothing.

"It's probably at home," Amber suggested.

"No. I looked everywhere this morning." The metal tag attached with two clutch pins, preventing it from simply falling off or coming unhooked.

"What if I can't find it?"

Amber shrugged. "We'll think of something."

"I didn't like his mood today. He seemed really mad. Why do you subject yourself to his anger? You should have told him the truth instead of covering for Leslie. He probably keeps a record of mistakes."

"I can handle him better. Besides, I shoulda checked. I'm the one with more experience. But I appreciate you wanting to fight the fight for me, Cass. That's nice. You seem full of fire this morning."

Cassidy swallowed. How long did the glow of afterglow last?

Amber winked and jumped up on the packing table. "So now that we're alone, you have some talking to do, missy. What's up with you and C.C.?"

Her stomach somersaulted. "I want to ask you about him."

"Geez. You two are so interested in each other, I wish you'd hook up already."

"What makes you say that?"

She waved her hand. "He asks me about you. You call me to get messages to him. Why don't you just cut out the middleman, me," she pointed her fingers at her chest, "and have at it?"

Heat crept from the pit of Cassidy's gut to ignite her cheeks and she looked away. But not before Amber noticed.

"Hmmm, maybe you already have. Time to spill, Jill. 'Fess up."

Wringing her hands together she eyed Amber. "Did you and him have a thing together?"

Amber's mouth dropped into a perfect oval. "Me and C.C.? What would he want with someone like me?"

It was her turn to look surprised. "What's wrong with someone like you? You're smart and witty and beautiful under the five shades of hair color and two pounds of eye makeup."

Amber threw her head back and laughed. "I'll take that as a compliment. But I'm not in C.C.'s league. I love flirting with him and he's done me some favors, kinda saved my life if you want to know the truth, but we've never had a thing." She raised her fingers to put quotation marks around the word. "What makes you ask?"

Cassidy studied the scuffs on her sneakers. "Just something Rosie said about you and him, you know, um, together, in a backseat."

Amber frowned. "You want to know if I ever had sex with C.C.?"

Cassidy picked at her thumbnail, sorry now that she'd broached the subject. Amber raised her eyebrow, eliciting a tinkle from the tiny star. "You can't even look at me and ask your question. What's going on? Sing, Bing."

Cassidy wet her lips and raised her gaze. "I saw him over the weekend. I more than saw him. But if you hope to be his girlfriend, I won't see him again."

Her voice cracked as she spoke, knowing in her heart she would find it difficult not to crawl into Clay's arms again. Her loyalty to Amber would have a hell of a fight against her desire for Clay, but she wouldn't betray her only friend.

Amber leveled that scrutinizing stare at her, the one that sliced right through her. "You're like that cube, Cass, the one with all the colors and you have to twist and turn it just the right way to get it to match." Her hands mimicked the action.

"I can't figure you out. If I had slept with C.C., I wouldn't tell you because he is a decent man and I wouldn't do anything to ruin his reputation. The only time I've been in his backseat is when he arrested me."

For a split second, Cassidy's breathing suspended.

Amber's head bobbed. "Yeah, I thought that would shock you. It's not common knowledge around here so if you squeal, I'll get fired. I don't think I could do anything to convince the old man to keep me if he knew I was on probation. So please keep your trap shut. I like to think me and C.C. are friends — if I needed help and called him, he'd come. So that's something. He's a good cop and, I think, a good man, too."

She arched one eyebrow and regarded Cassidy. "He seems to have an eye for you. That's opportunity knocking in my book. You said you saw him this weekend. Where? I just spilled my guts, Cass, you gotta share."

Cassidy nudged her glasses up her nose. "Well, since we're sharing secrets, I'd rather no one here knows, but he moved me out of Fortieth Street."

"Good for him." Amber pumped her fist in the air. "You didn't belong there. Where'd he move you to?"

"Into a building he owns. In return for rent I'm doing odd jobs, running errands, and helping maintain the place."

"That sounds like a fair deal."

"It's more than fair. The apartment I'm in is beautiful." She fell silent.

"And?" Amber swung her feet out and back from the side of the table. "There's gotta be more. Why did I have to get a message to him last week?"

She recounted the ride to the store with Clay and repeated Rosie's comments. "I didn't want her to see him picking me up."

Amber nodded. "That was a good move on your part. I knew you were a smart cookie. So why does working for C.C. and living in the same building as him make you blush like a virgin and have you so concerned about my relationship with him?"

Cassidy studied the well-worn path in the carpet between the front counter and the backroom, avoiding Amber's inquisitive stare. "We sort of had a date Saturday night. Nothing fancy, but it felt like it might be, I mean, maybe it could turn into something more. We, um, if you and he . . ."

Amber straightened her back, planted both fists on her hips, and laughed out loud. "Well, now the tables are turned. I'm curious as hell if you slept with him, but I'm not going to ask because either you've suffered heat stroke under these fluorescent lights or you're reliving the night and enjoying it as much as the first time around."

She did a little dance. "I can see the two of you together. It's a nice fit so I say good for you, girlfriend. He's quite a catch and probably just what you need."

Cassidy stared at Amber. "Why do you say that?"

"I've told you before, I think you're hiding something or running from something or in trouble. Whatever it is, C.C. is the man to help you resolve it."

The door chimed and she winked. "I do hope someday you tell me how he looks naked. I could live on that vision forever."

A tall woman with long brown hair stood waiting at the counter. She exuded cold, like a walking ice sculpture, zeroing in on Cassidy. Instinctively, Cassidy took a step back.

Amber cleared her throat. "Good morning. How can I help you?" The woman disregarded Amber and, instead, spit words at Cassidy.

"Stay away from my husband. Understand?"

Cassidy's knees buckled and she grabbed the back counter for support.

Amber stepped into her line of vision, shielding Cassidy from that arctic glare. "And you are?"

The woman riveted icy globes on Amber. "I'm not talking to you." She moved to her left to once again glower at Cassidy.

But Amber wouldn't be bested and she stepped to her right, blocking the woman's line of sight again.

"I'm talking to you," Amber hissed, emphasizing the first and last words. "Unless you have something to ship or wish to purchase office supplies, I don't think you have any business here."

Robotically, the woman refocused on Amber. "This doesn't concern you, honey."

Amber folder her arms in front of her and tilted her head in a side-to-side motion. "I've decided it does concern me, honey. Who the hell are you anyway?"

The woman's lips puckered together as if she'd eaten a lemon. "Lauren Cestra."

Amber dropped her hands to her hips. "Well, listen, Lauren Cestra. Either buy something or leave before I call the police. That would be Officer Clay Cestra, I believe. Know him?"

That startled Lauren. Her jaw dropped open and she took one step away from the counter.

The door chimed and a man entered carrying a small box to ship. Amber pointed to the door and spoke low and slow. "Out. Now. Or I call."

Lauren leaned to catch Cassidy's attention. "This isn't over." She turned, strutting out on three-inch heels and swinging her long hair behind her.

As soon as the store was empty Amber turned to Cassidy. "What was that all about?"

"I'm not sure. Clay told me he wasn't married."

"Well somebody forgot to tell the ice queen. Are you going to tell Clay about her?"

"Sure. Don't you think I should?"

Amber shrugged. "What do you think?"

"She has no right to come in here and tell me what to do or who to see. And Clay said they are divorced so she has no right to him either."

Amber smiled at the answer. "You are a fighter, aren't you Cass. You go girl, stake your claim."

Lauren was undaunted. If there was one thing she learned from her six-month stint in the county jail, it was how to get what she wanted. More often than not, all it took was money, and she definitely had more than those two little snots in that shipping store.

Her purpose had been to read the riot act to the little whore sleeping with Clay. Despite the other twit's interference, she had at least placed her on notice to stay away. If Clay Cestra thought he could discard her like last year's sweater, he'd better think again. That damn court order may force her to avoid contact with him, but it didn't address interaction with his play things.

Up until now, his handful of relationships with other women had been flirtatious and frivolous. But his affair with Miss Cassidy Hoake was escalating like a runaway train, and she was determined to derail it.

As distasteful as it was, she returned to the county jail for a visit with her former cellmate, Barbie Trumbolli. Barbie had at least one more year of her sentence to serve and because of her bully tendencies, which she flaunted rather than suppressed, early release for good behavior was not in her future.

Unlike Lauren. A smile creased her face. She'd been the model prisoner. Well, at least the prison officials said so.

Sitting in the dingy visiting area waiting for Barbie, she shivered in disgust. The room needed scrubbed from ceiling to baseboard. A healthy dose of disinfectant wouldn't hurt.

She'd been assigned to share Barbie's cell and their first meeting turned into one hell of a catfight, with her clawing at Barbie's face and screaming threats she couldn't remotely back up. Pure adrenaline fortified her to stand toe to toe with Barbie, refusing to back down from the verbal assaults and the shove against the wall.

She'd shoved back and then advanced on Barbie, breathing hard, staring eye to eye for the longest minute of her life, and snarled, "I'm not your bitch."

The end result was she'd earned Barbie's respect. Barbie smiled, winked, and said, "You'll do. I don't want some pansy sharing my space."

That marked the beginning of their friendship and Lauren's jail-survival education. She learned how a couple extra bucks could add a dessert to the meal trays, slip a bottle of nail polish into her pocket, and allow her to wear her own lingerie. Jail issue underwear was beyond horrendous.

When she shared her wealth with Barbie, they became allies. Barbie offered protection from the other inmates, who resented Lauren's perks. In return, Lauren deposited a sizeable amount in Barbie's jail account when she was released.

Like Lauren, Barbie had faced attempted murder charges that were reduced to assault. Unlike Lauren, who was mortified to be confined, Barbie's world revolved around organized crime, and violence seemed second nature. It was as if her stature within the family had risen because of her conviction and subsequent jail sentence.

Barbie beamed when she entered the visitor's room and spied Lauren sitting at the table. "You clean up real good, Baby Sis."

"How are you, Barbie? Still ruling the roost?"

"You bet your ass I am. I'm surprised to see you here. You miss me so much you voluntarily came back to this shit hole?"

She eyed the guard, turned back to Barbie, and winked. "I wanted to talk to you about a conversation we had a while back, about how I could get a good cup of coffee."

Barbie narrowed her eyes. "I thought you were a Starbucks girl."

Lauren plastered a smile on her face. "What if I wanted to try something different, more robust? You know, a little darker and more dangerous."

Barbie matched her grin. "How much darker?"

"I'm looking for a killer cup of coffee." She tossed her hair over her shoulder and laughed, wanting the guard to witness a simple, friendly reunion.

"Girl, it's so good to see you," Barbie responded, throwing her head back and laughing as well. "I know the perfect coffee shop. My cousin runs the place. He'll help you with anything you want to order. Just ask for Mittens."

12

Tony DelMorrie sucked on a cigarette, pinching his left eye closed to block the smoke drifting upward. He shifted in the front seat. His frame was too large to spend so much time slumped behind a steering wheel.

Checking his watch he calculated it at nine hours. His stomach growled and he had to take a piss. Where the hell was she?

The tip he got from his cousin's mistress had better pan out. Cassidy's trail had gone cold more than a month ago in some small town in Tennessee. Christ, he'd hated that hole. But he hadn't given up. No way. After his cousin called with the word that she was in Ohio, he'd driven all night.

He couldn't have missed her, even if she was disguised. His view of her bedroom window was clear. There hadn't been a light on in that apartment since he'd put eyes on it before the sun came up this morning. He'd searched it yesterday. She mighta been scared off finding it like that, but he still figured she'd come back to her own place before the start of a new work week. The little whore was probably shacked up with somebody.

He picked up the name tag between nicotine stained fingers

and wiggled it, catching the light's reflection. He'd waited this long. It was no time to get careless. He'd give it another day or two. If she didn't show up, he'd find The Packing Place.

Clay rubbed his eyes. Hell. When he began an archive search for Cassidy's name on *The Arizona Republic* website he never expected to find it linked to a murder and the mob. He stared at the photo of her surrounded by men in suits rushing her into a courthouse back door. Long, red hair floated behind her and, he noticed, no glasses.

"Eyewitness Cassidy Hoake is escorted by detectives into the courthouse under protective custody," the photo caption read. He skimmed the story details. It all seemed in order. She'd witnessed the crime and testified.

He moved the cursor back to the search box and typed "Tony DelMorrie." Clay was familiar with the name and the family's underworld reputation. DelMorrie had carried on in his father's footsteps, promoting prostitution and racketeering.

Reportedly, DelMorrie personally "disposed of" family business problems, a deviation from the norm for mob bosses, but authorities had been unable to charge him with two murders they suspected he committed. He was too shrewd to get caught.

Apparently, he'd let his emotions get the better of him with his girlfriend. The paper said he and Jill Diamond had lived together for more than a year and had a major argument the morning Jill Diamond died. The story reported that DelMorrie gunned her down as she was entering a local convenience store. It was careless and impromptu and in front of a witness—not DelMorrie's style. Police arrested him based on the testimony of the eyewitness, Cassidy Hoake.

Clay continued reading and there it was, the reason Cassidy was always looking around, constantly watching, forever evaluating her surroundings. DelMorrie had posted the one-million-dollar cash bail designed to keep him in jail and skipped town.

Why the hell had bail been approved on a murder charge for a man like DelMorrie, someone police suspected of other murders? That was unheard of. Granted, the high dollar amount would keep the average murderer behind bars, but not DelMorrie, not with his connections. Why had the prosecutor agreed to bail at all? It didn't make sense, unless DelMorrie's influence reached right into the prosecutor's office or the judge's chambers.

He read further. Arizona authorities were looking for him and Cassidy. She'd disappeared after her car exploded and police found her townhouse ransacked. There was some speculation about whether or not she was alive. A separate story included an interview with the presiding judge and his plea urging Cassidy to contact him and ensuring her safety. He didn't seem to think she'd been harmed.

The judge? That certainly was peculiar. Judges seldom gave interviews. They were supposed to remain impartial.

Another smaller article quoted the lead detective on the case. "We urge Ms. Hoake to take every precaution until we have detained Mr. DelMorrie."

Why wasn't he urging her to turn herself in? Something wasn't right. At the end of the article, the detective said he, too, feared Cassidy might be dead. Jesus.

"Jack's finally asleep," his sister said, coming up behind him. She placed her hands on his shoulders and peered at the computer screen. "Did you find anything?"

"Yeah, Mags. She's in trouble. Big time."

"You're in trouble," Leslie agreed. "Even if we order a new one on the sly, it won't be here for at least four or five days. Tomorrow, he'll be looking for the name tag."

Amber struck a key on the keyboard as if it were the final note of a piano concerto. "There. It's ordered and charged to the store account for luggage tags. Now, I have an idea."

She removed her name tag and laid it under the copy machine cover. Once she had a color copy of the tag, she returned to the computer and typed Cassidy's name in a matching font. Rising, she switched on the laminating machine.

"We can make this look like your badge. There is an old sweater in the backroom. If you wear that when the old man is here it will partially conceal it. Try not to let him get a good look at it. Stay at the counter waiting on people when he's here. It should work. Don't tape it on until tomorrow though. He already knows you don't have it today."

The remainder of the day passed remarkably quickly. Although Amber clocked out at four, she waited a half hour until Cassidy was finished and offered her a lift home.

"Is your lease up in the rat hole, Cass?" she asked as they drove.

"No, I have another week. It was a monthly lease."

"Do you still have the key?"

"Yes. Why?"

"I was thinking it might be a nice little hideaway for me and someone special, you know? A place where we might be alone that none of our friends could find us."

Cassidy's eyebrows rose. "I didn't know you had someone special."

Amber laughed. "Well, after I take him there and have some time alone with him he might be special. What do you say? I promise not to trash the place."

Cassidy's pulse jumped. Someone already trashed the place. "It's a hole, just like you said. There isn't even any furniture in there."

"That doesn't matter. Relax, Cass, all I want is some place private."

"I don't know Amber, it might not be safe."

"Maybe not for you, but I know people down in that neighborhood. I can pass as one of them. Will you loan me the key and let me have some fun?"

Against her better judgment, Cassidy dug into her purse and retrieved the Fortieth Street key. "Just be careful, okay? Turn here," she said, pointing.

Amber whistled as her car chugged up the driveway to the Cestra Chalets, a trail of black smoke spewing from the exhaust pipe.

"Whooeee, girlfriend. You have made it to the big time."

Cassidy laughed, directing her to the rear building. "It's only temporary. I'm in that one."

As the car slowed, Clay emerged from the front door, smiling as he walked down the steps and eliciting a second whistle from Amber. "Now that's something to come home to."

Cassidy's heart flip flopped. In tight jeans and a sky blue T-shirt spread as thin as film across his chest, Clay looked delicious. Every part of her body applauded the view.

He ambled to the driver's side and leaned in the window, smiling as he eyed Amber. "Green?"

Amber laughed. "It's called Neon Kiwi. You like?"

Clay shook his head and chuckled. "It's definitely you, hon. Thanks for giving Cassidy a ride home. Looks like you're burning oil."

"Yeah, I know. I have to get it fixed."

"What day are you off this week? I'll make an appointment at my buddy's garage. He'll take care of you."

"I don't have the money right now, C.C."

"Don't worry about it. I'll check Cassidy's copy of the schedule and set something up." He withdrew his money clip from his pants pocket and tugged a twenty free, handing it in the window.

"Take this for gas money. Are you able to ride her home tomorrow, too?"

Amber winked. "For another shot of you in a skin tight T-shirt, I'll drive her anywhere you want me to." She waved as she backed up and drove off.

Clay reached out his arm. "Hi. I've been thinking about you all day. Come here."

Cassidy scanned the smattering of cars in the parking lot, then eagerly stepped into his embrace and raised her eyes to his. How she had come to depend on this man so quickly, to want him so desperately, she wasn't sure. The only time she felt safe was now, in his arms. The feeling overwhelmed her.

He kissed her lightly on the forehead. "I want you to come over to Maggie's. We want to talk about Arizona."

She fought to keep her knees from buckling and stepped out of his arms. Looking around again, she cleared her throat and pushed her glasses up her nose. "What about Arizona?"

"That's what we want to discuss."

"We?"

"Me, Maggie, and Dan. C'mon." He extended his hand for her to take.

Crap. She wasn't ready to confront the devil yet. It was one thing to resolve to stand up to him while riding a bus, totally another taking that first step to start the process. She wanted a little more time. This whole feeling of empowerment was still in its infancy.

Her flight instinct barreled full force to the front of her brain. It was the only way she knew how to survive.

"How about if I change my clothes and then come over?"

Clay smiled. "How about if I come with you?"

Her head snapped up. "What's the matter, Officer Cestra? Don't you trust me not to run?" She didn't feel as mean as her words sounded. She actually felt lightheaded, like she might faint.

Clay pursed his lips. "To be perfectly honest, Miss Hoake, I don't. The look in your eyes screams panic. You want to bolt."

It was a standoff. Her, hands on her hips, defying him to say more. Him, returning the stare without the attitude.

She studied a car backing into a visitor's parking spot. The muscles across her shoulders grabbed each other, bursting into an instant headache. The hairs on the back of her neck edged up.

"Can we discuss this inside?"

Clay motioned toward the door. "After you." They walked into the building and headed toward the stairs.

"You're really going to follow me to my apartment? Really? You don't think I can change my clothes and walk over to Maggie's on my own? I'm insulted."

Clay smiled, a slow easy smile that seared its way into her heart. "You're trying to pick a fight with me. Good strategy but it won't work. I'm following you because I like seeing you without your clothes. How's that?"

He stopped at her apartment door. She raised her chin defiantly, but tears threatened to spill and she looked away.

"C'mon, honey. I know about the shooting. I know about Tony DelMorrie. That's who you're hiding from, isn't it?" He spread his hands wide. "See? I know the truth and I'm still here. I think you've been running so long, you don't know how to stop. Please, Cassie. I want to help. So do Maggie and Dan. I asked you the other night to trust me and I'm asking again."

He gently squeezed her elbow and she raised her face to meet his gaze. "We can work this out together. We'll get through it."

She blinked back her tears. "We?"

The corners of his mouth edged up. "I already whispered you're not alone anymore. Maybe I need to say it louder."

His eyes scanned her face. "We're definitely a 'we' now."

Inserting the key into the doorknob, Cassidy glibly threw her words over her shoulder as she entered her apartment. "I'm not sure Mrs. Cestra is on board with that idea."

Seconds earlier, her heart had been in her throat. Now, seeing the stunned look on Clay's face, she relaxed. She wasn't the only one with problems. Obviously, he had his own demon.

His eyebrows shot to his hairline. "Who?"

"Your wife. Tall. Stunning. Icy cold. She came to see me today to tell me to stay away from you."

The door slammed behind him as he strode to her. Clutching both her elbows he riveted his gaze on her. "First of all, she's not my wife. We are divorced. Secondly, I want you to stay away from her. She's dangerous."

Something about the look in his eyes erased the levity she'd felt moments earlier.

"I'm not the one seeking her out, Clay. She came looking for me. What are you telling me? That now I have two people to fear?"

He released her arms and automatically walked to the sliding glass doors to scan the parking lot. He was familiar with the tenants' vehicles and noted, almost subconsciously, that all of the cars presently in the lot belonged there. She wasn't waiting outside.

What was he telling her? What did he dare tell her?

"Clay?"

Turning, he noticed the dark circles beneath Cassidy's eyes for the first time, the strain on her face. Throwing Lauren into the mix would add to her fears. But she had to be warned.

"There is a restraining order on file, Cass. She's dangerous."

Her eyes widened and she lifted her hand to her throat. "She needed an order against you? Why? What did you do to her?"

No one ever expected a cop to need help defending himself against a woman. He flexed his right hand open, closed, open, closed.

"No, honey. The restraining order is against her, not me. I

have a two-inch scar just above my kidneys where she stabbed me."

He moved his hand to his back, gently touching the now-healed wound. Sometimes, he could feel that blade slicing into him again, akin to a box cutter separating a seam and releasing the contents like a volcanic eruption. He could still hear her high-pitched shriek, recall stumbling under the full force of her weight when she jumped on his back, and remember the rage unleashed by her actions, a fury that had simmered for a full year, simmered to boiling and exploded in uncontrollable anger.

His hands went to her throat, his anger out of control, his desire for revenge overtaking him like a flesh-eating disease.

"She tried to kill you?" He recognized stunned disbelief and panic in Cassidy's voice.

"It was mutual, honey." He'd wanted to kill Lauren, would have without a second thought if his colleagues hadn't burst through the door and rescued him. Him, not her. He'd been the victim of mental, verbal, and ultimately physical abuse. He flexed his hand, tightening and releasing his fist.

He moved toward her and she stepped into his embrace. God, even after a day at work she smelled wonderful. He buried his nose in her hair, captivated by the flowery scent. Heat surged through him as he ran his hand down her back to caress her bottom. He wanted her close, under his skin if he could manage that.

As if sensing his need, she melted into his arms, and raised her mouth to meet his. The kiss, sweetly tentative at first, exploded into blistering passion. They tore at each other's clothes and dropped to the floor, Clay fumbling for a condom as she wrapped those glorious legs around his hips. He plunged into her, needing to possess her, needing to make her understand.

"I'm not going to lose you, not to her, not to DelMorrie, not for any reason. I'll kill to keep you," he croaked.

He exploded inside her while she clung to him, gasping from

her own orgasm. She'd whispered something, he was certain. Barely audible. He rose up on his elbows and pushed sweat-soaked hair off her forehead. Her eyes remained closed, her mouth in a half-smile.

He traced her lips with his fingertip and whispered. "Hey, you." Slowly, her eyelids lifted, revealing shining brown orbs. "Say something."

She kissed the finger at her lips and smiled. "I'm afraid you just made love with a fugitive, Officer Cestra."

He grinned. "Tell me something I don't already know."

Her smile disappeared and her eyes darkened. Her breasts rose when she inhaled, brushing her nipples lightly against his chest. He didn't think she was going to say anything at all, and then, a second deep breath.

"I want to, Clay," she whispered, "I really do. Just give me a little time, okay?"

He touched the tip of her nose with his lips. "We have all the time in the world, hon."

She shivered. "I don't think so."

Something jolted him awake. Christ, he'd fallen asleep in the front seat with his head sitting on his chest and now his neck was stiff. One more reason to hate that Hoake bitch.

Swinging his head in tiny circle eights, he grimaced while he stretched out the kinks. Blinking, he focused on the apartment window and sat bolt upright. A new light shined inside. Vaguely, he could make out a shadow moving. Finally.

Tony eased out of the car, one stiff leg followed by the other, shoving himself off the seat with his hand. It wasn't only his neck, his whole damn body was stiff. He leaned against the car, waiting for the blood to circulate down to his feet, and glanced over his shoulder at the window again. Definitely movement. She was home.

From the backseat, he retrieved a black ball cap, which he jammed onto his oversized head and forced low over his eyes. He slipped into a black windbreaker, yanking the collar up to his ears, then retrieved his Berretta 9mm, screwed on the silencer, and checked again that the serial number had been obliterated.

He'd imagined playing out this scene several different ways in the weeks he'd tracked her. He'd love to punch her in the face a few times, maybe break her nose. Grab her by that long hair and swing her to the floor, drag her around a bit. Maybe pin her down and fuck the living shit out of her before he lodged a bullet in her brain. Anything to let her know she had crossed the line, that she couldn't get away with trying to put him in jail, that she'd lost and he, Tony DelMorrie, had won.

But as he crept down the hall toward apartment one-twelve as silently as a man his size could, he just wanted it over with. He wanted her dead. It couldn't be simpler.

Under the windbreaker, sweat soaked his undershirt, plastering it against his stomach, and his armpits felt sticky. He needed to catch his breath. All that sitting had weakened his leg muscles. He hadn't walked a great distance, but he was winded. He paused in front of her apartment, bending over to slow his accelerated heartbeat.

Some kind of crappy, loud music boomed from behind the closed door. It didn't surprise him that her taste in tunes sucked. Concealing the gun against his thigh, his finger hovering above the trigger, he knocked.

Jesus. The stupid bitch must not have heard. He pounded harder.

"All right! All right! Hold your horses, Slick."

The door swung open. "Who are—"

"Fuck you, Hoake. I win." Tat. Tat. Tat. Tat.

She dropped like a rock. The recoil jarred his hand slightly, but the silencer kept the sound muffled. With the music blaring, the neighbors couldn't have heard.

Opening his hand wide the gun slipped from his grip and bounced on the carpet with a dull thud. He turned and ran toward the exit. This time, adrenaline surging through his veins made it an easy sprint. Up the stairs two at a time and out the door.

He forced himself to slow to a walker's pace and surveyed the parking lot. Perfect. Not a soul in sight. As casually as possible, with sweat dripping from his underarms and his bowels churning, he walked to his car and squeezed into the front seat. Careful not to look around, he started the car and slowly drove out of the parking lot.

Once on the main road, he tugged off the ball cap, tossing it behind him, and allowed a small smile. It was done. Ding dong, the bitch was dead.

He'd never forget that look of surprise on her face. Never. She'd done a good job of disguising herself, he'd give her that. When the hell had she put purple and green streaks in her hair?

13

It was settled, she was going back to Arizona.

But not alone. After more than an hour of heated debate that included multiple curses, and threatened to turn into a loud, ugly argument between her and Clay, she agreed to let him take her back in what he called "personal protective custody." A cop and a witness.

Clay said he trusted his police chief and assured Cassidy their travel arrangements could be made quietly and kept confidential. Not even she would know the details. He cast the trip in a romantic light, counting off the different states where they could spend the night and grinning mischievously.

But before he did anything, he wanted to reach out privately to the detective in the news article who had seemed to be cautioning Cassidy to stay hidden, so their departure would be delayed a couple of days. That would give him time to work out his schedule and allow Cassidy the chance to give notice at The Packing Place that she was leaving. When this was all over, she hoped to resume her accounting career.

Clay's initial sense was that someone high up "on the inside" was on DelMorrie's payroll so he planned to tread lightly. Both he and Dan speculated that the bail arrangement implicated someone in the prosecutor's office or the judge's. Or both, for all they knew. The detective appeared clean, but Clay planned to check him out and Dan had an Arizona sheriff connection they trusted. It seemed like a simple enough plan.

Cassidy agreed the Arizona detective had seemed genuinely concerned about her from the minute she perched on the edge of a metal folding chair beside his desk and detailed her eyewitness account of Jill Diamond's murder. She was comfortable with Clay contacting him discreetly but affirmed his doubts about everyone else.

Recalling the discussion, Cassidy smiled. None of Clay's arguments about the law, her civic and moral duty, or his legal obligations to turn her in had persuaded her. It was the way he'd cradled Jack in his arms, rocking him to sleep, and the dark color his eyes turned when he said, "If you want us to have a chance together, you have to go back. I'm a lawman. All of it has to be legal."

Everyone in the room fell silent, waiting for her response. Maggie's words from their first meeting echoed in her ears—it was time for her to make a choice. Seeing Clay cuddle the baby, she'd let her imagination transform the scene into one where he held their child in a life they shared. She'd proven she could take care of herself. Now, she wanted to take care of someone else.

In a déjà vu state, she carefully wrapped her mother's clock in a bath towel while Clay stood at the door with her packed duffel bag. He'd convinced her it would be safer if she stayed in his apartment while he plotted their return. Automatic timers on different lights in Cassidy's unit would maintain the appearance that someone still occupied the space.

The idea of staying with him appealed to her for several reasons. First and foremost, she felt safe with him. Their connection went beyond the incredible sex they shared. They talked about social issues, world events, and news bulletins when they were together. When they were joined as lovers, they shared dreams worthy of Dorothy's Oz. In his arms she was beautiful, sexy, and empowered. She shared his confidence that together, as Clay recited over and over, together they could beat Tony DelMorrie.

"Can I ask you something, Cass?"

She looked up to see Clay regarding her with hooded eyes. "What?"

"You told me you were from a suburb outside of Pittsburgh. Was that a lie?"

"No. That's where I was born and raised."

"So how'd you end up in Arizona?"

A sigh escaped her. The similarities hadn't occurred to her until just now.

"I followed someone there, a man. Someone I thought was the guy for me. Mr. Right. Just like you, he wanted us to stay together, offered to take care of me, said he loved me."

Her words straightened Clay's spine.

"He wasn't as handsome as you, not as muscular, not even as strong in character. But he swept me off my feet and, just like I'm trusting you, I trusted him."

Clay's response was pained. "I'm not sure I like the comparison you're drawing."

"Sorry. It didn't dawn on me until this minute."

"So where's this guy now? Why didn't he help you? Are you still in touch with him?"

The heartbreak she'd felt the day he moved out seemed a lifetime ago. She'd vowed never to trust a man again, never to live with someone without marriage vows. But she doubted marriage vows would have kept him out of that other woman's bed.

And yet, here she was, packing to move in again with another man. Apparently, she hadn't learned much from the betrayal.

She clutched the bundled clock to her chest. "Maybe staying with you isn't a good idea, Clay. Maybe I should call Amber."

Clay opened his hand, letting the duffel slide to the floor. He walked toward her but stopped and sat on the edge of the sofa. "Are you still involved with him?"

He was certain his blood pressure spiked to stroke level. The ringing in his ears had to hint of an impending seizure or something fatal. If she said yes, he'd be crushed. He flexed his hand and studied Cassidy.

She half smiled and moved to balance on the edge of the coffee table in front of him, sitting between his knees and clinging to her mother's clock.

"You're wondering how I could make love to you if I'm involved with someone else, aren't you?"

He couldn't move, didn't blink.

"That's not it at all. We were over long before I witnessed Jill Diamond's murder. I was on my own, not making a whole lot of money but doing okay. Saving to move back to Pittsburgh.

"The thing is, I trusted him, just like I'm trusting you. I believed him and moved in with him, just like I'm doing now. It was a horrible mistake. I can't make it again."

Okay, his heart restarted and his lungs resumed expansion and contraction efforts. This wasn't about him and her, it was about some asshole who'd hurt her.

"You think all men are alike?"

Her focus dropped to her feet and she whispered, "I'm not sure I can afford to find out."

"And if we have a fight, do you think I'm going to shoot you dead?"

She gasped as her head snapped up. "No! No, why would you say something like that?"

He reached out, laying his hands on her knees and moved his thumbs in a gentle caress. "If you can compare me to some butt wipe who hurt you, you can compare me to Tony DelMorrie who shoots women when they make him angry. If you paint all men with the same brush, that has to include me. Or, you could look only at me, see only me, and give me the benefit of the doubt. Do you think I'm like those other men?"

"I know in my heart you are not." She looked down again, her voice quivering as she spoke.

He reached and gently raised her chin, forcing her to see him. "What else does your heart tell you?"

Now, he watched tears pool in her eyes. "It's a pretty scary thing you want me to do, you know."

"What's that? Give a guy a chance? Maybe knock down the walls once and for all?"

One tear escaped and made a slow descent down her cheek. "No, silly. This isn't about you. I'm scared about going back to testify."

"That's where you're wrong, Cass. This is all about me and what you feel for me. You have to start by trusting me. If you do that, everything else will follow. If you aren't going to trust me, this isn't going to work. We'll probably both get killed."

Her shoulders lifted and she leveled her gaze at him, making good eye contact. The cop in him liked that.

"You're right, I'm sorry. I know this is different, that you are different. It was unfair of me to say what I did. You couldn't make love to me the way you do if you weren't sincere. I won't doubt you again."

Relief washed over him. Without total trust, he couldn't protect her. She had only a hint of the extreme danger they were heading for. If his suspicions were right, the level of corruption spilled into the exact offices he was leading her to.

"Thank you. C'mon, I have to work tonight. Is there anything else you need from here?"

She shook her head. He retrieved the duffel, locked the door behind him, and held her hand as they walked to his apartment.

Clay's home stunned her. It was designed identically as his sister's and as clean and bright. Even the sofa pillows were plumped.

"Clay, your home is lovely."

He carried her bag into the bedroom. "Make yourself at home. I have to change and get moving."

She surveyed the room and stepped into the kitchen. Tentatively, she opened the refrigerator and a grin erupted across her face. It was chock full of food and beverages. Her voice could echo in the emptiness of her refrigerator shelves.

Clay returned from the bedroom, dressed in his uniform and her stomach did a happy dance. He looked totally edible and she told him so. He grinned as he reached to the top of the china hutch and retrieved his gun. She came to him and he planted a brotherly kiss on her forehead.

"I'm short on time. You'll have to explore on your own. Help yourself to anything you want. Don't hesitate to call me or Maggie if there's a problem. You should be fine."

She walked beside him to the door and he embraced her. "I can't tell you how good it feels knowing you'll be here, kinda like you're at home, waiting for me. I'm gonna like playing house with you. What time do you work tomorrow?"

"I start at ten. Amber opens."

"Good. I'll come home first and pick you up. I can drop any samples for shipment when I take you in. I'll call and check on you later." He kissed her sweetly.

"I hope you're as happy as I am that you're here."

"If you didn't have to leave for work, Officer Cestra, I'd show you how glad I am to be here. Don't worry, I'll be waiting for you to come home to me."

"Promise?"

"Promise."

His smile was lecherous. "Seal it with a kiss."

Cassidy rose on her tiptoes and locked her lips with his, plunging her tongue into his mouth and pressing her body into his for a long, slow kiss.

Clay released her and stepped backwards, blinking rapidly. "Jesus, Cass, kiss me like that and I'll have to call off."

She was pleased the kiss had the effect she'd hoped. He plucked his keys off a decorative hanger beside the door, removed his hat from the wooden hall tree and dropped one final kiss on her lips.

"See you tomorrow morning, hon."

Lauren walked confidently into The Drip Stick, her head held high. This was the seedier side of town, but Barbie had warned her not to appear nervous or the neighborhood delinquents would be all over her. A group of them were leaning on the building, clucking their tongues and howling when she walked by, and she ignored them, realizing that, in actuality, she was excited by this adventure into the underworld, titillated by the danger. She strode to a round table for two, wiped the chair with a napkin and sat.

She stood out like a diamond watch in a discount store, in her two-piece red designer suit and matching pumps. Red was the color of power and she exuded it.

She regarded a stocky, dark haired man with bulging muscles and a towel in his hand who approached her, one of those all brawn no brain types.

"What'll it be for you tonight, ma'am?"

"I'd like an espresso with a shot of Bailey's, please."

"One carajillo, coming up. Anything else?"

"Yes. My friend told me I should try the red velvet cake that Mittens makes. She says the frosting is to die for."

She recited the phrase exactly as Barbie had instructed, wondering if the stooge standing in front of her knew the code. Surely, people who dealt in this kind of thing were smarter.

The waiter's eyes roamed from her face to her hands, assessing the rings on her fingers and the gold dangling from her wrist, evaluated the designer clutch on the table and returned his gaze to hers. "I'll see if we have any in the back."

Heat engulfed her when she looked around to find the other customers staring at her. She was the center of attention and it turned her on. Somewhere behind her, the espresso machine hissed and she visualized warm, milky froth spilling down her breasts and pooling beneath her waist, firing up a sensory awareness she hadn't known since Clay held her. She wanted him back. There was no two ways about it, the little girlfriend had to go.

The waiter placed a cup and saucer in front of her and a plate with a red wedge of cake and a fork beside it. "See if you like this, ma'am."

Crap. Maybe he didn't understand the message. She'd expected to be whisked into a back room to meet some toothpick chewing bald thug who'd wink, shake her hand conspiratorially, and question her about the cryptic message. Wasn't that how code words worked?

Barbie had been specific about what to say but Lauren hadn't anticipated being served an actual piece of cake. She hated cake, but she ate it, barely keeping the sugary icing down, waiting for some kind of signal regarding the real reason she was there. The waiter cleaned various tables but kept his attention on her, finally returning when only crumbs littered the plate to stand in front of her.

"Would you like something else?"

"Yes." She recalled Barbie's directions to ask for the recipe. "It was the best I've ever tasted. I'd love the recipe."

He smiled. "Who told you about our cake?"

"Barbie Trumbolli."

He furrowed his brow. "How do you know Barbie?"

Smiling as she checked the nearby tables to see who might overhear, she said, "Barbie and I were roommates together last year at an all girls' extravaganza. I believe Barbie liked it so much she is still there. I need something for a special occasion and she suggested I come here for your cake recipe."

He regarded her for one long minute, finally nodding. "I'll speak to the chef in the kitchen. Maybe he'll share the recipe with you." He yelled for another waitress to cover his tables and disappeared behind a swinging door. Time crawled to a standstill while she sat, watching the other customers and wondering what she should do next. This plan did not seem to be working.

She jumped when the waiter's voice cut through her thoughts. "Come in back, ma'am. The chef is always interested in meeting fans of his cake."

She'd imagined meeting a Jimmy Cagney character like in the movie *White Heat* or a Clyde Barrow gangster type, not someone who looked like he stepped off of a Disney soundstage. Mittens was a little man with tiny hands, and she immediately wondered if gloves were too big for him, hence the moniker. He should have remained seated behind the table, where she wouldn't have realized his lack of height, instead of jumping from the chair like a jack-in-the-box and extending his miniature hand for a shake. She towered over him by more than a foot.

He grinned widely and bobbed his head like an animated cartoon character. Nothing about him threatened her and now she wondered if Barbie had misinterpreted their conversation.

His office was little more than a pantry, his desk a folding table situated in front of shelves lined with baking supplies. He'd jumped out of the only chair in the storeroom.

"Hello, hello. I understand you know my cousin Barbie. How's she doin'? When'd you see her last?"

She recounted her visit and Barbie's suggestion that she contact Mittens. "I spoke to Barbie about a problem I was having with, um, an ingredient in a cake recipe and she thought you might be able to help. She mentioned your killer icing. I can pay whatever the recipe costs."

Mittens flashed nicotine-stained teeth. "You've come to the right place. Icing is a specialty of mine."

14

C lay sauntered into the police station twenty minutes before his shift began. The bounce in his step and the lightness in his heart amazed him. Christ, he was as giddy as a kid on the first day of summer and Cassidy was the reason. Just thinking about her, he grinned like a dope.

He'd deal with the Lauren issue tomorrow, but that was nothing more than a mosquito that needed another swat. At least he hoped all it would take to back her off was a call from his attorney. After all, she was still on probation and he doubted she wanted to lose her freedom again.

Mentally, he dismissed her. She wasn't going to douse his smoldering thoughts about Cassidy tonight.

"You look happy to be here," Pat Tatman quipped, while he pecked the computer keyboard with two fingers.

Clay's grin widened. "Not happy to be here, just happy. You can take off if you want to clock out a few minutes early. I'll cover the last fifteen of your shift."

Pat didn't look up when he spoke. "Thanks but I have to finish this report before I leave. Another shooting at the Fortieth Street apartments."

Clay checked his mailbox, removing two pieces of junk mail. "Drugs?"

"Probably."

He reached for a clipboard to sign out his cruiser, noting that Car Twelve-Thirteen wasn't back on station yet.

The springs squealed when Pat leaned back in his chair. "Yeah, that unit was dispatched to the apartments. We need an ID on the vic. Had to rouse the apartment manager for the rental records. He's not back yet."

"No big deal." Clay wandered into the break room and poured a cup of coffee, then sat at a computer station and plugged in a search for *The Arizona Republic*. Probably too much to hope that Tony DelMorrie had been apprehended overnight. That kind of arrest would make national news.

Absorbed by the newspaper search, he was vaguely aware of the arrival of two fellow officers. Their words trickled into his concentration, ". . .facial identity impossible . . ." ". . .couple hours before they found her" "Hoake, H O A K E."

What did he hear? Clay walked to the doorway, listening as the patrolman shared additional information. "no driver's license on record . . . dental records won't work."

An uneasy feeling suddenly soured the freshly consumed coffee. "Who are you talking about?"

Pat looked his way. "There's a problem with confirmation on my shooting vic. Don't you know someone who lived in the Fortieth high-rise?"

Clay moved toward the trio. "What's the problem?"

Pat removed his eyeglasses and rubbed his eyes. "Four shots. Two above the neck, one facial. She's unrecognizable. The apartment manager wasn't much help. Said it didn't seem like it was the tenant of record. But the sight of her made him puke so who knows?"

Clay glanced down at the pages spread on the desk in front of

Pat, his eyes searching for the Victim Identification block on the report. The writing was too small to decipher.

"What name do you have?"

Pat returned his glasses to his face, picked up one of the sheets, and read out loud, "Hoake. C. Hoake. Age unknown."

The coffee threatened to come up. The warmth drained from his face and that buzzing in his ears resumed, the same noise he'd heard hours ago when he feared Cassidy was in love with another man.

"You okay, Clay?"

He reached for the report sheets. "May I see these?"

The details were minimal. A neighbor walking to her own unit passed the opened door of the apartment and saw the body. She screamed, ran to her apartment down the hall, and called police. A weapon lay at the woman's feet, its identifying serial numbers removed. Ballistics would likely find nothing.

The apartment number jumped off the page—one-twelve. Clay swallowed bile that threatened to gag him. "Your ID isn't correct. C. Hoake is Cassidy Hoake. She wasn't in apartment one-twelve last night."

"How do you know?"

His attention dropped to the box on the report marked physical description and his heart thudded. Dammit. The height and weight were estimates, which would be confirmed or corrected by the coroner.

The blocks for the facial description—eyes, identifying scars, piercings—remained blank. But the hair, the description of the hair was there despite the massive amount of blood matting it. Long and dark, highlighted with purple and green streaks.

Why was Amber there? "Son of a bitch," he whispered. "Son of a fucking bitch."

"Clay?"

Clay's emotions flooded his senses, drowning him in a genuine numbness of loss. Anyone who thought cops weren't affected by the daily incidents they handled was a fool. Why her? He'd really liked her.

He blinked, unashamed of the tears that welled. "This is Amber Malone. Age twenty-four. Place of employment, The Packing Place in Greenbrier." His voice wavered. "She's has one prior. My arrest. You'll find her other stats in my files. Same address. She hasn't moved since I arrested her."

Laying the pages on the desk, he shook his head. "This wasn't a drug shooting. She's been clean for more than a year." The three men studied him, taken aback by the rare emotional display.

Pat screwed up his face. "Domestic?"

"I doubt it. She was single and she didn't live there."

"Know the next of kin?"

He shook his head against the tightening in his chest. He teased her almost daily, went out on a limb to keep her out of trouble, and had relied on her to help Cassidy. Yet, he didn't know much about her, not even if she had a sibling or parents.

"Can you give me anything else?"

He didn't dare say another word, couldn't tell his co-workers that it was likely reputed mobster Tony DelMorrie who gunned down Amber thinking it was Cassidy. What was Amber doing at Cassidy's old apartment? Certainly she couldn't have known Tony DelMorrie, couldn't have been in on his hunt for Cassidy. She'd had too many opportunities to hurt Cassidy if that were the case. No, this was a case of misidentification and the second costly mistake DelMorrie had made.

His jumbled thoughts nauseated him. Tony DelMorrie was in town, he knew where Cassidy lived, he'd been at her doorstep. Where was he now?

Did he realize it wasn't Cassidy who he killed? He shot Jill Diamond in anger, deviating from the cautious, premeditated actions he was known for. When Amber opened that door, did he act impulsively and fire or did he see who it was first?

Either way, he had to follow through with it. How do you explain knocking on someone's door with a gun aimed at their head when they answer?

"Clay? Are you with me?"

"Sorry. What did you say?"

"Do you know where I can find Miss Hoake? She might be able to fill in some blanks, like why this woman was there and who might have wanted to hurt her."

His heart drummed in his ears. His oath as a law officer battled with his desire to protect Cassidy. He'd promised he would.

"I'll have her in here tomorrow morning for you to interview. Do me a favor, Pat, and go with that for now. Here. Tomorrow at nine." He had to get out of there. The buzzing in his head hadn't ceased. "I'm heading out on patrol. Tomorrow. Nine-hundred hours."

He reached for the car keys and ignored the gaping mouths of his co-workers. He needed fresh air now. The urgency to hear Cassidy's voice, assure himself that she was safe, overwhelmed him.

How was he going to break the news about Amber? How was he going to impress upon Cassidy that it was imperative she stay where she was, that the safest place for her was with him? And how, dear God, was he going to keep her safe?

She couldn't sleep. Surrounded by Clay's possessions, curled into his sofa, Cassidy felt wide awake and alive. Her mother's clock occupied the center of Clay's mantel as if it was designed for the space. She smiled when it chimed one o'clock and didn't flinch when her cell rang seconds later. It had to be Clay, calling to check on her and say goodnight.

Reaching for the phone, the idea of her mother and Clay ringing into her life at the same time turned her insides into jelly.

"Hi, hon, did I wake you?"

"Nope. I'm having trouble crawling into your bed without you so I'm watching TV on the couch. I just may sleep here tonight."

Clay cleared his throat. "Cassidy, would you do me a favor if I asked?"

She laughed. "I am not getting into that bed without you. I'll be fine here for one night."

When was the last time somebody cared about her like this? Not since her mom.

She knitted her eyebrows, realizing silence prevailed on the other end of the line. "Okay, grumpy. What's the favor?"

"Go stay with Maggie and Dan tonight."

She sat upright. There was something about his tone.

"Is something wrong with Jack? What happened? Clay, tell me."

Through the phone, she heard him inhale, hesitating before he answered. "Amber's dead."

An involuntary scream escaped her throat.

"She was shot, honey, in your old apartment. We don't know . . ."

The room began to spin. ". . . will be safer . . ." Her stomach heaved and she jumped to her feet and ran to the kitchen sink ". . . just until I . . ."

She disconnected the call. She couldn't listen to another word, didn't want to hear that Amber, her friend, was dead on account of her. She knew her old apartment wasn't safe, knew in her heart that it had been Tony DelMorrie who trashed it searching for clues to find her.

A warning voice had cautioned her, even as she handed her apartment key to Amber. It might not be safe, she'd told her friend. But Amber waved aside her warning with typical nonchalance. And now, she was dead.

Oh God. He found her, Tony DelMorrie had found her. For all she knew, he could be outside right now, waiting.

It had been her biggest fear. Not for her own safety, but for Clay's and Maggie's and the baby. She'd set them in harm's way.

"Will you keep danger from my door?" Maggie had asked.

Dear God, she hadn't. Instead, she'd brought it directly to the doorstep.

Turning on the cold water she rinsed her mouth from the faucet. No time to think about it, she had to go. How fortunate that she hadn't unloaded her duffel except for her toothbrush and paste. She grabbed those from the bathroom, tossed them in the bag, and zipped it closed.

Surveying Clay's room, she spied a gallon jug in the corner three-quarters full of coins. Clay must empty his pockets every night and toss his loose change in the jar. She rushed to the kitchen and frantically searched the drawers until she found plastic storage bags. Back in the bedroom, she emptied the coins into two bags.

Looking around, she reasoned that he had to have more money stashed at home. Groaning at the invasion of his privacy, she riffled through his drawers and closet. Nothing. She ran to the office. Opening and slamming desk drawers she found a box marked petty cash in a lower drawer. She didn't count the bills, just crumbled them into her fist and shoved them in her jeans pocket. Not only was she a fugitive, now she was a thief.

Snatching up the pen she scribbled on a piece of mail, "I.O.U. $–C.H."

She hurried into the living room for her shoes as her mother's clock chimed fifteen minutes after the hour. Dear God. She was going to puke again.

She rushed into Clay's office and lifted a blank sheet of paper from the printer tray. Her hand trembled as she scrawled across the page, "I'm sorry." She propped it beside the clock.

Yanking one of Clay's jackets from the coat closet beside the door, she slipped her arms into the sleeves. The khaki cargo coat was huge on her, but it had lots of pockets and with a ball cap, she'd be pretty well covered.

There was no time to dwell on what she was leaving behind, no time to cry about what could have been. No time to think about how Tony DelMorrie had ruined her life.

Any life she might have made here was dead. Just like Amber.

15

C lay burst through his apartment door shouting
Cassidy's name, knowing there would be no response.
From the minute she'd hung up on him, he knew in his
heart she'd run. That was her trained response, like Pavlov's
pups.

That's why he rushed back to the police station and issued
two be-on-the-lookout advisories, one for Cassidy and one for
Tony DelMorrie. The alert for DelMorrie included the information that the suspect, wanted in connection with the Fortieth
Street shooting and an out-of-state murder, was armed and
dangerous.

He sped with sirens blaring to The Chalets, but the delay in
leaving the station had given Cassidy the window required to
disappear. He instantly spotted her note next to the clock on the
mantle. His heart dropped. She'd lugged that clock across the
country, protecting it from damage. Dammit. It hinted at how
quickly she fled.

He didn't have much hope that the BOLOs would locate
either Cassidy or DelMorrie. He had no idea what DelMorrie
looked like now. He could describe his appearance months ago,

based on the newspaper photographs, but had he changed his looks? Based on the newspaper picture, Cassidy had.

The BOLO description for her was equally generic. What was she wearing when she left and which way did she run? Two hiding places came to mind and he requested police units check out both — Amber's apartment and The Packing Place. She had keys for the packing store and Amber's roommate would likely harbor her. Had Cassidy made any other friends besides her co-workers?

He couldn't obtain a list of the store employees at this hour. Would she try to leave town? How much money did she have? And where the hell would she go?

The bus station smelled like urine. Cassidy nestled her duffel deeper into her lap, warily eyeing the raggedy man snoring on a bench in the far corner. Only one other man occupied the deserted terminal, a tall, African-American man who paced the walkway outside while talking on his cell phone. Despite the dim exterior lighting, a glint of light reflected off his neck jewelry each time he pivoted.

She hadn't bothered to retrieve her phone from Clay's kitchen counter, fearing that, even though it was a drugstore pre-pay, they could ping the cell towers and locate her. Without it, though, she was as alone as if on a desert island.

Most travelers made their arrangements online in advance nowadays, booking bus trips early and taking advantage of discount prices, but she hadn't had that luxury. So she was spending an uncomfortable night waiting for a person to arrive at five forty-five, according to the posted hours on the glass-enclosed cubbyhole designated as the office. Her destination was unknown. The bills from Clay's petty cash box totaled three hundred, twenty-seven dollars.

Where the bus took her didn't matter. She would buy a one-hundred-dollar ticket to wherever one hundred dollars would take her. The self-serve kiosk couldn't answer that question, stalling her escape. She had no other choice. A plane ticket was out of the question and she was afraid to hitch a ride.

Her objective was to escape Tony DelMorrie and navigate her way back to Arizona because ultimately, Clay was right. It was time to wake up from this nightmare. Enough was enough. Tony DelMorrie could kill her, like he murdered poor Amber, if that's what it came to. But he was done dictating how she lived. Testifying against him would be justice for Jill Diamond, but now it was more personal. She wanted vengeance for Amber.

Her throat closed, tears welled in her eyes, and she bowed her head. Amber befriended her from day one. And now she was gone. "I'm sorry. Amber," she whispered, gulping back a sob.

"You okay, Sugar Plum?"

Her head snapped up and her heart escalated to her throat. The black man towered over her, the now silent cell in his hand. His features were sharp, clearly defined cheekbones and bright eyes. His black T-shirt hugged his chest beneath an open black leather jacket and he smelled of soap. Not the average bus terminal bum.

Nevertheless, he frightened her. "I'm-I'm fine, thanks."

"What's a fine young thing like you doing in a bus depot all alone in the middle of the night?" He smiled, revealing straight white teeth.

"Waiting for my boyfriend. Please, I want to be alone."

Still grinning, he winked. "You want me to wait with you?"

She sat up straighter. "No, thank you. Please leave me alone."

He held up both hands, fingers pointed to the ceiling. "Okay, Sweet Muffin. It simply looked like you could use a friend."

He backed up three steps before turning and walking outside the terminal door, raising his cell to his ear as he exited.

"Where to?" the Greyhound employee asked, stifling a yawn.

"How far can I go on a hundred-dollar ticket?"

He rolled his eyes. "You're kidding me, right? Which direction?"

"Pardon me?"

"Which way are you headed? North, east, south, or west?"

Cassidy answered confidently. "I'll take the first bus going anywhere west."

He ran his fingers across a spreadsheet. "Today, with a C-note, you can get about two states away."

She dug into one of the inside pockets of Clay's jacket, counted out the bills, and slid them into a sunken tray beneath a barred window. The clerk robotically punched a few keys and returned a ticket to her that would take her into Illinois. She had about an hour to wait.

Shoving the coveted ticket into her jeans, she lugged her duffel into the ladies' room. Turning up her nose at the stench, she used the facility, cursed at discovering the faucet didn't release water, and resumed her seat on the hard wooden bench.

As the sun rose, the terminal became a hub of activity. With the arrival of each bus, exhaust fumes permeated the air, threatening to turn her stomach. What she wouldn't give for a cup of coffee.

"He stand you up?"

The black man stood in front of her holding two small coffee cups. He extended one toward her. "It's from the machine, but it's better than nothing."

"No, thank you."

He threw back his head and laughed. "Suit yourself, Princess." He balanced the cup on the end of the bench and strolled outside.

He looked like a pimp, probably surmising that she was some

young girl running away from home and he could entice her into his world. If he knew what she was running from, he'd probably run, too, in the opposite direction. She scanned the windows and didn't see him, then reached for the Styrofoam cup and lifted the thin plastic lid. The steam from the hot black coffee moistened her upper lip. She preferred her coffee with cream and wondered if he had dropped something in it, a sleeping pill or date rape drug.

The aroma was tempting, but she snapped the lid back in place, returned the cup to the end of the bench, and dropped her head into her hands. Within seconds, a pair of boots stepped into her line of vision on the floor. This guy was really starting to scare her.

"You promised you would be there when I got home."

Clay's rich voice wrapped around her like a covered flannel blanket. She raised her head to find him standing stone-faced in front of her in full uniform.

"Clay? What are you doing here?"

"What are you doing here, Miss Hoake?"

The formality didn't escape her and a part of her heart splintered. "I have to leave, Clay, I can't . . ."

"You have to come with me, Miss Hoake. I would prefer voluntarily, but I can cuff you if you resist." His right fist opened and closed rhythmically.

Tears sprang to her eyes and her heart shattered. The man who had made love to her so exquisitely wasn't the man standing in front of her any longer. Chalk up another thing Tony DelMorrie killed.

The black man leaned against the wall, his cell at his thigh, watching through half-closed eyes, feigning disinterest. Most of the people in the bus station openly stared, anticipating a confrontation. The man behind the glass beamed. This would likely be the highlight of his day. Clay waited.

"I haven't done anything wrong." She heard the childish

sound of her words. "On what grounds are you arresting me?"

From her seat, he towered above her.

"I'm not arresting you, Miss Hoake, I'm asking you to come with me voluntarily." He glanced toward the black man and then leveled his gaze at her. "I could charge you with solicitation if you insist."

She gasped, his icy words chilling her soul. Cassidy stood, willing her knees not to buckle, and Clay clutched her left elbow.

He wouldn't look at her, didn't say anything as they made their way to the police car parked outside the front door, its lights flashing. There was no use trying to check the tears that fell slowly from the corners of her eyes and roamed down her cheeks. Clay floated his hand over her head and recited automatically, "Watch your head," when she bent and slid into the backseat.

He slammed the door, walked around the rear of the vehicle, and slid into the driver's seat. He unhooked the radio from the dashboard and spoke a combination of letters and numbers, informing dispatch he was on his way in.

They rode in silence. She massaged her forehead with her fingertips, hoping to ease the pounding headache that had exploded hours earlier with Clay's phone call, and cried.

She cried for Jill Diamond and Amber. She sobbed for her mother, who'd whispered with her last breath that she would always be with her. And she cried for herself, for all that she had lost from that day on. She cried because now she had lost Clay and she knew in her breaking heart that she would never know what it was like to have this man love her.

The police station was abuzz with activity when they arrived. Clay held her elbow and guided her around the dispatch desk, moving her toward the back. She tried to maintain a steady step yet keep her head down. She must be a sight to the curious onlookers. Her mascara surely had run, her cheeks were wet, and her eyes probably swollen. When they approached the ladies' room, she paused and turned pleading eyes to him.

"Go ahead. The window isn't big enough for you to crawl out, if that's what you're thinking." His words dripped with sarcasm.

Dropping her duffel on the floor as a signal to him that she wouldn't run, she leaned on the door. She was done running. If only Clay would listen to her, let her explain. She used the facilities, grateful for the warm water washing over her hands, and stepped back out into the hall where Clay waited like a statue.

He gestured down the hallway and they walked to the end and into a small room with a table and three chairs. It was exactly like she'd seen in the movies, one chair on one side and the other two facing it. In the center of the gunmetal gray table was a ring with a large chain attached to it and a dirty ashtray. Clay slid the single chair out from the table and looked at her expectantly.

"May I stand?"

"No. Sit."

She obeyed and watched Clay speak into an intercom in the corner of the room. "She's ready, Pat." He turned, crossed his arms over his chest, leaned against the wall and stared at her. It reminded her of the look his ex-wife shot her the day Amber faced her down at the store. His was just as chilling.

She recognized the officer who entered the room as the policeman who stopped them the night they drove to her apartment for her clothes, the night another dead body lay outside the Fortieth Street apartments. He must specialize in murders.

He extended his hand. "Miss Hoake, I'm Pat Tatman. Thank you for coming in."

She could hardly speak when she shook his hand. "I didn't have much choice."

He shot a quick glance to Clay in the corner, cleared his throat, and smiled. "Well, thanks anyway. What can you tell me about Amber Malone?"

∾

Tony DelMorrie was a creature of habit and when that routine was interrupted, it ruined his entire day. That's what happened this morning, when he carried the newspaper into the bathroom for his morning constitutional, settled down with the sports section, and caught the front page headline out of the corner of his eye.

"Murder Could Be Mistaken Identity." What the fuck?

Amber's smiling face stared back at him from the page. He didn't know her, but that purplish-red streak in her hair rattled him. Dropping the sports section he snatched the front page off the tile floor and read the article beneath the photo. The story hinted that the shooting was an orchestrated killing gone awry and that the dead woman was in the wrong place at the wrong time. The story did not identify who the actual apartment tenant and intended target might be, but he was no dummy. She would have had to show ID to rent the place, so the cops knew whose name was on that lease.

Hell, they probably knew where Cassidy Hoake was this exact minute. Maybe they even had her in custody to keep her safe.

Zipping his pants, he cursed. He had hoped to get in and out of here under the radar of the Tanzini family. This was their turf and he was here without their knowledge or permission. That was mistake number one. Even in the underworld, there was a code to follow. You didn't go trampin' onto someone else's turf without askin'.

Rule number two was no hits without consent. This would not sit well with the boss, Johnny Tanzini.

He cancelled the manicure and massage he'd scheduled today. Damn, that was his reward to himself for writing the final chapter on Jill Diamond's accident. He'd been looking forward to proper pampering before making his way back home. But the news article made it clear his business wasn't finished. This was twice now he tried to do away with that bitch. He wasn't screwing around anymore. The third time would be the charm.

16

Pat Tatman wrapped up his interview by asking Cassidy not to leave town and for her contact information, including an address where he could reach her. She stuttered, glanced at Clay, and then shrugged. "I, um, I was staying with a friend, but I'm not sure that is where I will be going forward."

"I'll give her a place to stay at The Chalets, Pat. You can list my address and let me know when you need her again."

"Thanks, Clay. Miss Hoake, it was a pleasure and again, I'm sorry about your friend." He stood, his hand outstretched. Cassidy rose as well and reciprocated. Pat strolled out of the interview room, leaving the door open. Cassidy rubbed a spot on the table, refusing to look at Clay.

He wanted to throttle her. The old Clay, the one with anger issues, would have slammed the door shut and ripped her a new one for being so stupid. The safest place she could be was with him. She obviously didn't see that as an option, so all her words, their lovemaking, their talk of a future together, meant nothing to her.

He was a fool to trust her, to let her into his heart. Well, hurt me once, shame on you. Hurt me twice, no way José. "Let's go."

He strode past her to the door and waited, turning when he didn't hear her behind him. Seeing her with her head hung, trying to hide the wet rows on her cheeks jerked his heart. He couldn't let her tears affect him, wouldn't be swayed by them. She was the devil in an angel's body but evil none the less.

"C'mon, Miss Hoake." *Keep it formal, stay focused. She took off. She didn't trust you.*

Cassidy retrieved her duffel bag from beneath the table and came to a stop beside him, sniffling. "What now?"

He placed his hand between her shoulder blades to direct her out of the room and down the hall toward the exit, ignoring the tingling in his fingers and the urge to yank her into his embrace and hug her tight. Cassidy closed that door last night when she ran.

"I've been up all night. I'd like to sleep before I come back out on my next shift." He flashed back to the last time he worked an all-nighter and then rushed home to make love to Cassidy and fall asleep in her arms. *Dammit.*

She stared at the pavement as they walked toward his truck. "What about The Packing Place? I have a job there."

"You can't go back there. When they found out about Amber this morning they assumed you were with her and that you got scared and ran. I didn't tell them differently."

She waited until he turned the key in the ignition to ask. "Where are we going?"

Time to lay it on the line one last time. "We're going back to my home, Miss Hoake. I'm not going to chase you again. So, when I fall asleep, if you run, you'll be running for your life. All I can say is good luck."

"I won't run again. We both know what happened to Amber, even if neither one of us is telling Officer Tatman the whole story. My plan was to go back to Arizona. You convinced me that's the right thing to do. I care about you and I don't want you hurt. If Tony DelMorrie is that close, he'll follow me and leave you and Maggie alone. I didn't run out on you, Clay, I ran to protect you. I won't leave again, I promise."

Countless emotions clogged his throat, checking his angry retort. But that didn't quash the hurt.

"You make empty promises, Miss Hoake." Backing his truck out of the parking space, he headed toward the Chalets.

Curled in a ball on the sofa with the television volume barely audible so as not to disturb Clay, she berated herself. Running away from him was a dumb thing to do. Too bad she didn't realize that before she ruined everything with Clay. He was a protector by nature, as well as professionally. For her to disregard his protection had been a slap in the face.

And that didn't even take into account the feelings he professed, a deeper connection she'd tossed aside like a wet sock. Well, it was broken now, probably beyond repair.

She drifted off, once again sensing that here, with that man in close proximity, she was safe. She roused when she heard Clay banging around in the kitchen.

"Did you eat something?" he grumbled without locking up.

At least he was speaking to her. She shook her head as she watched him crack eggs into a pan, add seasonings, and slide four pieces of toast into their slots. "Can I help?"

Without a word he turned, yanked a cabinet door open and slid open his silverware drawer. She took the hint and removed plates, forks and knives and arranged them on the dining room table. She added two cups with saucers, retrieved the salt and pepper from a spice rack in the corner, and ripped two paper towels from the holder, folding them to serve as napkins. She sat at the table with her back to the kitchen and waited. Maybe it was better if they didn't talk.

Clay dished up scrambled eggs and toast with jelly for them, sat to her right and lifted his fork.

"I'm sorry, Clay. I wish you would yell at me or something, anything except ignore me."

He never looked up from his plate. "It's better if we don't speak, Miss Hoake." He balled up the paper towel and dropped it onto his empty plate. "I have to go out. Please clean up the mess I made, I don't have time." He pointed his index finger at her face. "And don't leave this apartment."

Minutes later, he was gone. Dutifully, she cleaned the kitchen then showered. With nothing else to do, she curled into the corner of the couch again and watched mindless television until a knock on the door interrupted.

Maggie rushed in with Jack asleep on her shoulder and offered a one-armed hug, which Cassidy gratefully accepted. Maggie was the only person showing her any warmth, something she desperately needed at the moment. She felt as isolated as she had sitting alone in the bus station.

She whispered so as not to wake the baby. "Clay will kill me if he knows I'm here, but I had to see for myself that you're okay." She ignored the tears that rimmed Cassidy's eyes. "I can't stay. He's only running a couple of errands."

She closed the door but didn't advance further into the apartment. "Where did you run to?"

Cassidy hung her head. "The bus station."

"Oh, Cassidy, you poor thing. I understand you were probably scared beyond belief, but that was a dumb move. Honey, you have to let us help you. You have to trust us. I know it's been a while since you put your faith in someone, but it's time now. Clay is one of the best. You must believe that and let him help you through this."

She looked around cautiously, even though they were alone in the apartment.

"They're going to relocate you soon, so I don't know when I'll see you again. Please be careful and take care of yourself. Everything will work out, I know it." Maggie kissed her lightly on the cheek. "Be safe."

Cassidy shook her head to clear her brain and process Maggie's words. She reached to grab Maggie's arm.

"Wait, Maggie. What are you talking about? Who is going to move me?"

Maggie knitted her brows and stared at her as if she had two heads. "The police."

"Move me where?"

"I don't know where. That's the point of police protection. Didn't Clay explain all this?"

A quivering smile creased her lips. "Clay is barely speaking to me."

Maggie nodded. "He gets like that when he's mad, all brooding and introverted. He'll sulk for a while, but don't worry, he'll come around. I just wanted to give you a quick hug and wish you luck. I gotta run." She offered a second hug and was out the door.

So much for providing safe haven. Clay was pawning her off on some protection unit, leaving her safety to strangers. She had briefly entertained the idea that returning to his apartment together was an indication that he still cared. Now she knew. This was just a stop along the way.

She heaved a despondent sigh and curled into her spot on the couch. At least when they moved her somewhere else, he'd be out of harm's way. It was probably a good plan.

"Yeah, it's Mittens. I'm reportin' in." He'd called Lauren twice already, both times with no news. Her idea to stake out the apartment was wasting his time.

"Nah, I haven't seen her. She ain't been nowhere near her place and she didn't show up for work today. I was in there, talked to the manager myself. If they know where she is, they ain't sayin'. Lot of cryin' goin' on in there. One of their coworkers croaked. I don't know, I didn't ask."

Why the hell would Lauren care what happened to one of Cassidy's co-workers? She should keep her eye on the ball if she wanted to play in the big leagues.

"I got eyes on the place anyway. But I think this is a dead end. I'm gonna relocate and find your ex-."

She didn't like that idea. "I think he's a key to finding her, that's why. If he was tappin' that, he'll still be sniffin' after her." Her tirade on the other end of the phone made him smile. That remark hit a jealous chord.

"Take it easy, will ya? I'm the professional here, let me handle it. I'll be in touch."

17

Clay eyed the prior night's drunken driving samples nestled in the front seat console. He hadn't wanted to take it to The Packing Place with Cassidy in the truck and, knowing he had errands to do today, he waited until now to ship them.

An enlarged picture of Amber hung on the rear wall behind the counter with a sign that read, We'll Miss You. It appeared the employees had signed it and written personal notes. Amber would have appreciated the irony, since most of them gossiped about her behind her back. Rosie stood at the counter clutching a ball of tissue in her right hand.

He wondered how real her tears were. She probably doused the tissue with onion juice so it would look like she was upset. It was a trick Amber said she once used for a dead uncle she claimed molested her.

He opted to be polite. "How are you?"

Rosie choked back a sob. "This is such a difficult day for us. Amber was such an asset to this store."

He dipped his head, suppressing a gag, and nodded,

snatching a pen from the cup holder to complete his shipping form.

Rosie continued. "I know you and Amber were quite close. I'm sorry for your loss." He remembered Cassidy's story and concealed his smile, instead asking, "Have you heard from Cassidy?"

What made him ask that, he wasn't sure — that cop's instinct, maybe, but her answer catapulted those instincts to high alert.

"No and you're the third person to ask. I didn't realize she was so popular for being so new. Another man was in here this morning as soon as we opened. He was a big man, said he was a relative and he was trying to locate her."

"What did you tell him?"

It was apparent the question was an affront to her integrity. She straightened her spine and all sense of grief disappeared. "Sir, I am not at liberty to divulge personal information and I didn't in this case either." She pointed her nose to the ceiling and crossed her arms at her chest. "I didn't tell him anything."

"What exactly did he want to know? I'm asking as a cop investigating Amber's murder and Cassidy's involvement, Rosie."

"He said he knew about the shooting at her apartment and that he thought Cassidy was in trouble and he wanted to find her and help. He asked where Cassidy was staying and when I said I didn't have that information, he wanted to know what time she was scheduled to work again. I told him I wasn't sure because we are reworking the schedules for the funeral."

"Is that true?"

This might have been the first time he'd ever seen her smile. "No. We're going to close the stores for the funeral. But I didn't like the way he asked his questions." She rubbed her arms. "He made me squeamish."

"Did you tell him anything else?"

Her glare answered his query.

"Did he say if he would be back or leave a number to call if she came in?"

"No. He just looked around, went to the end of the counter to peer into the backroom, as if I was lying, and then left."

"You said I was the third. Who else made inquiry?"

She shook her head. "I've never seen him before either. He was a little man with dark hair. He just asked if Cassidy was here and if I knew when she would be in. When I said no, he left. He had a bouncy step, like he was walking on the balls of his feet."

Clay wrote on the back of his business card and handed it to her. "If either of them comes back, especially the big one, will you call me immediately? My cell number is on the back. Do it discreetly but do it while he's here if possible."

Taking the card, she nodded. He slid the signed shipping receipt across the counter and turned to go.

"Tell Cassidy I hope she's okay."

Glancing over his shoulder, he smiled. "Thank you, Rosie. You're not so bad after all."

There was no use unpacking if she was going to be moving again. Cassidy emptied the coin bags back into the gallon jug and returned the remaining petty cash to the box. She wondered if she could get a refund for the unused bus ticket and restore the rest of Clay's cache. A tiny voice hoped he hadn't noticed she stole it, maybe hadn't realized how low she'd stooped. But he was a cop and he was trained to notice those things, so it was doubtful.

Fighting desolation, she wandered to the sliding glass door, glancing longingly at Maggie's windows. Now, more than ever, she needed a "girl" friend, someone who would simply listen without judging to her reasons for disappearing, perhaps challenge her rationale without arguing, and, at the same time, understand her logic. If nothing else, offer a hug.

As if in response to her wish, her mother's clock chimed, bringing a sad smile to her face. She closed her eyes and whispered, "I hope you're watching over me, Mom, because I sure need some help."

As she opened her eyes and resolved to take whatever cards were dealt to her, a movement in her peripheral vision caught her attention and she glanced far to the right at the back entrance of the building. Casually leaning against the wall beside the door smoking a cigarette was the man from the bus station. She recognized the black leather jacket and the ever-present cell phone in his hand.

Good Lord, he'd followed her. But how could that be? She'd spent a couple hours at the police station before coming here with Clay. Surely, he hadn't waited all that time. Was he one of DelMorrie's men? That was doubtful because she remembered numerous derogatory quotes DelMorrie made in various news articles about people outside his family. He didn't differentiate between sex, race, or religion. He despised everyone.

When Clay's truck cruised into the parking lot, the black man walked casually to a car, tossing his cigarette in the hedges. He waited for Clay to cross in front of him then drove away.

Clay didn't seem to notice him. She barely gave him time to enter the apartment when she asked. "Clay, did you see that black man in the car?"

"What black man?"

He didn't even look at her. Apparently, the time away hadn't made him more communicative.

"He was in the car you just walked in front of. Is he a tenant here?"

"I didn't notice. We have people of all colors in The Chalets, Cassidy. What kind of official identification do you have?"

She furrowed her brows. "What?"

"Do you have some type of ID? Maggie said you have a driver's license. I need it."

Anger replaced trepidation. "Clay, I'm certain I saw that man at the bus station. He spoke to me. Twice. I think he's following me."

He exhaled loudly, as if she exasperated him. "What do you think he did? Follow the patrol unit to the police station and wait outside for who knows how long just to track you here? I'm sure he isn't the same person. You probably saw Curtis. He's a weight instructor who lives in the building. Big guy. Works the afternoon shift. What about some ID?"

She locked her jaw, hating his dismissal of her concerns. Her chest rose and she elevated her chin. "For your information, I have a valid Arizona driver's license and an excellent driving record."

"Please give it to me. We were going to move you tonight, but that's changed. You'll have to stay here again. You should probably sleep in the spare room. The bed has to be more comfortable than this couch."

No invitation into his bed. She ignored the heaviness in her chest. "The sofa is fine, thanks."

He took her license into the office and awakened his computer. She followed him and after several long, silent moments, verbalized her anguish. "I'm not wrong about that man and I don't appreciate the way you just blew me off."

Clay didn't respond.

Cassidy cleared her throat. "I've returned the money I took to the petty cash box and the bus ticket is on the desk. I hope you can get a refund. I understand you're angry with me, but may I please ask you something?"

He swiveled in the desk chair to face her.

"Do you know anything about funeral arrangements for Amber?"

"No."

"Did she suffer?"

"No. She probably didn't have time to realize what was happening."

"Will you attend the funeral?"

"If you're thinking about going, Cassidy, forget it. We'll have a surveillance team in place because we suspect the shooter will show up looking for you. And you and I both know who that shooter is. It's a kind thought for Amber, but you can't go."

He turned back in his chair and focused on the monitor, adding over his shoulder, "I didn't mean to blow you off about the man you saw. I just don't think it's anything to worry about."

Effectively dismissed, she returned to the living room. Tears weren't even an emotional outlet any longer. She was cried out. All that remained was simmering anger.

Clay left for work and she endured a restless night on the sofa. Her hands cupped a mug of hot coffee as she leaned on the kitchen counter the next morning when he returned, carrying a bag of fresh pastries.

"You look like hell. Did you sleep?"

"Not really." She couldn't count the number of times she'd tiptoed to the sliding glass door and peered into the darkness searching for that man in the parking lot.

"You should rest today. We're getting on the road early tomorrow, like about four in the morning. You'll need to be up and ready by then."

He tossed a second bag on the counter. "For you." He walked away.

Inside was a shoulder-length blond wig with full bangs. With the hairpiece still in her hand, she walked to Clay's bedroom door to find him packing a valise on the bed.

"What are you doing?"

"I told you we leave tomorrow."

"You're going with me?"

He stopped and looked at her incredulously. "Who did you think you would go with?"

"I thought . . ." She didn't finish the sentence, instead lifting the wig slightly and whispering, "Thank you."

He was being hard on Cassidy but keeping her scared might keep her on her toes. And he remained angry at her for leaving the way she did, for not trusting him. He had to admit, though, he admired her strength. Had she really planned to travel all the way back to Arizona by herself, walk into that police station and say here I am, not knowing if there was anyone in the building she could trust? That took balls.

Zipping the valise, he smiled in anticipation of the one-on-one time ahead of them. She may not be interested in him romantically, which still hurt, but she'd be a lively travel companion.

Strolling into the living room, he found her curled into the corner of the couch.

"What are you watching?"

She shrugged and muted the volume. "Nothing much. I don't know how people watch TV all day. I'm about to go out of my mind."

He shoved his hands in his jean pockets. He could probably ease up a little.

"You've been cooped up in this apartment for two days. Want to get out of here?"

She swung her feet to the floor, her eyes wide. "Really? Yes, please. I'll get my shoes."

He eyed her small, tight bottom as she walked into the spare bedroom where her duffel bag sat, silently berating himself for banishing her from his bed. Just because he was angry with her didn't mean he didn't appreciate an attractive woman. And he remembered quite clearly what was tucked into those jeans — soft, firm cheeks that fit nicely in his hands. He adjusted his pants as she returned, grunting uncomfortably. Not all of his parts were mad at her.

She stared at him expectantly, like a child waiting for permission to go outside. "Where's the wig?"

A momentary look of surprise flashed across her features before she returned to the spare bedroom. Minutes later she stood in front of him again.

"Glasses?"

"I don't really need them."

"I surmised that myself. But they are a good add to the disguise."

Dutifully, she retrieved the glasses from the bedroom. He inspected the transformation, ignoring the twinge of titillation. Long blond hair with bangs that barely edged over the red frames.

"Do you wear lipstick?"

"Not often."

"Some nice red stuff would work. Let's go see if Maggie has any." He opened the door then walked beside her out of the building and across the common area. Cassidy inhaled deeply, relishing the smell of autumn. He laughed when she kicked the leaves along the walkway like a five-year-old.

Maggie swung open the apartment door and did a double take, then smiled and coaxed Cassidy into her arms. "It's so good to see you. I've been worried about you. Let me look at you." She nodded approvingly. "This looks good."

Cassidy welcomed Maggie's proffered warmth. As if in silent communication, neither said anything to hint at their earlier meeting. "It's good to see you, too. Thanks."

Clay scooped up Jack from his blanket and said over his shoulder, "She could use some bright red lipstick, Mags. And anything else you think will add to her new look."

Cassidy noted the monotone in his voice, no different than if he were referring to a stranger.

"It's called lip gloss these days, caveman. Follow me, Cass."

Moments later, after the women emerged from the bathroom, Clay cleared his throat. "I'm not a big fan of blonds but, ah, you look pretty good." He ducked his head, but not fast enough to hide the blush on his cheeks, and turned away, cooing to the baby.

Cassidy's heart leapt. Maybe, just maybe, she could regain his trust, and then his friendship. She wanted to count these two people as friends. Maggie winked at her and moved into the kitchen, returning with three glasses of iced tea.

"What time are you leaving?"

"Early."

"You'll check in at the station so I'll know from Dan that you both are okay, right?"

"You'll be asking your husband to violate department protocol, but yes, we'll check in."

She focused on Cassidy. "And you'll do everything Clay tells you to do, right? Because if you don't, and something happens to him, I'll never forgive you."

Cassidy nodded. She would protect him to the death.

18

Tony DelMorrie wiped his sweaty forehead with a napkin. He'd fucked up when he ignored the underworld code of behavior. So here he sat, picking red velvet cake that had been as dry as popcorn out of his teeth and waiting for the boss, Johnny Tanzini. At least they were equals on the pie chart of power.

The Drip Stick was Tanzini's base, a coffee shop cover for his illegitimate businesses. He'd think Tanzini would be smart enough to sink some money into the joint and make it look like something. It was a hole. But most of the tables were full, so it must be popular.

All heads turned when Tanzini entered the room. Some nodded in deference. Christ, the man had a giant barrel chest and shoulders that reached to his face. The guy had no neck, he was just one bulging muscle. He must live in the gym. Who the hell had time for that?

"How you doin'?" Tony mumbled. He rose and extended his hand.

"Good. You?"

"Good." The chair groaned beneath Tanzini's bulk when he

sat. He could probably splinter it between his thighs. "Talk to me, Tony. What are you doin' in my town?"

He'd expect respect on his home turf and he had to show it to Tanzini. Mindful that they were in a public place and one never knew when the Feds were listening, Tony chose his words carefully.

"I had this problem in Arizona that I tried to take care of, but it didn't happen. I followed the problem here, thinking I could take care of it without bothering you."

Tanzini's expression hadn't changed. He simply stared, waiting for more. "I meant no disrespect to you or your family by coming here without lettin' you know." Tony felt sweat beads dotting his forehead again.

"I still have to take care of the matter at hand, but I can handle it. You don't need to concern yourself."

Tanzini removed a toothpick from an engraved holder and leaned back, lifting the front legs of the chair off the floor. "Let's discuss this."

The meeting had not gone well. Tony strolled out of the coffee shop, his demeanor belying his anger. Tanzini didn't like a stranger shootin' up his territory and wasn't convinced Tony could settle matters successfully. He gave Tony twenty-four hours to find Cassidy Hoake or he would step in. Either way, she'd be taken care of, but now the DelMorrie family pride was on the line. How would it look back home if word got around that he'd come to Ohio and botched a hit, or worse that Tanzini, a rival family, had cleaned up his mess? How was he supposed to wrap it up when he didn't know where the fuck she was? Shit. He was screwed.

At least Tanzini, out of respect for his position as a boss and an equal, had offered protection and one of his soldiers to assist in locating Cassidy, since Tony was unfamiliar with the city. It galled him to accept the handout, but if it helped find her, it was worth it. He'd owe Tanzini big-time though. Fuck.

She just finished tucking her hair beneath the wig when Clay poked his head in the spare room. "I swear you sleep in your clothes. Here, don't forget this." He extended the drugstore cell phone she'd left at his kitchen sink.

"Are you ready? We'll grab some coffee on the road."

He handed her his cargo jacket, the one she'd borrowed when she escaped to the bus station. "I believe this is your coat of choice."

Wincing, she slipped her arms into the sleeves while following him outside into the darkness. An uneasy sensation crept over her in the eerie silence, like a spider crawling up her back. Clay walked to an unfamiliar car, loaded her duffel and his bag into the trunk, and then touched the key fob to open the automatic locks, motioning for her to get in. He tucked a smaller briefcase behind the driver's seat.

She buckled her seatbelt. "Whose car is this?"

"It's a rental."

"Where are we going?"

He turned the key and looked at her. "You don't get carsick, do you?"

"No, why?"

"We'll be driving for a while."

"Clay, I'm nervous enough without added drama. Please tell me where we're going."

"To the airport."

She considered his words, wondering what the exact plan was. "Are we leaving the car at the airport?"

"Yes."

"What time is our flight?"

Clay eased the car out onto the deserted street. "We don't have a flight yet."

Her head jerked up. She could barely make out his features in the lights from the dash panel. "We're going to the airport, but we don't have a flight to board? Please explain your plan to me."

"You might as well get comfortable. We've got about a six- or seven-hour drive ahead of us, depending on how many times you need to stop. I didn't trust making travel arrangements from the police station. Too many unknowns. We're driving to the Indianapolis airport. We'll book a flight there."

"You don't trust the people you work with?"

Clay shrugged but remained silent.

"I thought you made arrangements with the Arizona detective. You said you felt comfortable about him, that he was on my side."

Clay's smile glowed in the dash lights. "I do think he's on your side and I think we can trust him. That doesn't mean I have to tell him everything, especially our travel plans. He thinks we'll be there this weekend. I'm not taking any chances."

The gravity of his words smothered her like a pillow. It was just her and Clay on this mission to bring justice for the murders of Jill and Amber. Together, they might live or die. The feeling was crushing, almost claustrophobic. She reached for the button to roll down the window and let the cold air beat her face.

Clay adjusted some knobs on the dash. "Are you too warm?"

It took a minute, maybe two, to regain her composure, to be sure if she spoke, she wouldn't break into a sob and spill her fear all over their laps. The suffocation of it was that tangible, so encompassing, she began to perspire despite the cold air rushing into the car. Finally, she eased the window closed.

"Are you all right?"

She inhaled deeply, trying to stabilize her heart rate. "No Clay, I'm scared beyond belief."

He glanced at her, and then refocused on the road. "Scared is good, honey. It will keep us both on our toes."

His voice hardened a bit. "It's too late to change your mind, Cassidy. If you're thinking about running, forget it. There are other people involved now, people willing to risk their lives to help you."

She knew that. Him for one, and Maggie and Dan. In a sense, their lives depended as much on her as she did on them. "I'm not changing my mind. I know I messed things up between you and me, but you said if we were ever going to have a life together, I had to make this right. I know that's not going to happen, but I also realize that if I'm ever going to salvage my own life, I have to do this. You don't have to worry about me running again. I'm just afraid."

Clay leaned over and squeezed her knee. "I read once that a brave man, or in your case a brave woman, is one who dares to look the devil in the face. I think you're pretty brave to have been through all you have. And I've got your back, hon. Why don't you try to get a little more sleep?"

Silently, she gave thanks that his mood had improved. His touch seared through her jeans, radiating down to her toes and up her thigh. How could she sleep with so much heat beside her?

"I can drive for a couple hours and give you a break."

"Thanks, but that's not how it works. I'm fine."

"Can we talk then?"

He hesitated and then smiled. "Sure. What do you want to talk about?"

In the darkness, with only the inside dials casting their faces in shadows, her guard came down. The emotion that welled up so quickly in her throat surprised her, as did the tears. "I can't stop thinking about Amber. I should've never given her the key to my apartment. That day you and I went there and all my clothes were dumped on the floor, I knew, I just knew, Tony DelMorrie had been in there. I didn't tell you then. Maybe if I had, Amber would still be alive."

She wiped her runny nose with the back of her hand. "I liked her so much, Clay. She was so down to earth and so in tune with me. We were so different and yet, I think we could have been good friends. She was really smart, you know. She suspected from the first time she saw me that I was hiding something. Did you know that?

"I think there was something fishy going on with her and Mr. Keaseling. She protected all those girls from him, covering for them when they made mistakes and bearing his anger, and most of them were mean to her. It is so unfair that now she's dead. I feel so guilty, Clay. I should have never let her go to my apartment."

"You didn't shoot her, Cassidy. Tony DelMorrie did. You can mourn Amber and you should. You're right, she was one of a kind and she deserves to be remembered. But you didn't kill her. You have to keep that in mind."

"I wish I had been a better friend to her. But I was too terrified to allow her close. I will always regret not telling her how I felt."

"She knew, honey, she knew. She cared about you too, giving you all those lifts home and watching out for you. She had your back from the first time I saw you in the store."

"She cared about you too, you know."

He smiled. "In her own way, I think she did. I liked her, too."

"She told me once that she thought if she called you for help, you'd be there for her."

This time, the corners of his mouth dipped in a sad smile. "She was right, I would've helped her with whatever. I'm glad she knew that."

About five minutes passed in silence before Cassidy spoke again. "It's one more reason why I want to do this, Clay, why I want to testify and see Tony DelMorrie behind bars where he belongs. I owe it to Amber."

"Me too, honey, me too."

Thankfully, Clay turned the conversation and Cassidy's mood lightened over the next six hours as they chatted about music, old television shows, favorite foods, and books. He entertained her with stories about growing up with Maggie, and she in turn told him about her childhood.

Learning that she was a CPA on the path to make partner surprised him as did the information that she'd been pretty well off, too, until she fell under the spell of the man she followed to Arizona. They avoided discussing Jill Diamond's murder and what sent Cassidy to the streets, just as they didn't discuss their relationship, whatever it was.

"What exactly are the travel plans?"

Clay shrugged. "We're winging it. Why?"

"I live out of this duffel bag. Laundromats are my friend. I'll need one soon."

Clay's brow furrowed. "That's probably out of the question. Don't worry, we'll figure out something."

They arrived at a small hotel one block off the main interstate in Indianapolis shortly before noon. Clay declared he was pleased with the time they'd made and complimented her on how well she traveled. She'd go anywhere with him, she wanted to reply, but she thought better. He switched off the ignition.

"Please go along with whatever I say or do, okay? No questions, no volunteering information. Simply follow my lead." She nodded.

He reached for her hand as they walked through the parking lot to the lobby and her heart soared. She was grateful the oversized eyeglasses and bangs hid her eyebrows, which catapulted when she heard Clay register Mr. and Mrs. King and produced

valid driver's licenses for both of them. He handed her a dupli-
cate of her Arizona license, which now identified her as
Eliza King.

She didn't speak until they stood inside the room, eyeing the
king-sized bed. "We're sharing a room?"

Clay deposited their bags in the corner, carried the briefcase
to the desk, and removed a handgun, placing it on the nightstand
to his left.

"One room is safer and more cost effective. Are you uncomfortable doing that?"

"No, it's just, um, all this one-on-one time with you has me a
little confused, I guess."

He withdrew a pillow from beneath the comforter. "There
isn't anything to be confused about. Don't over think it. I'm pretty
tired so, if you don't mind, I'd like to nap for an hour or so. You'll
have to stay in the room, I'm afraid, but if you keep the sound low,
the television won't bother me."

He kicked off his shoes and stretched out across the
comforter, bunching the pillow beneath his head. Within
seconds, she was listening to soft snores and rhythmic breathing.

Cassidy retrieved the remote control and climbed onto the
bed beside Clay, propping up her pillows for support. His face
was softer in sleep, the physical stiffness emanating from him
during the car ride gone.

Maybe, when all this was over, he'd relax again with her and
they could start over. She released the thought as quickly as she
entertained it. She was his current police assignment, a fugitive
he was delivering to the authorities and nothing more. He'd just
said as much. There was no sense pretending otherwise.

Clay slowly emerged from the fogginess of sleep, blinking as he
focused on unfamiliar surroundings. The television droned low

and Cassidy sat propped against the bed board, her head drooped onto her chest. Her slow breathing was soothing, much like when he cradled a sleeping Jack on his shoulder.

She'd removed the wig and glasses which, to him, signified her intentions to stay. This woman was following him blindly, agreeing to do whatever he asked without question, and trusting him to keep her safe from death. She literally had no one to turn to except him.

Sometime during their interstate ride, he'd forgiven her for running out on him, even acquiescing that her reasoning might be valid—at least in her mind. Maybe it was the interest she showed in his childhood and subsequent police life, or the way she threw her head back and laughed at his stories, or the sadness in her voice when she recounted her mother's life and death and mourned for Amber.

At every turn, it seemed, she'd had a mountain to climb and she'd done it mostly alone. At some point in their lengthy conversation, he became certain she wouldn't run again, would never lie to him, and would probably die for him. In return, he wanted to protect this woman from all that was evil and when this was over, he might ask for a second chance at a relationship with her. All the basics were there: trust, honesty and mutual attraction. Now all they needed was time.

He tried to ease up without waking her but the minute he moved, her eyes fluttered open. She smiled, raising her hand to the back of her neck to massage the stiffened muscles.

"Feel better?"

He nodded. "You?"

She grimaced as she squeezed her neck. "A little."

He scooted closer. "Turn your back to me. Let me help." Gently, he began massaging her shoulders, running his thumbs along her neck, pressing into knotted muscles while relishing in the silkiness of her skin. She groaned, piquing his desire. He leaned toward her, resting his forehead on the back of her head.

"I'm so sorry, Clay," she whispered. "Please forgive me." The pulse in her neck thumped beneath his fingertips.

Eyes closed, he whispered into her hair. "I don't want to lose you. And I don't intend to."

Abruptly, he released her shoulders and swung his feet off the other side of the bed, ignoring the liquid eyes she turned on him.

"Right now, I'm a cop and you are my assignment. There is police protocol to follow. I have to keep my head clear and keep my focus on that." He reached for his briefcase.

"But we're going to sleep together?"

A slight smile turned his mouth upward. "Thousands of married couples go to bed every night together and never touch each other. I think we can handle it."

Thoughts of sleeping beside her created butterflies in his stomach, which he mentally tamed. Cassidy stood with her hands on her hips, grinning widely.

"Tell me, Mr. I-Follow-the-Rules. Since when does police protocol allow a male officer to escort a female prisoner? That seems odd to me. Do you spend the night with all of them?"

Returning to the bed with his laptop in hand, he laughed. "Well, you're not exactly a prisoner, remember? But no, normally you would be escorted by a female officer, and I've never spent the night with a prisoner of the opposite sex."

She spread her hands wide and grinned, making it clear to him she was enjoying the contradiction of his words. "Then how is it you were approved to take me on this trip? What exactly did you tell your chief?"

Slow heat crept over his cheeks. He cleared his throat. "That's classified information. Let's just say this is a special assignment involving exigent circumstances. Would you rather I call in a woman to escort you? I can, you know."

Her jaw dropped. "You'd leave my safety to strangers? I thought you cared about me."

His entire face reddened. "Miss Hoake, please stop making

this more difficult than it already is. I do care about you and when this is over, I'll show you just how much. But not until it's over, understand?"

He positioned his pillows against the back of the bed and motioned for her to sit beside him, their shoulders touching.

"Now be quiet and let's see if we can fly somewhere."

Mittens tapped his right foot on the floor, waiting for the call to connect. Every time he called her, Lauren let the phone ring and ring before answering. What could she be so busy doing all the time that she couldn't answer the damn phone?

She'd learned quickly that he wouldn't leave a message. Never leave a traceable trail was a rule set in stone. Finally, she answered.

"Yeah, it's Mittens. I'm reportin' in."

"And?"

"I ain't found her yet. I been keepin' eyes on your ex- 'cause I think he'll lead us to her. But my source in the police station ain't seen him either."

"What am I paying you for?"

Her words were cold enough to freeze his ear to the receiver. "Look, things like this take time. And I'm only one guy workin' on my own time. If you want to up the ante, I can bring more men in on this."

"Money is not an issue."

Mittens did a little dance in his seat. This bird was ripe for the plucking. She was committing a cardinal sin, thinking emotionally instead of rationally. And he could reap the benefits.

"Okay, good. You open your wallet and we'll finish this faster."

19

Tony DelMorrie understood now why he had capos to handle the more unsavory parts of his business dealings. He wasn't cut out to chase people, he didn't know the first thing about tracking someone who seemed to have totally dropped off the radar screen, and he didn't like being pressured by a fellow paisano.

He'd lucked out following Cassidy Hoake across country, mainly because he knew she was from Pittsburgh and suspected she'd head in that direction. And once he blew up her car, her only mode of affordable travel was by bus. It was easy to flash a Ulysses and ask for information. Those people who worked in bus stations didn't lay eyes on a fifty-dollar bill too often and were all too willing to earn it.

But now, he was stymied and Tanzini's clock was ticking. Where the hell was she? He hadn't bothered staking out the funeral of the dead girl. Hoake was too smart to show up there. He'd waited at the bus terminal after persuading the clerk to disclose her travel plans, but the Illinois-bound bus drove away without her. What was that about? She paid a hundred bucks for that ticket.

He had a meeting with Tanzini at eleven tonight and he sure as hell didn't want to report that he hadn't taken care of the matter. He headed to The Packing Place one more time. Maybe one of those ladies would be interested in a little cash under the counter for information.

They had time to kill until their eight o'clock flight. Cassidy was partially disappointed that she wouldn't be sleeping with Clay and somewhat relieved that temptation was being removed from the picture.

He cursed, disconnecting a call for the second time and dialing a third number.

"Is something wrong?"

"I can't find Dan. Only he and the chief know what we're doing right now." He paused before speaking into the phone. "It's Clay. I need to speak with Dan Armstrong. It's important."

He waited then spoke again, relaying their flight numbers and travel details. "Got it. I'll text you when we're at the airport." He disconnected the call and turned to Cassidy.

"Are you hungry? I'm sorry, I can't take you out, but we can order something in."

His phone rang before she could answer. Listening to his one-sided conversation sent shivers down her spine.

"Yes, Rosie . . . is he still there . . . what did you tell him . . . no, you did fine. I'm sending someone over there at closing just to be safe . . . I appreciate it. Thanks."

Without looking at her he redialed the phone, reaching Dan on the first try this time. Cassidy rubbed her arms to ward off the sensation of all the blood in her body draining away, leaving her feeble as she listened. A man fitting DelMorrie's description had questioned Rosie about Cassidy's whereabouts. Clay suggested beefed up patrols around The Packing Place.

"I agree, he wouldn't be dumb enough to hang around there, especially since there is no indication Cassidy has been there. But at least we know he's still local and she's a state away." He agreed with something Dan said, said he would check in later, and disconnected the call.

Clay looked at her and smiled. "It's all good, hon. What do you want to eat?"

Despite sitting alone in his pantry office, Mittens bobbed his head and spoke out loud. "All right. All right. We got ya."

All that attention he'd paid to that mousy clerk in the police department had paid off. The fact that Cassidy Hoake and her cop were heading west was a complication, but he was certain the boss had some cross-country contacts and the distance would add to Lauren Cestra's tab, maybe even include a little extra for his own pocket. No one would be the wiser if he jacked up the contract amount. He dialed Lauren's cell number.

"Yeah, it's Mittens. I'm reportin' in. How ya doin'?"

Miss Frigid Ass dispensed with the social niceties. "I hope you have something to tell me this time." She was always all business.

"Yeah, I do. I found her. I told you your ex- would be sniffin' around that."

"She's with Clay?" She sounded surprised.

"Yep. Looks like they're takin' a little trip to the West Coast, but like I tole you when we first met, they can run but they can't hide, if you know what I mean."

"Clay has no connections on the West Coast. Why would they be going there?"

"Maybe they just want a little R&R together." She didn't get it. Her ex- had obviously moved on, although Mittens couldn't understand why.

Lauren Cestra had money and looks. What more could a man

want? She was a little stiff, but he bet he could loosen her up. A grin exploded across his face at the thought. He didn't understand how her ex- could have the hots for Cassidy Hoake. She was like a pauper compared to Lauren.

"Are you sure your information is correct?"

"Yeah, I got a reliable source in the police department. She gave me the flight information and everything."

"Wouldn't it be better to stop her before she leaves town? I want this over with as soon as possible." She spoke the words like a command.

"I know, but listen, this could work to your advantage if somethin' happens to her outta town. But icing this cake is gonna cost a little more now."

"I'm not giving you one penny more until I know you're going to hold up your end of the deal. And I'm through with cake metaphors. If you can't get this done, I'll hire someone who can."

Yeah, like she knew where else to go to hire a hitman. The woman had never gotten her hands dirty in her life. "Don't worry about it, Lauren. I got it handled. I'm gonna call my boss now about some long-distance arrangements. I won't know until I talk to him how much more it's gonna cost. Just relax. We'll meet soon at a little restaurant I know. I call ya."

He disconnected from Lauren and punched in Johnny Tanzini's number. "Yeah, boss, it's me. I been workin' on a little somethin' that we should talk about. A new cake recipe, if you catch my drift. You got some time to see me? Okay, I'll be there."

The plan was playing out better than Clay expected. Tony DelMorrie had no clue that Cassidy was on her way back to Arizona to tighten the noose around his neck. Her appearance would either lure him back into the hands of Arizona authorities or generate an all-out manhunt for him, planting his picture in every local police department, every post office, and on every news channel across the country. He wouldn't be able to hide.

Clay's phone vibrated in the center console cup holder. Glancing down, he barely made out the name on the screen, but saw that it was from Maggie. He wrinkled his forehead. She knew he was on assignment and how dangerous it was. What could be so important that she was texting him now?

Well, her message would have to wait until they arrived at the airport. He reached down and pressed the button to stop the repeating text alert.

Cassidy rode silently in the passenger seat, her hands clasped tightly in her lap. She was being a trooper. "You know, the long blond hair is nice, but I really liked the red in the newspaper picture." His stomach jumped at the recollection.

"My mother used to brag that it came from her side of the family. I probably never would have cut my hair if I hadn't been trying to look different. I have to admit, though, short and spiky sure is easy to take care of."

"Do you think you'll keep it that way when this is all over?"

Her lower lip quivered. "I'm afraid to think that far."

Clay followed the signs to the car rental return, driving to a stop in front of the office. "They have a shuttle from here to the airport. Come in with me."

He tucked his phone in his jacket pocket, surveyed their surroundings while he waited for Cassidy to collect her purse and slip into her shoes, and held her hand as they approached the glass doors. Only one other customer, an older man, stood inside.

Dirty, blue plastic chairs lined the wall in front of the windows. "Want me to wait there?"

"No." He drew Cassidy close and wrapped his arm around her shoulders. Over her head, he scanned the waiting room, noting the camera mounted in the far corner and a partially opened door to what he presumed was an office.

Cassidy watched him wide-eyed and whispered. "Is something wrong?"

Yeah, but he couldn't lay his finger on it. He shook his head. "Just a feeling."

Remembering Maggie's waiting text message, he removed his cell from his pocket and pressed the button to view the screen. He swore under his breath, stood taller, and looked around again. The change in demeanor didn't escape Cassidy's notice.

"What's wrong?"

The elderly man in front of them stepped away from the counter and the clerk turned her attention to him. "Can I help you, sir?"

Clay nudged Cassidy to the counter and completed the paperwork to return the car. A van waited outside, its motor running, to shuttle them to the airport. Before boarding, he inspected the inside, seeing only the gentleman who had been ahead of them in the rear seat.

He cleared his throat. "Sir, would you mind very much if my wife and I sat in that back seat? She is not feeling well, feeling a little sick to her stomach."

The threat of vomit usually motivated people to move, and the old man was no different. Cassidy's eyes questioned Clay but, to her credit, she remained silent. He helped her into the van, and they settled on the last bench seat.

Clay urged her into the corner and perched on the edge of the seat, essentially creating a shield in front of her. He was in full cop mode, his hearing heightened, his focus pinpoint accurate, adrenaline surging through his veins.

After they stopped in the departing passengers' lane, Clay whispered, "Stay in the van until I tell you."

He retrieved their bags from the rear compartment, tipped the driver, and made sure the old man was inside the terminal before leaning inside the vehicle. "C'mon, honey. Do you still feel like you're going to yak?" It was enough to send the driver around to the other side.

He helped Cassidy to the pavement and hustled her through the sliding glass doors into the noisy, congested terminal. She leaned into him as they moved and whispered. "Clay, what's the matter?"

Slowly, he reached in his jacket pocket and retrieved his phone, touched the screen, then turned it for Cassidy to see.

Maggie's text message read: "You've been compromised."

20

This was bullcrap. Tony DelMorrie bunched his shirttail into the waistband of his sagging pants. He was "The" Tony DelMorrie, head of a syndicate on the West Coast. Underlings answered to him, not the other way around.

Yet, here he was, obediently walking into The Drip Stick, answering Johnny Tanzini's summons. It stuck in his craw big time. What was he going to say? The little bitch was somewhere, but he couldn't find her? Might as well stand there with his dick in his hand like the stooge he'd sound like. Hate was too mild a word for his feelings toward Cassidy Bitch Hoake.

Holy hell, it was almost midnight and the coffee shop was crowded. How did these people sleep after guzzling all this caffeine? Two pieces of red velvet cake on serving plates passed him on a tray and he repressed his gag reflex.

A skinny waiter directed him to the far rear table, the one closest to the door that led to Tanzini's office.

"May I serve you some coffee while you wait?" Head to toe he screamed light in the loafers, making DelMorrie's skin crawl.

"Yeah, sure. Regular, black." Christ, he'd be up all night.

With twenty-seven freakin' varieties available, the waiter

frowned at the bland choice, but nodded and scurried to the serving counter. Moisture dampened his armpits. If the roles were reversed and this was his turf, he'd be ready to order an intruder out of town by the time the sun rose.

And then, he'd whack the guy before he walked out of the building, just as a matter of principle. And like it or not, he was an intruder on Tanzini's turf. He'd look like an ass backing out of this coffee shop when he made his exit, but that was his plan. Tanzini wasn't stupid enough to bring cops to his own doorstep to investigate a shooting, but DelMorrie wasn't going to let his guard down one minute, just in case. His body temperature hiked several degrees when the waiter motioned for him to go into the backroom. He prayed he didn't stroke out.

Tanzini rose from a wooden desk the size of a Camaro, his hand outstretched.

"Tony, welcome. Did you order some coffee? How about a cigar?" He recognized the black and gold band immediately when Tanzini eased a Cuban Cohiba from his jacket pocket. DelMorrie's bowels gurgled. Christ, he was going to get whacked right here.

Tanzini motioned for him to sit and he did, regretting imme-diately that he responded so obediently. They were equals, he reminded himself.

Tanzini smiled, showing more teeth than most and reminding Tony of a horse. "I've got some good news for you, my friend. We know where the young lady you are interested in is. In fact, it appears that she is headed into your neck of the woods. I think this could be the beginning of a fine partnership, Tony, seeing as how I have a vested interest in her now."

Tony blinked once, twice, processing what Tanzini had just said. "Non capisco. I don't understand."

"I'm saying we found your girl." Tony stared at the photo Johnny Tanzini slid across his desk of a couple slipping into a car at what looked like an interstate rest stop. He disregarded the man and focused on the woman.

An oversized jacket virtually swallowed her and with that long, blond hair and the huge eyeglasses, her face was barely discernible.

This meeting wasn't going at all the way he'd figured and he was confused, a feeling he didn't like. "Who are they?"

Tanzini taped the photo, his forefinger connecting on the woman's head. "This is Cassidy Hoake. Pretty good disguise, eh? He moved his finger onto the man's face.

"This is Clay Cestra. Police Officer Clay Cestra. That's a turd in the punchbowl because I'm not in the business of knocking off cops. But we can work out those details."

Tanzini checked the time on a watch the size of his fist. "Right now, those two should be boarding a plane to your hometown. Hopefully, your contacts can figure out where they are staying and," he placed his hands together as if praying, "with some luck, the little lady will meet with an unfortunate accident." He winked at DelMorrie. "You know what I mean?"

He bolted upright in his chair and snatched the photo from beneath Tanzini's lacquered fingernails.

"Holy crap! Are you sure?"

Tanzini nodded.

"Where's this taken? How long ago?"

Now Tanzini sat up straight, eyeing him warily. "We managed to discover their travel plans. It's unfortunate that the cop is involved, but he's been in her pants, which makes him part of the equation. Don't get so excited. Barney Fife is a complication, especially since he's escorting her back to testify against you.

"You have a shitload of dirty laundry hanging out there, a rather major snag that you neglected to mention. I don't appreciate you're not being honest with me. This has to be handled properly. But I think it's doable."

Tony needed a bathroom. Sweat pooled in the crevasse

between his thighs and belly. Damn, it was hot in here. At least Tanzini wasn't crazy enough to go after a uniform.

"You sure it's her?"

Tanzini nodded again. "We employ a solid source in the police department."

"And you say they are flying back to Arizona?" A poem from his childhood popped into his head, the one about the spider luring the fly, and he smiled.

Was she really walking — make that flying — right into his own backyard? Finally, things were turning in his favor.

He reached for the proffered cigar. "Don't worry, Johnny, my people can handle this."

For a moment, Cassidy feared she wouldn't be permitted to board the plane. In her driver's license picture, her long hair was wavy red and she didn't wear or need glasses to drive. What made her think of that just as she approached the counter, she didn't know, but she slipped off the glasses and tucked them in a pocket of Clay's cargo jacket.

The attendant studied the license, assessed Cassidy, reexamined the license, and raised her eyes again. Cassidy leaned into the woman, grabbing the top of the wig and lifting it slightly. "It's a wig. He prefers blonds. Really gets him hot, if you get my meaning."

She winked and tugged the hair back in place.

The attendant glared at Clay momentarily, then processed the ticket declaring loudly, "You should find a man who accepts you the way you are."

Cassidy suppressed a giggle watching the woman rudely validate Clay's ticket. They received boarding passes and seat assignments and made their way to the security line. Clay hadn't said a word since showing her Maggie's text message. His eyes scrutinized everyone, while his head pivoted from side to side.

If it could revolve in a full three-hundred-and-sixty-degree swivel, she imagined he'd be happier.

He hadn't released her elbow either and now he dragged her out of line. Leaning close to her ear, he whispered, "We're not getting on this plane. C'mon."

The warmth of his breath seeped down her neck, beneath her shirt, and into her heart. She'd follow this man anywhere.

"What's going on?" she asked between huffs, trying to keep up with his long strides.

Those eyes continued to canvass the terminal "I can't explain it now. Just trust me."

"I do trust you. I'll do whatever you say."

"Be careful. I might ask you to marry me."

She wished he'd looked at her when he said it, so she could see his face, see if he was joking or if there was even a hint of forever in his eyes. As it was, he propelled them through the airport at lightning speed, nudged her through another check-in line, and before she knew it, they sat in chairs at Gate B24 waiting for a plane to Cleveland. With their backs against the wall, he noticeably relaxed, but his perusal of their surroundings was constant.

He wrapped his arm around her shoulders, drawing her close so no one could hear him speak. "Something went wrong. I don't know what. It must be something inside the police department, otherwise that text would have come from Dan. The fact that Maggie sent it tells me I can't call him."

"Are you sure?"

Idly, he rubbed his thumb along the outside of her right ear and she closed her eyes to preserve the memory.

"Maggie has never sent a three-word text in her life. Her texts go on and on, like a high school essay. That's Dan's message."

"So what do we do now?"

Clay squeezed his eyes shut momentarily and pressed his thumb and forefinger to his forehead. "I'm not sure, Cass." His eyes dimmed and her heart lurched.

"Why are we flying to Cleveland? We just drove away from there. Isn't that the wrong direction from where we want to end up?"

"We're going back to Ohio because that's where the cavalry waits. I won't take a chance on unknown backup in Arizona. But it means I'm dropping you right back into Tony DelMorrie's reach." He released a frustrated sigh.

Words escaped her. She should be frightened out of her wits, but beside this man who emanated so much warmth and protection it wrapped her in a giant bear hug, she remained calm.

He misinterpreted her silence.

"I'm sorry, I let you down. You have a right to be scared. I assured you we could return safely and make this whole DelMorrie thing go away and I was wrong."

She turned soft eyes to him. "Clay, please. I'm not afraid, not with you by my side. I meant what I said. I'll follow you wherever you go and I'll do whatever you think is best. Don't waste time worrying about me. How do you think we were found out?"

"I don't know. If there is a leak, where? This was a need-to-know assignment. Only my chief and Dan know what's going on, and I swear on my life it's not either of them."

"But you had to talk to that secretary this afternoon to reach Dan. Maybe she overheard the conversation."

He swung his head to stare at her without really seeing her, no doubt mentally weighing the suggestion that the chief's assistant factored into this betrayal.

He shrugged. "I don't see it but maybe. What it tells me is we can't talk to anyone. We're on our own until Dan reaches out to us."

The gate agent called their flight, but Clay held her arm,

waiting until all of the passengers were on board before moving Cassidy to the portal. His head never stopped pivoting.

The hum of the engines and the sheer terror of the day combined to defeat her efforts to stay awake. She woke at Clay's gentle urging, sleepily realizing her head nestled on his shoulder.

Clay retrieved their bags from the overhead compartment and locked his hand on her shoulder while they moved single file down the narrow aisle and off the plane. At this hour, well after midnight, the airport was relatively empty.

Clay reached for her hand and she stared up at him. "What're we going to do?"

"Let's find a room for the night. I'm exhausted and if I'm too tired, it's dangerous for both of us. Tomorrow we'll rent a car and drive south."

"I hate to remind you, but it's already tomorrow. Will we drive to the police station or return to your apartment?"

Her heart tugged when she viewed the dark circles ringing his eyes and their muted hue. He looked tired and confused, like a lost little boy.

"We can't go to either of those places, honey. We are nomads at the moment. I hope Dan figures out how to communicate with us. I'm too fatigued to think rationally about what to do next. Tired isn't good, it will make me sloppy. We'll decide later, okay?"

She offered her best reassuring smile. "That's fine, Clay. We'll figure out something."

21

Clay slept until eleven, waking to discover Cassidy bent over her laptop, her fingers tapping the keyboard. He watched her, smiling at the wrinkles on her forehead as she concentrated.

"Hey you, didn't your mom ever tell you your face could freeze like that?" He stretched the kinks from his back and legs.

She rewarded him with a bright smile. "Good morning. Is this better?"

His manly parts applauded. "Much."

"I hope I didn't wake you."

"You didn't." She had showered and dressed in clean clothes. Her eyes danced with a little bit of makeup and her spiked hair framed her face. The complimentary newspaper lay in sections on the floor.

"What are you looking at that makes you frown like that?"

She winked at him conspiratorially. "I'm plotting our next move. Or at least trying to figure out our options."

Clay sat up, threw his legs over the side of the bed and ran his hand through his hair. "Oh? What'd you come up with?"

Her face beamed as she reported the different flights they

could take from Cleveland to Phoenix, consulting notes she'd written on the hotel tablet. She'd also mapped out several driving routes, in the event Clay opted for ground travel. With all that had happened and gone wrong, she wasn't giving up the fight. She was ready to start another journey with him into the unknown.

He conceded a new admiration for her. He'd asked her to trust him and she did, unconditionally.

"Of course, none of that could matter if Dan says we should return to the police station. But I haven't heard your phone vibrate."

He checked his cell phone for messages. Nothing.

"I'll shower and we can discuss our options while we eat. I don't know about you, but I'm starving."

Twenty minutes later, he stood before the full-length mirror tucking his Polo shirt into his jeans. Sleep and the hot water worked wonders. His thoughts were clearer and he was centered again. Cassidy reached for the room service menu.

"Why don't you go blond for me and we'll walk downstairs to the hotel restaurant?"

Her eyes lit up like a child's on Christmas morning opening a new toy. She jumped from the loveseat and retrieved the wig from the desk. Dutifully she added the glasses, turned with her palms spread wide, and grinned. "Ready."

After the elevator doors closed and they were alone she asked, "Is this a good idea?"

Clay shrugged. "Well, by now I suspect they know we weren't on that plane to Arizona. The advantage we have is that they aren't looking for Clay and Eliza King so they shouldn't be able to track us here. To our disadvantage, we don't know what is happening at home, so we can't go back there yet. I have a mind to just chill here for a day or two or until Dan sends word to us."

"What do you think is going on?"

"I wish I knew, hon."

"Can't you call Maggie? After all, you are her brother."

"No. Dan will make contact when it's safe."

He waited until they were seated and had ordered lunch before continuing. "Cass, do you know how to shoot?"

She gasped and clutched her hands to her throat. "No. I don't like guns."

He arched an eyebrow. "If you live with a cop, you have to learn to live with guns. Guns don't kill, irrational people with guns do."

"That's a political debate."

He canted his head. "You don't blame the car for a fatal traffic accident, do you?" She lowered her gaze to the tabletop.

"Ever handle a gun?"

Her head snapped up and she shook it, wide-eyed. "As long as I stay with you, why would I need one?"

"As much as I'm enjoying this time with you, ignoring the circumstances of course, I can't be with you every minute. Right now, if you need to use the ladies' room, you have to walk to the front of this restaurant and out of my sight."

"You could come with me."

He smiled at her quick solution. It was the first time he'd done that in days. They were running for their lives and she still could make him smile, like a bright ray of sunshine after a long, gray winter. He hoped they survived this and he could look forward to her sunshine every day.

"And call attention to both of us while I stand outside the bathroom door? I don't think so."

"Well then, I'll just hold it." Now he laughed out loud.

"I have a better idea. I have a small pistol in my briefcase. We'll review the basics of firearm safety and shooting back at the room. I want you to know how to use it in case of an emergency."

She swallowed so hard her Adam's apple jumped. "Are you going to make me carry it?"

"Not right away." Their meals arrived and the conversation ceased.

After lunch, she convinced Clay to send their dirty clothes to the hotel laundry, paying extra to have them ready by noon the next day. Now, she sat beside him on the bed, their thighs touching, her right arm rubbing against the muscles in his left arm as he explained the mechanics of the black mini-Glock forty-caliber pistol. He handled it like a feather, but clutched in her hand, her biceps strained to keep it level.

"Lock your wrist."

She did, using her other hand to level the weapon. Sleek and cold in her grip, she couldn't imagine actually aiming and firing the way Clay was demonstrating now.

"Are you listening to me?"

"Yes."

No. She concentrated on the nausea, willing her lunch to stay down, forcing herself to stay at his side, focusing her eyes on the weapon without really seeing, silently praying that she would never, ever have to do what he was explaining.

But what if that son of a bitch Tony DelMorrie stood before her, the man who had virtually ruined her life? If he stood in front of her threatening Clay's life or terrorizing Maggie and Jack, or if he screamed that he would end hers like he did the day she fled the convenience station? Could she pull the trigger then?

She'd resolved that he wouldn't dictate her life anymore, that he wouldn't keep her in the dark. She reminded herself that enough was enough. She squeezed her eyes shut and envisioned Amber, smiling, laughing, wiping sandwich sauce from her lips. Her heart tugged.

"Cassidy, answer me."

Instead, she raised the unloaded gun to the window, balanced her right hand in her left palm in a steady grip, and slowly squeezed the trigger. Click.

The decisive crack cut through the tension in the room.

"Don't worry Clay." She inhaled, renewing her resolve. "If I have to, I will."

The little shit had better be kidding. "What do you mean you lost her? You're shittin' me, right?"

Johnny Tanzini imagined Mittens squirming on the other end of the phone. He shoulda known better than to leave this kind of job to the manboy and some sweaty goombah he didn t know.

"Our info was solid, Boss. But they didn't get off the plane. Maybe she got sick or somethin'. Tony says he got eyes on every flight settin' down in Arizona, and we got our guys watchin' every plane coming back here."

"Yeah, well, Tony's been followin' her all over the freakin' United States and he ain't caught her yet. I don't set much stock in his abilities."

"I hear ya, Boss. I know you ain't happy but look at it this way. They ain't got no place to go but back home. That's where we control the situation. No fuckin' pansies from the West Coast interferin'."

"Maybe. But remember, I ain't whackin' a cop, you hear me? Just her. She's the target. You kill a cop, we'll have every freakin' police agency all over us, includin' the legit businesses. He's off limits. Say you understand this, Mittens. Tell me you ain't gonna fuck this up."

"I hear ya, Boss. Just her in the crosshairs. Got it."

His pinging phone vibrating on the nightstand awakened them. Cassidy sat up, dragging the sheet and blanket to her shoulders. She slept in her panties and one of Clay's T-shirts, having sent most of her clothes to the laundry. The shirt bunched around her waist.

Clay reached for his cell, which cast the only light in the darkened room, touched the screen, and smiled. He turned the screen to Cassidy.

"E.T. Go home!"

"Is it from Dan?"

Clay checked the screen. "No, it's from Maggie. Something is still wrong. But something must be right or she wouldn't have sent this text."

"Are you going to respond?"

"No. Go back to sleep."

"Does it mean we go back home tomorrow?"

Clay snuggled under the covers and plopped his arm across her stomach, stretching alongside her, electrifying every nerve ending in her body.

"No. It's the code to go to the safe house."

"Where is the safe house?"

"You'll see tomorrow. Go back to sleep."

"Will you stay there with me?"

He raised his head from the pillow and stared at her through the darkness. "Of course I'll be there with you. Why would you ask that?"

She slid beneath the covers, settling them at her chin. "I keep waiting for you to turn me over to someone else, Clay. That would be the safe, smart thing to do."

He dropped his left leg over both of hers and snuggled closer. "No one ever accused me of being smart. I have too much invested in you to turn you over to someone else. You feel incredible under these covers and it's all I can do to keep from rolling on top of you right now and making love to you. I'm not letting that go. Go to sleep, hon. It's going to be fine now."

Lauren shuddered when her elbows stuck to the plastic red and white checkered tablecloth. Mittens had commanded this meeting at Ron's Ragu Room, an Italian restaurant in a section of town she never ventured to. She doubted all four wheels would be intact on her Mercedes when she returned to it.

The waiter lugged a gallon jug of the house red to her table and handed her an oversized menu encased in vinyl, equally as sticky as the tabletop. She ordered the rigatoni, just as Mittens specified, and an iced tea, passing on the wine. Her taste ran toward, dry, fine cabernets, not brewed-in-the-backroom-by-the-barrel concoctions. Besides, she needed to keep her head clear.

She inwardly grimaced when she saw Mittens bounce in the door, nodding and shaking hands at every table, but forced a smile and pasted it on her face. He acted like a movie star greeting his fans, patting the men on the back and kissing the women on both cheeks, throwing his head back to laugh loudly and too often. There was something to be said about being a big fish in a small pond, but someone needed to tell Mittens he was a minnow in a fishbowl. Definitely small time.

Surveying the food on her table, he smiled. "Whaddaya think? Ain't it the best rigatoni you ever ate?"

She smiled, remixed the sauce-covered noodles of the untouched entrée with her fork, and nodded. "This place is fantastic. A well-kept secret."

His head bobbed. "Yeah. You're right."

Automatically, a waiter brought him a tumbler of wine. Mittens drank half of it, smacked his lips, and withdrew a chair. "Let's git down to business. Did you bring your wallet?"

She smirked. "Not so fast, Mittens. The last time we spoke, you didn't know where she was. I told you, no money until I see some results."

He nodded and bobbed his head some more. That kind of action would give her a headache. "I know, I know, we had some complications. But that's all changed. My source in the police department came through for me. In fact, your ex- and," he paused, glanced from side to side and cleared his throat, "your friend should be arriving at a designated location even as we speak."

"Where?"

"Ah, I can't reveal the exact address. But it's what they call a safe house. Actually, it's not too far from here."

She leveled her gaze at him. "And do you have a plan?"

He grinned stupidly and spread his palms wide. "Of course I do. But it's better if you don't know the details."

Her temper was short. "I'm paying for the details, dammit. Tell me."

The price was twenty thousand. Lauren would have gladly

doubled that to extinguish Clay's little slut. She wasn't convinced this little man could accomplish it even as she slipped Mittens a bulky envelope.

"Half now. Half when I read the obituary."

He dipped his head in acknowledgement, salivating as he eyed the packet but smart enough not to grab for it and gawk at its contents.

"When this is all done, why don't you and me have a celebration dinner here together? We make a pretty good team, I think."

A shudder snaked down her spine. She'd shower the minute she walked in her front door. His expression was ludicrous, his eyes twinkling and the grin dissecting his little face into two tinier halves. She'd like to laugh out loud but she didn't dare offend him. Not yet.

She smiled the phony sophisticated smile she'd perfected in her teens. "We'll see. How soon do you think you will complete our business arrangement?"

The quicker she could hurt Cassidy and console Clay over his loss, the better. She'd already fantasized about their reunion once she offered him an understanding shoulder to cry on.

"Soon. I'll reach out to you. Meantime, you enjoy the rest of the meal. They give ya a lot, don't they? Take it home. It's just as good warmed up the next day. Don't worry 'bout the check. Dinner's on me."

She reached for her designer clutch and stood. "I've eaten way too much already. I'll wait to hear from you."

Mittens stood as well, clucked like a chicken, and winked. "Later, babe."

She felt his eyes on her back as she exited the restaurant, along with most of the men sitting at the other tables. She was beautiful and she knew it. She had more class than anyone in that place. Now all she needed was Clay.

Mittens bounced through the double doors into the kitchen, his cheeks hurting from the face-splitting grin he couldn't suppress. Ten thousand smackers nestled safely in his suit jacket. He'd picked up the envelope like it was nothing, cool as a cucumber, like he handled that kind of dough every day and smoothly slid it inside his coat.

Then he'd winked at Lauren and watched her tight ass walk out the door. Like nothin'. The bulging bills rested against his heart, generating a bulge of another sort. Man, it was like takin' candy from a baby. As soon as one of the boys called from the safe house to say Cassidy and the cop were there, boom! Ten thousand more buckos in his hands.

Johnny Tanzini had nixed his original idea to whack Cassidy when she stepped out of the car. Too noisy and too risky, he decided. Instead, they'd cut the power lines to the house. While the cop was in the basement checking the circuit box, they'd sneak in the unlocked back door wearing their high-tech night vision goggles and find her. Mittens liked this plan better. It was more exciting, more like something Al Capone would do.

He simply had to bide his time and wait for the phone call. What the hell was takin' so long? They shoulda been there by now.

Patting the envelope inside his coat reassuringly, he emerged from his small pantry office and returned to the dining area. He looked up like he always did when the hinges on the front door squealed and then froze, caught in a moment of surprise, uncertainty, and fear all in the same instant.

Long blond hair, fat red glasses and a coat she could swim in. Holy Mother of Jesus he was lookin' at Cassidy Hoake. The behemoth beside her was enormous, ten times bigger than the picture he'd seen in Johnny Tanzini's office, but it was him, Lauren Cestra's ex-.

Goliath surveyed the dining area and motioned Cassidy toward a booth against the wall.

Mittens jumped back behind the kitchen door and observed them through the crack. Cassidy reached for a menu, speaking unheard words. The cop still surveyed the room, assessing every table with narrowed eyes like some giant overlooking his land below.

He snatched a wet towel from the kitchen sink and strolled through the swinging doors, laying his hand on the kid's chest heading toward the table to stop him. "I got this one."

He bounced to the table for his first up-close look at them both, as lightheaded as if he was high on drugs.

"Hi, welcome to Ron's Ragu Room. Can I start you off with some house wine?"

Through the fog in his brain he saw the cop focus on his face, saw Cassidy's lips moving as if in slow motion, and realized her words sounded distorted in his ears. Involuntarily, he stepped one pace backward. He should drop the towel, reach to his ankle holster and come up shooting, firing his automatic right in the big man's face. Two pops and then the girl. Bang! Bang! Deader than roadkill.

But Johnny Tanzini had declared the cop off limits and this restaurant was one of his semi-legitimate businesses. He wouldn't appreciate a table shooting, especially not one involving an off-duty police officer, and Tanzini likely would not understand if Mittens argued there was no way to kill the girl without wiping out the hulk, too.

His lifetime goal was to become a made-man, to be accepted into the Tanzini family, but this wasn't the way to do it. No, a public execution like this would surely backfire.

"Are you all right?" the cop asked.

What the hell, he was in a stupor. The room spun and his legs had morphed to rubber, his chest so tight he could barely breathe.

"Yeah, sorry. For a minute I thought I recognized you." Jesus, his voice cracked like a girl's. "How ya doin' tonight? Can I recommend the rigatoni? It's the best. What can I get for youze?"

The cop eyed him, making him feel inadequate. Three shots, that's all it would take.

"I'll have some coffee."

Cassidy Hoake smiled at him. Much warmer than Lauren's phony grin. "I'd like some iced tea, please."

"Comin' right up. I'll give you some time to look over the menu." He pivoted and sauntered toward the drink station, his heart thrumming in his ears. He better call Tony. Right now.

23

Clay twisted in the booth, following the waiter's disappearance through the swinging double doors into the kitchen. What was that about?

"What's the matter?" Cassidy whispered. A bus boy arrived with paper placemats and silverware and Clay turned back to face her.

"Is everything all right?" She caught her bottom lip between her teeth and waited for his answer.

Something about that waiter bothered him. Or was he so mentally fatigued, he'd turned the corner from protective care-taker to obsessive companion? Not likely. They were in a public restaurant in a part of town Cassidy had never been to. The chances of someone recognizing her were nil. Something about that waiter was out of sync.

Cassidy's face bunched together in concern. "Clay? Is every-thing all right?"

"Yes. Just getting paranoid, I guess. What are you going to order?"

But it wasn't paranoia, it was that sixth sense. That waiter's hand trembled when he wiped the wet cloth across the table. His voice warbled when he spoke. He thought he recognized them? Recognized who? Cassidy or him? From where? The man resembled some knock-off hoodlum. How would he know them?

The bus boy returned with their drinks. "What'll you have?"

"Where's the other waiter?" Clay asked.

The kid shrugged. "In the back, I guess. This is my station anyway."

Clay straightened his shoulders and nodded toward Cassidy. She ordered a pasta dish and salad. "Make that two." He followed the waiter's path to the kitchen, looking away only after he'd moved through the swinging doors, and then turned to find Cassidy staring at him intently.

"What is it?" she whispered.

"I can't put my finger on it, Cass." He pressed his neck muscles between his thumb and forefinger, squeezing to relieve the pressure.

"I'm at a loss as to why in the hell we haven't heard from Dan. He should know better than to go silent like this for so long. We're defenseless, hanging out here like sitting ducks. We're close to our safe house destination. We should've heard from him by now."

"That brick house we drove past three times, is that where we're going?"

He nodded.

"Why did we drive here instead? Shouldn't we have gone to the house? Isn't that what Dan's message said to do?"

Heavy circles ringed her eyes and the strain of the day creased her forehead. He wasn't helping matters, acting so mysterious, dragging her to this restaurant without explanation, keeping her in the dark. But when he didn't see the signal to enter the house, it spooked him. And set every cop nerve on edge.

Not knowing what else to do and realizing they were both tired and hungry, he'd opted for this neighborhood eatery. Maybe he should have driven them directly to the police station instead. Exhaustion could be wreaking havoc with his judgment.

"There should've been a light on in the front room."

It was as simple as that, the tiniest hint that something was amiss.

"Maybe we were too early, or it burned out."

"No, that's not it, Cass. I can't explain it, so don't ask me."

She offered a weak smile. "It's okay, Clay. You'll figure it out."

There was her blind trust again, following his lead without question, placing her life in his hands. Had it been a mistake, thinking he could protect her like some one-man army instead of enlisting help from his fellow police officers?

Had he wanted her to perceive him as her hero, the man who swoops in and saves the day and, because of his ego, he'd led her to imminent danger instead? He eyed her, sitting patiently, returning his gaze, ready to blindly fight the unknown.

She had no doubts, why did he doubt himself? He was good at what he did and he'd never questioned his instincts before. This wasn't the time to start.

He glanced toward the round windows on the kitchen doors and saw the smaller waiter duck out of sight. Something definitely was not right.

"I'm sorry, Cass, but we're not staying here. Stand up as casually as you can when I signal and walk straight to the car. I'll be right behind you."

She didn't question him, just nodded, reached for her purse, and didn't flinch when he eased the gun from the back of his waistband and concealed it along his side. On his signal, she slid from the seat and headed toward the door.

Clay followed, grabbing her elbow and rushing her to the car. He didn't wait to open her door, just whispered "Hurry" and ran around to the driver's side. Looking into the rearview mirror as he peeled out of the parking lot, he spotted the small waiter standing at the front of the restaurant, waving his arm and yelling into his phone.

They sped out onto the street and merged into traffic. Clay extracted his cell phone from his pocket and handed it to Cassidy. "Find the last number called. It should be Dan's. Text the message, Jack jumped over the candlestick. Do it quickly, Cass."

Her fingers trembled, working to betray her efforts to tap the letters on the screen, but she followed his instructions. A tiny whoosh indicated the message was sent.

"Is it safe to text Dan?"

"Honey, I'm not sure what is safe anymore."

All thoughts of dinner dissolved into her fear of the moment. Clay was driving too fast, clutching the steering wheel with both hands. Her mouth was dry, her throat tight, her chest caught in a vice-grip. The car zoomed along a street that seemed familiar. "Where are we going now?"

"We don't have a choice, we have to return to the safe house. That message can only be issued from there. But we're not going to stay at the house."

Well, that was confusing. Why would they drive someplace they couldn't stay? She didn't dare ask. Clay looked like a madman behind the wheel, executing turns faster than he should and stepping on the accelerator at a yellow-lighted intersection to speed through it. And then just as suddenly, they slowed to a crawl and she recognized the cobblestone street where the safe house was located. At barely a two-mile-an-hour pace, the car eased down the street toward the driveway on the right side of the house. There were more cars parked along the curb than when they drove by earlier. Maybe more of the residents on the street were home now. Funny that they didn't park in their driveways.

Clay turned off the ignition. "Pay attention to me. When we

walk in the front door, we'll walk straight to the end of the hall and turn right into a bedroom. We won't turn on any lights so keep hold of my hand. A large dining table and chairs will be on our right. That's the only furniture in the room so you shouldn't trip over anything, especially not if you stay directly behind me. Whatever you do, Cass, follow my lead."

She whispered her response. "Don't worry, Clay, I will."

"I'm going to drop you out the back bedroom window and I want you to stay low to the ground and wait for me. We'll crawl right back here to the car. I'll be right behind you."

With key in hand they walked up onto the front porch, opened the door, and stepped inside. Stale, musty air assaulted her nose. Clutching her right hand, Clay dragged her forward and she stepped intuitively through the dark room. In a matter of minutes they were poised at a rear window, which Clay eased opened.

Outside, several car doors slammed. It was an easy drop from the window to the ground, but Cassidy fell to her knees, then edged backward to give Clay room to land. They hunched down and crept to the car.

Clay held up one finger, motioning her to wait, and slipped out of his jacket. He laid it across the back window, opened the driver's door, and reached inside, switching off the interior light.

"Get in," he ordered, retrieving his coat and scrambling into the driver's seat.

"Where's my briefcase?" Despite being enclosed inside the car, he whispered, and Cassidy likewise responded, "Here. Right here."

He blindly searched the inside and removed the pistol she'd practiced shooting in the hotel room, extending it toward her with a parental glare.

Tentatively, she grasped the weapon, ignoring the sinking feeling in her stomach and the tears that blurred her vision.

"Keep it with you at all times, so you can grab it quickly. Don't stash it in your purse or at the bottom of your duffel bag. Hide it in a pocket you can easily reach.

"If you're in danger, squeeze the trigger and make it count. Don't think about it, don't hesitate. Understand?"

She nodded.

"Stay here."

Her heart raced when she realized he was easing out of the car, leaving her alone in the dark. She bit her lip to stymie her words and reminded herself that she trusted this man. But she couldn't quell her high-speed breathing.

Twisting in the seat and squinting to focus, she watched Clay's shadow creep to the edge of the drive and slink back. He settled into the front seat and she waited.

And waited, wondering when he would turn the key in the ignition, where they would run to now, what would happen next. She couldn't stand the silence.

"What'd you see?" she whispered.

"There are a couple thugs milling around out there, like they are trying to organize. I'm not sure what they're waiting for. Dan should have gotten that text by now. I don't understand why police units aren't here. That's like a Code Red in a hospital. But we can't afford to wait.

"In a minute, we're going to tear out of here like a bat out of hell so buckle up. I don't know where we're going, Cass, and I hope to hell no one follows us because we're on our own."

"And if someone does?"

"We chance it and drive straight to the police station. You ready?"

She tugged the shoulder harness tighter and whispered, "Hope you don't mind if I close my eyes."

Clay chuckled, turning the key in the ignition. "Hope you don't mind if I do too."

Clay threw the car in reverse. Tires screeched and the smell of burned rubber saturated the night air. The power with which he stomped on the gas pedal thrust Cassidy forward, forcing the seatbelt to painfully cut into her shoulders. Clay shifted into drive and her head snapped back from the surge like she rode the Jack Rabbit at Kennywood Amusement Park, reminding her momentarily why she hated roller coasters.

The car lurched out of the driveway, eliciting yells from several men who appeared to be walking en masse toward the house. She couldn't make out what they hollered.

Clay swung the steering wheel in an arc and sped down the street. Two hands clutched the wheel as he eyed the rearview mirror.

"Son of a . . . hold on."

How fast could they drive through a residential neighborhood before someone called the police? Maybe that's what he was hoping for. Pure fear kept her from asking. Any minute she expected a g-force tug on her face. Trees, cars, and houses whizzed by. The car tires squealed when he navigated a corner, calling to mind the sales expression "turns on a dime." She tightened her grip on the door handle and braced her feet on the floor.

Suddenly, flashing lights were charging toward them head-on, approaching them just as fast as they traveled. Red, blue, and white bulbs exploded in her line of sight, spinning and popping, and the high-pitched wails of multiple police sirens pierced the air. She jammed both feet into the floorboard as if the brake pedal was on her side and she could stop the car.

But Clay stopped it for her, barked for her to "Stay!" and jumped out of the driver's seat with his hands in the air like a felon, yelling, "Go! Go! Go! Go! Go! Behind me! Blue Chevy."

Four police cruisers sped by him and one halted in front of their car. The siren cut mid-squeal and Dan leaped from the passenger seat, ran to Clay, and embraced him, pounding his back. Only then did she release the door handle and swipe her sweaty palms across her jeans.

She'd never seen so many police in uniform in one place. They were everywhere, their radios cackling in code, their heads moving in constant surveillance. One officer walked to her side of the car and she made ready to get out, but he turned his back to her and stood at attention, blocking her view out the window. The butt end of a rifle protruded beyond his right hip.

She settled back into the seat, trying to make some sense out of the radio transmissions filling the air. Finally, Clay crawled back into the front seat, leaned over, and squeezed her knee. "You okay?"

"What's happening?"

"They caught two of the men who were at the house and they apprehended whoever was chasing us in the car. He has ten thousand dollars in his pocket, but he's not talking. The other two seem like lackeys. They are probably just following orders and won't know much. Everyone is being hauled to the station for interrogation. Right now, it's not clear who they are or if they are connected to Tony DelMorrie, but I don't believe in coincidences."

He ticked off his thoughts on his fingers.

"First, they knew our flight details and then they knew we were going to the safe house. There has to be a leak inside the department. Dan still thinks that's the safest place for you, but I disagree. I'm not willing to take you back there, not knowing who to trust. What do you want to do, Cass?"

She swallowed hard. "What do you mean?

"I haven't done such a great job so far. Nothing has gone the way I planned. If you'll feel safer at the police station, surrounded by cops, we'll go back."

She studied his face, wishing she could see those laugh lines that brightened up his eyes. He looked so tired, so defeated.

"You've protected me so far, Clay. If you don't think it's safe to go to the police station, then we won't go back there." He raised weary eyes to her and the silence stretched between them like a bridge begging them to cross. Slowly, almost imperceptibly, Clay leaned toward her, leveling hooded eyes on her lips. She inched toward his face, sensing a new beginning.

It was the most tender kiss she'd ever experienced, sweet and much too brief.

Dan pounded on the rooftop and appeared at the driver's window. "You ready to go?"

Clay raised a questioning eyebrow at her. "Lead the way," she whispered. He smiled and turned to Dan.

"We're not going to take the chance and return to the station. When we stop, I'll let you and only you know where we are. Meantime, you figure out who their mole is."

He ignored Dan's objections and shifted the rental car into drive. "I'm afraid you and I are spending another night in a motel room, honey. We'll grab some takeout along the way. I don't know about you, but I'm hungry and tired."

She nodded. "You're going to let Dan know where we are when we get there?"

He glanced at her quickly and then looked out the windshield. "No. I'm not telling anybody where we end up."

From his hiding spot behind some schmuck's front yard hedges, Tony DelMorrie watched the car drive away and cursed. He'd planned to park and walk the final two blocks to the address Mittens had called in, when a flood of police cars woke up the whole neighborhood and forced him to drive to the curb and stop. He'd gotten out of the car to watch the scene unfold.

Fortunately, the house whose yard he crouched in remained dark. The owners must not be home.

The action reminded him of a raid on one of their numbers joints—lights, sirens, and cops everywhere. He felt sorry for the poor dope who jumped out of the car with his hands up until he realized it was the cop escorting Cassidy Hoake. He watched fascinated as four cars surged ahead and others arrived, the fuzz swarming the area like flies at a picnic table. From what he could make out from the garbled radio conversations, they nabbed Mittens. That little shit better keep his trap shut.

His thighs had cramped and his back pulsed in protest against the unnatural squat position he'd been in forever. He doubted he could straighten up without pain, but he forced his muscles to move because the cop and that Hoake bitch were driving away.

Despite the cool air temperature, sweat rolled down the sides of his face. He crawled through the grass toward the sidewalk, ruining a good pair of dress pants. One more cause to hate her. Gawd, he'd lost count of the reasons.

He stood, grateful for the two large maple trees that virtually cast the entire yard in darkness, straightened his clothes and walked nonchalantly to his car. Just a resident going out for some milk.

He eyed the fracas as any curious onlooker would do, and even raised his hand in acknowledgement in case any of the cops were watching. Snickering, he unlocked the driver's door and eased into the seat. What a bunch of idiots.

Smiling, he made a U-turn and casually drove to the end of the block, laughing out loud when he saw the car with Cassidy and the cop make a right turn. Wherever they were going, Uncle Tony was right behind.

24

W hat a low-baller. He drove her to a sleep-cheap motel. Maybe it was all he could afford on a cop's salary. She didn't deserve better anyway.

DelMorrie backed into a parking spot at the far end of the lot and switched off the headlights. He mentally reviewed his options. If the cop left Hoake in the car while he went to the office to check in, he'd drive up, shoot her through the passenger window and take off.

If they both walked inside and he had a clear shot of her from here, he'd take it. If the cop blocked the shot, he'd wait until they came back for their bags, zoom up and blast her to kingdom come. He'd been shooting a gun since he was ten, detonating every tin can his mother emptied. He'd perched them upside down on the cyclone fence that enclosed their backyard and little by little was able to step farther back and still hit the target. This would be a cinch.

Clay shifted into park but kept the car running. "Stay here, crouch down if you can. I'll register and be right back. It's better if the clerk thinks I'm alone."

The fear in her heart must have etched itself on her face because he paused, stretched across the console, and squeezed her thigh. "Don't worry, hon, it'll be fine."

She nodded, once again so overwhelmed by all that had happened she was speechless. She pressed the switch to lower the window, silently begging the fresh air to decrease her elevated body temperature and calm her nerves. Clay sauntered across the parking lot as if he didn't have a care in the world and entered the glass-walled motel office. A young man and woman stood at the counter and Clay stopped a short distance behind them, waiting his turn.

Remembering his directive, she unbuckled and slouched in her seat. A minivan driving into the parking lot to her right caught her attention and she turned to watch in idle curiosity, wondering if its occupants were as exhausted as she. The driver touched his brake pedal and the taillights glowed, shining a red spotlight on a man stepping out of a car beyond the van. She blinked and eased up to see more clearly.

It was him. DelMorrie. His fedora rode low on his forehead and his coat collar stood high, but he was a big man and enough of his face was revealed to recognize him. He looked first to his right, then left, then hunched over and scurried to the line of cars in the row where she was parked, crouching while he advanced forward.

She was all thumbs and she cursed when the cell phone dropped to the bottom of her purse. Balancing it on her thigh she touched Clay's name on the contact list screen with trembling fingers and typed. She studied Clay, counting the endless seconds until he felt his phone vibrate, reached into his back pocket to retrieve it, and read her message. DELMORRIE.

Clay spun around and charged out of the office as she threw her left leg over the console and hauled her body into the driver's seat. She jammed the car into drive and sped forward, at the exact moment gunfire erupted like a cannon in her ears. Two, three, maybe four rapid-fire shots.

The back window shattered and her nightmare found voice in a scream so forceful, her vocal chords strained. In the rearview mirror, Clay dropped to one knee.

Blindly, she drove to the end of the row of cars and yanked the wheel to the left, hearing more shots. She navigated a wild U-turn and drove straight toward Tony DelMorrie, right in the middle of the parking lot, his arm extended. She screamed a second time when the headlights illuminated Clay sprawled on the ground and DelMorrie doubled over but still aiming at his target.

Howling Clay's name like a banshee, she clutched the wheel and crushed the gas pedal to the floor, the car lurching forward like a rocket toward DelMorrie.

Dumbfounded, a deer caught in the headlights, DelMorrie twisted to assess the car speeding toward him, repositioned his weapon, and fired the second Cassidy smashed into him with the front bumper. The windshield shattered, the car careened out of control and two hundred and fifty pounds of dead weight bounced onto the hood, spiraled over the roof, and rolled off the trunk.

She crashed into a parked car. Momentarily stunned, she shoved the driver's door open and fell out onto the ground in time to see DelMorrie roll to his side and rise to his knees, his gun still locked in his grip and aimed at her. The echo of her own scream clashed with Clay's voice shouting her name. As if in slow motion, she turned in Clay's direction, watched him spiral up to his knees, raise his hands, and shoot.

Boom! Boom! Boom! Boom! Boom! Rapid shots, like a machine gun volley, pounded the night air.

DelMorrie folded into his middle, his head falling toward the ground, his arms flailing outward, fingers splayed wide, the gun releasing from his grasp in a slow drop. A spray of giant blood drops spewed from his chest and stomach and, when Clay squeezed the trigger once more, his head shot back, his neck snapping like a twig. The momentum knocked his body backward and his back hit the pavement with a dull thud, his legs and feet flying up into the air as if he'd fallen onto a trampoline, his face distorted, his eyes as wide as baseballs, and his lips puckering into a bloody kiss.

Eyes bulging open, arms spread wide, palms up, DelMorrie lay sprawled on his back beneath a light pole, motionless.

She couldn't hear anything, deafened by the gunfire and the fear coursing through her body, her nose burning from the smell of sulfur, tears blurring her vision.

"Clay! Clay!" She screamed, seeing him face down on the cement. "Somebody help." Scrambling on hands and knees, Cassidy flashed back to the day she crawled for her life from the convenience store, praying for God to help her. Now, she ignored the parking lot debris cutting into her palms and her blue jeans shredding as she scurried toward Clay, calling his name and pleading, "Please God. Don't let him die."

Faintly, the distant screech of police sirens sounded in her ears. When the motel office came into view, she saw through the shattered picture window the couple huddled in the corner and the clerk barely peaking over the counter.

A puddle of blood slowly seeped from beneath Clay's left thigh. "Clay? Clay?" She reached for his arm to roll him onto his back and shrieked at the dark, stain spreading across his stomach. His eyes were closed and she laid her hand on the sticky shirt hoping to detect a heartbeat. "Clay?"

Barely a moan. "Cassidy?"

"Oh thank God. Clay, be still, I can hear the police cars."

"DelMorrie?" he whispered. She raised her head and stared at the lifeless form.

"Dead. I'm pretty sure."

He blinked, coughed, spitting up blood, and grabbed her arm hard enough to leave finger marks. "Don't trust anyone. No one but Dan. Understand?" His eyes fluttered closed and his head clunked to the pavement.

Mittens knew his rights. He didn't have to tell these cops anything and he was entitled to a phone call. His only problem was, who to call? He didn't dare call Johnny Tanzini, that would be suicide.

Something was going on out in the main part of the police station. Whatever it was, it was causing a commotion in the whole building. The two detectives trying to play good-cop-bad-cop had disappeared, leaving some young rookie standing guard outside the door, the radio on his hip going crazy with garbled transmissions.

He yelled over the noise. "I gotta use the head." He wanted to see what was going on outside of this room. "Hey! At the door. I gotta use the head real bad."

The cop outside opened the door and leaned in. Geez, he was a baby who didn't look old enough to shave. His buddies had harassed Mittens about the pencil thin mustache above his lip but at least he had one. Not this kid.

"Hang on, little man. You're not the priority at the moment."

"Well unless you want me pissin' in that wastebasket in the corner, you better make me a priority."

Baby Cop spoke into the microphone hooked to his shoulder and then motioned to Mittens. "Okay. You can use the facilities and then make your phone call. We're cutting you loose."

He bounced to his feet, surprised by the change of events. Something real big must be going on. He scanned the room hoping for a clue on his way to the john but no luck. When he emerged, Baby Cop escorted him to the corner with a small metal table, folding chair, and phone.

"Can I have some privacy, please?"

Baby Cop moved a few steps back, glaring at Mittens. By now, he knew Lauren's phone number by heart.

"Yeah, it's me, Mittens, I need a ride. I'll meet you on the corner of Main and Abigail in fifteen minutes."

She wasn't happy, but he didn't care. He wanted out of this police station and back on Cassidy Hoake's trail. That would right everything with Johnny and redeem his reputation with the family.

"It'll be a couple minutes," he informed Baby Cop. The kid simply nodded.

Mittens narrowed his eyes, studying the frenzy in the room. Some kind of shootout somewhere. It sounded real bad. He checked his watch again and stood. It didn't matter if he had to wait longer on that corner, this room was starting to close in on him. And then, as clear as if they were delivering the message to his own ears, Mittens heard the voice transmission he knew would save his life broadcasted from the radio on Baby Cop's hip.

"This is Unit Four Eleven. I'm transporting Cassidy Hoake to the station now."

Praise the saints. They were bringing her right to him.

She wanted to ride in the ambulance with Clay, but because she wasn't a relative, they wouldn't let her. Dan embraced her briefly and assured her he'd keep her informed of Clay's condition. It frightened her that Clay lapsed into unconsciousness just after whispering his warning.

She overheard bits and pieces of talk between the ambulance crew and the hospital expressing concerns about a collapsed lung and the large amount of blood loss.

She sank deeper into the folds of Clay's oversized cargo coat trying to ward off the goose bumps. Without Clay protecting her, she felt naked. Vulnerable. Dan's presence wasn't the same. He insisted they had to debrief her so she waited inside his police cruiser, the red, blue, and white flashing lights casting the area in a surreal disco scene.

She braved one glance to the spot where DelMorrie lay as the car rolled past him, a sheet now draped over his body. Her nightmare was over, but it hadn't sunk in yet. She was numb.

They drove to the police station in silence after Dan radioed in to say they were en route. How would she even begin to make a statement? So much had happened and she was uncertain if she should tell all. Clay's cautionary words stayed in the forefront of her mind.

Pat Tatman waited for her when they arrived, taking her arm to assist her exit from the backseat of the police car and signaling to Dan. Instead of the barren interrogation room she occupied last time, he escorted her to a small lounge with two overstuffed loveseats and a counter full of coffee, tea, and cocoa products. She declined his offer of any of them.

She massaged her hands, trying to edge some warmth to the tips of her icy fingers. "Have you heard anything about Clay?"

"Only that it's pretty serious, but they're doing everything they can. He's in good hands. As soon as I hear more, Miss Hoake, I'll be sure to let you know. Meanwhile, I'd like to discuss what happened tonight. Maybe we can talk first before you write it all down."

"I'm not sure, Officer Tatman. Clay came running out of the motel office yelling for me to drive out of there and the shooting began. I floored the gas pedal, but when I saw that Clay had been hit I turned around and the only thing I could think was to run down the man with the gun."

She rubbed her forehead with her thumb and fingers hoping to shield her face with her hand. She'd thought her life of deceit was over but she was lying again.

"That wasn't a very smart thing to do, Miss Hoake. You could have been shot."

"I only wanted to help Clay."

He nodded. "I understand. Did you know who Clay was shooting at?"

"No, no I didn't. I didn't really have time to look at him to see who it was. Officer Tatman, it's been a really long day for me, a rough couple of days, actually. I don't think I'm up to writing a statement tonight. My thoughts are all jumbled and I'd like to return to the hospital to be with Clay. Is it possible that we could do this tomorrow?"

"I really should take your statement while the events are fresh in your mind, Miss Hoake."

She mustered a sad smile. "I understand. But believe me, I can barely think clearly. Please. I'm not going to forget what happened tonight, not one minute of it. Can't we delay this until tomorrow?"

He stared at her, his lenses magnifying his eyes to twice their size. She squirmed under the intense glower. It seemed like an hour passed before he sat back and nodded. "I suppose, if you don't think you can do it tonight, we can start fresh tomorrow. Where will you be staying?"

Good question. Did she still have an apartment at The Chalets? "I'll be at the hospital until they throw me out. Then I'll stay at Clay's."

His eyes grew even wider. "You have a key?"

"Yes." It was another lie, but it didn't matter. Maggie would probably let her in, and if not, she'd sleep in one of the pavilions in the common area. Maybe she could pick the lock on the pool house. Right now, it was imperative she get out of this room, away from guns and uniforms and crackling radios, and breathe fresh air before she passed out.

"Well, if you're going to Clay's, you might as well drive his truck home. We were talking about dropping it off at his place so you'd be helping us out. Would you mind?"

"Not at all, officer. I'd be happy to and thank you for understanding. I promise I'll return tomorrow."

Cassidy cringed when the truck's gears squealed, reminding her how many years it had been since she'd driven a stick. Every clutch had its own feel. It was just a matter of capturing that touch. She sensed Clay all around her, the way the leather seat cupped her bottom and the feel of the grip wrap on the steering wheel holding her hands. She was tuned into him, his cautionary words echoing in her ears and his ever-present awareness of his surroundings ingrained in her brain. A pair of headlights in the rearview mirror appeared to be following her.

She turned down two side streets, essentially weaving off and on the main road to the hospital, and the car remained behind her, even though it stayed a safe distance back. But she was certain someone was tailing her.

The police? Why? She told them she was going to the hospital to be with Clay and where she'd stay once she left his side. There was no need to keep her under surveillance. They wouldn't have let her leave the police station if they were concerned about where she might go, and certainly not driving Clay's truck.

Tony DelMorrie was dead. She no longer needed to hide from him. The reality of that nightmare ending was still an unbelievable blur.

So who could possibly be so interested in her? She weighed her options. She could retrace her route and return to the police station for another round of questions about why she suspected someone was following her and who it might be. The thought deflated her. She couldn't walk back into that police center with its heightened level of activity. Not tonight.

She could veer onto the next residential side street and park the truck, essentially halting the convoy. But that option left her alone on an unfamiliar street to confront a stranger. That was a bad plan.

A better idea was to proceed to the hospital where the parking lot was well lit and, presumably, there would be human activity. A more public place offered more protection.

She breathed slowly, enveloped in a sense of calm. She must be overtired not to be nervous or scared. Or, more likely, she was ready to be done with fear.

Exit signs for the hospital snapped her to attention. The emergency entrance was probably the busiest area, and the safest. She waited at the stop light, noting in the side mirror that three cars back, the silver car also had a turn signal blinking.

She navigated the turn and chose the emergency lane designated for cars only. Inching alongside the curb, she studied the silver Mercedes while it traveled the lane to the parking area. A man rode in the passenger's seat, but her glimpse was too brief to recognize him. That meant two people tracking her, not just one.

Turning her attention to the emergency entrance, where a steady stream of emergency personnel and visitors moved in and out, her stomach lurched.

There he was again, the black man from the bus station. Sauntering out of the sliding glass door, he stopped short when he saw her, pausing as if he recognized Clay's truck. He waited and watched.

What should she do? Lay on the horn until hospital security arrived? Her stalker would likely take off when she sounded the alert and she would resemble a madwoman claiming she was being followed.

Perhaps the activity around the entryway would prevent him from approaching her. The hospital was the only safe place for her to be, and the only way to get there was to turn off the engine and step out of the truck. *You can do it, Cassidy.*

She dropped the keys into Clay's coat pocket. When metal hit metal she remembered the pistol. She gulped and lowered her hand into the pocket, gripping the gun. Opening the driver's door, she extended her left foot to the ground, looking in the black man's direction as she did. Oh sweet Jesus, he was walking toward her.

In a panic, she looked to her left and realized the Mercedes had turned around and was circling back, a police car directly behind it. Panic rose to close her throat.

Under the bright parking lot lights, she saw the passenger and, worse, recognized the driver. Clay's ex-wife wore a maniacal look on her face, her forehead and eyebrows pinched together and both hands clutching the wheel. The man beside her—the waiter from the diner—grinned widely, his arm extended out the window aiming a gun at her.

Clay's instructions sliced through her fear—don't hesitate. She dropped to the ground, yanking the gun from her pocket and steadied the weapon in her hand. Shots rang out, one pinging beside her into the rear truck fender, the other coming from somewhere behind her, and she squeezed the trigger. She recalled Clay's caution about the gun's recoil and, even as her arm jolted upward, she controlled the movement with her left hand, and fired a second time.

The Mercedes swerved violently and, from inside, a high-pitched wail echoed.

And then, the black man was beside her, gun drawn, huge hand shoving her to the ground.

"Stay down on the ground. Behind me. Don't move."

She fought the bile rising in her throat as thick blue-jeaned legs backed her against the truck in a squat position and work boots shoved into her body, effectively trapping her to the spot.

Pandemonium erupted in the parking lot. Feet stomped the pavement like stampeding horses and radio transmissions from the police cars interrupted and cross-talked orders, but she couldn't discern the words and from her position on the ground, trapped against Clay's truck, she couldn't see. Fear wrenched her belly tight.

"Silver Mercedes. Southwest corner. Go! Now!" her long legged jailer yelled. Suddenly he turned and grabbed her by the arm. "C'mon, we need to get you inside."

He yanked her from the ground, shoved her around the opened truck door, and propelled her toward the hospital entrance. She shrieked, wrenching her arm from his grasp. "No. No more. You can't frighten me anymore."

Her outburst stunned him, giving her the opening to raise the gun and point it directly into his face. She gulped for air, aware that the pistol shook in her hands, but determined once and for all to fight to the end.

Tires screeched and Cassidy and the black man turned in unison to see the Mercedes zooming toward them, the passenger still leaning out of the window to aim at them.

"Get down," her stalker yelled, dropping to his knees. Cassidy sank to her knees, raised her gun, zeroed in on the steering wheel and squeezed the trigger, once, twice, again, and again. The car crashed into a light pole, its horn blaring and steam spewing from the crumpled hood. She kept her aim on the wreckage, the gun wobbling in her hands.

Kneeling beside her, the black man also fired three rounds before reaching out to ease his hand over hers, smiling that bright, white smile as he lowered her weapon.

"It's okay, Cassidy, it's okay. It's done."

She struggled to catch her breath.

"Are you all right, Sugar Plum? Your face is bleeding. You and parking lots are having a real bad time tonight, aren't you?"

She had no voice to speak, couldn't slow her rapid breathing, and failed to squelch the tears.

"Sorry I had to be so rough, Princess. We'll get you inside and have the docs take a look at you." He stood and reached for her hand.

"Who, who are you?"

She could swear his eyes twinkled.

"Marcus Bassman. Come, sweetness. I'll help you up."

"I saw you at the bus station."

If it was possible, his smile grew wider. "Yes ma'am." He reached and gently lifted her to her feet, clinging to her when her legs refused to support her bodyweight.

"And you were at the apartments."

"Yes ma'am. You want me to find a wheelchair, Pumpkin? You don't seem to have your sea legs."

A sharp pain shot through her side and she clutched his meaty forearms. "It's hard for me to breathe."

"Let's get you inside. You're a pretty good shot. Clay must have taught you. He's going to be proud when he hears how well you did."

She gasped. "What did you just say? Who are you?"

He winked and grinned. "Detective Marcus Bassman, at your service. Me and Clay go way back. We're best friends. We've known each other since high school and went through the police academy together. You were never really alone, Sugar Plum. When he wasn't with you, I was."

Marcus kept his arm around her waist and slowly, they walked toward the hospital entrance. "But, at the bus station . . ."

"I work undercover, honey. That bus station is part of my territory. Clay alerted me the minute he started looking for you, and I called him the second you walked in there. You don't think he was going to leave you out there on your own, do you? That man loves you too much."

25

Doctors and nurses poked and prodded her, sent her for X-rays, and discovered she had two broken ribs plus numerous cuts and bruises. Her right cheek was already a dark mix of blue and purple and had begun to swell, impeding her vision slightly. They taped her torso and suggested pain medication, which she declined.

The only medicine that would ease her pain was Clay. True to his word that he wouldn't leave, Marcus had remained on guard outside her examining room, and finally she rode in a wheelchair he deftly pushed toward Clay's room.

Marcus assured her Clay would recover from the bullet wounds to his thigh and his side, which doctors called a clean entry-exit wound. They'd operated and Clay was resting in a private room. But she needed to see for herself. And his words, that Clay loved her, had sent a surge of hope through her heart.

Clay sat propped upright against the pillows, tubes running from his nose and wrist. He'd been asleep, but he managed to smile once he saw Cassidy and stretched his arm over the edge of the bed. Marcus moved the wheelchair close, allowing Cassidy to reach and cling to his hand.

Her new friend repositioned himself to the opposite side, carefully embraced Clay, then sat on the edge of the bed. "What's with the hospital gown? You need to rock some jams, bro. I'm thinking purple might be your color."

Clay offered a feeble smile. "Purple's your shade, bro."

The color drained from his face at the effort required to turn his head toward Cassidy.

"How are you? They wouldn't tell me anything once I woke up from surgery. I've been worried about you."

Her heart leapt. "Never mind about me." She swallowed a lump of emotion. "Are you going to be okay?"

"I'm going to be fine. I'll need some rehab work on my leg, but the doctors said the muscles prevented more severe damage. Same with my side. All those hours at the gym with Marcus paid off, I guess."

She glanced at Marcus. How could she have feared that handsome, smooth face? "You've got some explaining to do about Marcus, mister. I was scared to death of him."

Clay nodded. "As you should have been. He works hard to look fearsome when he's undercover. Of course, his ugly mug always scares me." He flashed another weak smile at his friend.

"What happened after I passed out?"

Marcus winced. "There's a chapter to the story you don't know about, Clay. It didn't end with you killing Tony DelMorrie at the motel." He rose and closed the door.

Clay looked confused. "What do you mean? What happened?"

"The chief's secretary panicked when she heard you took a couple bullets and confessed that she'd been telling someone your information, someone other than Tony DelMorrie."

"She was the leak? I can't believe it. She seemed so loyal to the Chief."

Marcus agreed. "She fell into some financial trouble and asked the wrong people for help." He cleared his throat. "There's more, Clay. There's news about Lauren in all this. I'm not sure how you're going to take it."

Clay furrowed his brows and shook his head slightly to signal he didn't comprehend.

"She's dead, Clay."

His grip on Cassidy's hand tightened when he heard the words. He blinked once, twice, and again shook his head as if to clear his thoughts. "What? How?"

Marcus laid his hand on Clay's arm. "It seems she hired a hitman to kill Cassidy, that little squirt we picked up at the safe house with the pocket full of money. That's how they knew you were there. He was tracking you. We hauled him into the station, but with all the commotion you caused at the motel, the chief's secretary said to release him and no one questioned it. They didn't know he was the contract hitman though, so you can't blame anyone. We didn't put two and two together until we found them in the car."

"What car? I don't understand."

"It's a lot of detail we don't need to discuss right now, my friend. But I'm glad I was still tuned into Cassidy and when I heard she was on her way to the hospital, I stayed."

Cassidy tore her gaze away from Clay to stare at Marcus. "You were waiting for me?"

"Sure, Sugar Plum. I told you, if it wasn't Clay watching you, it was me. Pat radioed when you left the police station. We had an unmarked unit behind you the whole trip, partly on my orders and partly because Pat thought you were somehow complicit in all this. You were easy to follow in Clay's truck, especially since you told Pat you were coming to the hospital.

"I was here with Clay, so I waited. It wasn't long before our unit realized the Mercedes was following you too."

Marcus laughed and pointed to her. "You must have suspected it as well. That's what those little detours down the side streets were about, weren't they? Clay must be rubbing off on you."

Cassidy sensed her cheeks turning red. Clay laced his fingers with hers and whispered, "Is that right?"

She nodded. "I didn't know who, but I was pretty sure someone was following me. At first, I thought I should drive back to the police station. Then I decided there would be enough activity at the emergency entrance here to protect me plus I wanted to see you. I was so worried about you and they hadn't given me any information at the station."

Clay released her hand and attempted to ease into a more comfortable position, grimacing from the movement. Marcus jumped up and lifted him into place, adjusted the pillows, and ordered Cassidy not to move when she tried to help. In a weakened voice, Clay whispered, "Tell me the rest, Marcus."

"We ran the license plate and knew it was Lauren." As if filling in the blanks for Cassidy, he added, "Most of us are familiar with their domestic history, so we suspected she was either on her way to the hospital to harm Clay or she was after you. Mittens was a bonus."

Cassidy screwed up her face. "Mittens?"

"Mittens is a small-time thug affiliated with the Johnny Tanzini family. He had ten thousand dollars in his pocket. He jumped out of the car and tried to run after taking those shots at you which, by the way, Clay, left a nice round hole in your fender." He laughed when Clay didn't seem amused.

"I shot him in the buttocks as he was running. He's squealing like a pig two floors below us. He's even offering up information about Tanzini and his businesses, trying to save his own hide."

Marcus paused, but Clay wanted the rest of the story. "And Lauren?"

"We don't know yet how those two connected. She must have picked him up at the police station. My focus was on the shooter leaning out of the passenger window. Lauren was dead before the car crashed into the light pole. It appears when Cassidy aims at a target, she hits it."

Cassidy gasped and her heart plummeted. A heavy wave of sadness enveloped her. She turned tear-filled eyes to Clay and broke the silence that shrouded the room.

"I'm so sorry, Clay."

Clay's eyes darkened. "Don't say that, Cass. You did what I told you to do, what I would have done in the same situation. It's sad that it had to end like that but I'm grateful that I didn't lose you. I couldn't live without you."

Cassidy caught her breath. Did that mean what she wanted it to mean?

Marcus stood. "You two have some fences to mend. I'm leaving so you can do that privately." He kissed Clay's forehead and shut the door behind him.

Clay regarded her with watery eyes. "I owe you an apology, Cassidy. I always said Lauren needed professional help. I should've taken it more seriously when you told me she showed up at The Packing Place. I was too focused on Tony DelMorrie."

"It's understandable, Clay. He was the obvious threat."

"No, it's inexcusable. I'm a professional, but I let my emotions cloud good police judgment. Because of my feelings for you, I convinced myself that only I could keep you safe and that was dangerous for you."

"That's not true. For one thing, you had Marcus standing in the background. And it was always my choice to follow you. I'm not some weakling that you ordered around. You asked me to trust you and I did. My choice. It was as simple as that."

The corners of his mouth lifted. "Well, I do think we make a pretty good team. But you didn't always trust me, remember? You ran from me."

Cassidy sat up straighter in the wheelchair, her heart racing. He still didn't get it. He didn't understand her true motives. "I never ran from you, Clay. I left you because I wanted to protect you. I ran because I knew that Tony DelMorrie would follow me and that would keep you safe."

Clay reached for her hand. "You could've been killed."

She shrugged, blinking back the tears that welled in her eyes. "I would've died to protect you. I would do it all again, because I'm in love with you. I know with everything that has happened, you probably don't want to hear that. But before we go our separate ways, I want you to know I wish things had worked out differently."

He arched his eyebrow. "Are you leaving me again?"

"What? No. I just assumed . . ."

"Honey, you crawled under my skin almost from the first moment I met you. And then you wormed your way into my heart. I took two bullets trying to keep you, I'm not letting you go so easily now. If I have to fall out of this bed right now to my knees to ask you to stay by my side, I will. I'm in love with you, too, and I want the chance to share your life."

Her heart catapulted. "You do?"

"You're the oxygen I need to live, Cassidy. Stay and grow old with me."

A wave of fullness engulfed her. Finally, she had everything she'd ever dreamed of. She couldn't suppress her smile. "Don't worry, Clay, the only running I'm going to do from now on is into your arms. You're going to have a devil of a time getting rid of me."

— End —

If you enjoyed this book, please leave a review on Amazon.

More from This Author

INTRODUCTION

Off the Grid for Love

CHAPTER 1

The mouth of the gray metal gun, aimed directly at her midsection, looked as round and as wide as a beer can. Everything else blurred in her vision.

Snippets of last week's FBI training session flashed through her mind and the agent's words replayed in her brain. He'd called it "situational awareness."

"Stay alert," he'd lectured, *"and take note of everything around you. Be aware of what's happening."*

At this moment, staring at the handgun, Mackenna McElroy became aware of several things. She was scared speechless. All noise around her morphed into a monotonous drone, like a swarm of locusts. Her underarms were sticky with perspiration and she smelled her own sweat. The strawberry yogurt she ate for breakfast threatened to resurface, right on the neatly printed envelope that demanded she empty her cash drawer and not make a scene. Her heart thrummed so loudly in her ears, she barely heard the robber's words.

"Do it!"

His command was a sandpaper whisper. No, more like a snake's menacing hiss. Cold green eyes stared at her from beneath the rounded bill of a blue ball cap tugged so low on his forehead, it covered his eyebrows. An unfamiliar insignia decorated the front. Those eyes still hadn't blinked. Was he a robot?

A slow inhale filled her lungs with tepid air and she swallowed the boulder clogging her throat. The FBI agent had instructed them to stay calm, if ever they were face-to-face with a bank robber, and surrender the money. She eyed the weapon peeking out from beneath the envelope bearing her instructions, which casually covered the top of the thief's hand. Was his finger on the trigger ready to shoot? *"Don't risk your life,"* the agent had cautioned.

Mackenna stepped back on her right foot and opened the cash drawer, sweeping her hand across the counter surface, effectively whisking her pen to the floor. To her right, her co-worker Sandy remained oblivious to her plight, chatting happily with an elderly woman about winter finally ending. On her left, Matt studied a printout of his customer's checking account.

"No dye packs. Please hurry up."

A courteous bank robber. She'd have to remember that. Lifting the spring-loaded bill clips one at a time, Mackenna emptied the slots. Remarkably calm hands eased the collection of singles, fives, tens, and twenties into an ordinary looking bubble mailer. It mutated the flat envelope into a bulky lump. The room spun like a carousel, yet her hands remained steady. Every person in the bank faded into the background and time stopped. There was only the gun pointed at her belly and those ice green eyes.

She allowed the cash drawer to hang open, hoping Sandy would notice the violation of bank procedure and realize what was happening.

"Close your drawer, please."

Wow. This bank robber was polite and smart. She shut the drawer and regarded her assailant.

"Thank you, miss. I hope I didn't scare you."

He pivoted, a soldier executing an about-face, and then released an ear-piercing scream like a wild animal before pointing the gun to the ceiling and firing a shot. The room erupted in screams and he bolted for the door, hunched over like a running back carrying the ball. Mackenna pressed the alarm button at the edge of her desk and sank to the floor into welcomed darkness.

～

Voices buzzed. Her nose burned from an ammonia whiff that clogged her throat and stung her eyes. She flailed her arms in the air and struggled to sit up. The odor choked her.

"Give her some air."

"Back up."

"Are the paramedics on the way?"

Gagging, and then coughing, she swiped at her nose with the back of her hand and raised watery eyes to her co-workers. The room still spun like a merry-go-round with their faces parading by. Her boss. Matt. Sandy. Strangers. Sirens blared in the distance.

She gasped for air and motioned for everyone to step back. "I-I'm all right. Please. I'm fine."

The bank manager's arm snaked around her waist. "Let me help you up, Kenna. Are you hurt?"

Never had he called her by her nickname, always maintaining a boss-employee relationship and addressing her as Miss McElroy. She'd always regarded Mr. Gleaner as somewhat feminine but he lifted her off the carpet as easily as he might retrieve her pen, which remained on the floor near Sandy's station. Gently, he settled her into someone's roller chair and tucked her hair behind her left ear. Those errant strands always loosened from the ponytail she wore for work every day. Blue eyes leveled on her.

"Kenna? Speak to me. Are you hurt? What's my name?"

He grinned when she whispered, "Mr. Gleaner." Her throat felt raw and her pulse raced. The veins in her neck hammered a bass beat to some unheard rap song.

"The paramedics are here, sir."

"Bring them back. Kenna? Would you like some water?"

She nodded and a plastic bottle of natural spring water materialized in front of her. Mr. Gleaner unscrewed the cap. "Just a sip, okay? The paramedics are here. I want them to check you out."

"I'm fine, sir. I just fainted."

"Humor me, Kenna." He rose to his full six-foot height and

ordered Sandy and another woman to assist her into his private office, directing the paramedics to follow. The women each clutched an arm and helped her stand. That's when she saw the sea of blue swarming the bank. Police were everywhere.

Bank protocol dictated that the doors are locked immediately after a robbery and she saw the elderly woman who'd been talking with Sandy and Matt's customer being interviewed by uniformed officers. Police questioned several other customers as well, and allowed them to leave one at a time. Her turn likely would be soon.

Once her blood pressure dropped to a more normal reading and the effects of the smelling salts wore off, the paramedics pronounced her healthy. Outside the glass office door, Sandy wrung her hands and shook her head in response to a policeman's questions. Mr. Gleaner hovered, casting anxious glances toward her. He rushed in when the paramedics opened the door and said he could enter.

"Are you sure you're all right, Kenna?" When she nodded, he placed both hands on her shoulders. "Are you up to telling us what happened? The police are here and some agents from the FBI." He squeezed her shoulders lightly. "I can give you some more time if you think you need it."

She'd never thought of him as anything except a strict bank manager, a stickler for the rules, and a son-of-a-gun when someone's cash drawer didn't balance. Now, he seemed almost tender. It was possible she banged her head when she fell.

"I'm fine, sir. It's okay."

He stepped to her right side. "I'll stay right here with you. If you need to rest, just let me know."

The questions seemed endless. Even though she recalled the awareness training as the robbery was happening, she'd noticed so little. Except for the blue ball cap, the robber might as well have stood at her window naked. She couldn't describe the clothes he wore.

She didn't think he had facial hair. Was she certain? No.

Height? Tall. Towering in the frame of the teller's window. But he'd been smart enough to double over and dart out the front door, rendering the measuring tape at the bank's entrance useless.

He definitely held the gun in his right hand but she hadn't actually seen his hands once she stared down the cavernous gun barrel. The few words he muttered hadn't revealed an accent. All she recalled were the piercing green eyes and the gray steel he'd slid beneath the mailing envelope.

Yes. She'd glimpsed the gun. No. She had no idea what kind it was.

No, she didn't know him. Didn't recognize him. Pretty sure she'd never seen him in the bank before. Couldn't tell them anything more.

It felt like she hadn't disclosed any useful information at all. But the FBI agents and the police seemed satisfied with her responses, despite urging her to contact them if she remembered additional details. Mr. Gleaner glided his hand across her shoulders and bent so that his face was next to hers.

"The bank will be closed for the rest of the day. Why don't you leave early and go home? I have to stay otherwise, I'd drive you."

Mackenna narrowed her eyes to stare at him. It'd taken a gun pointed at her for Mr. Gleaner to treat her like a human, instead of a math android. Or had she suffered a concussion and hallucinated? He continued to speak. "And take the day off tomorrow." His hand squeezed her left shoulder. "I'll call and check that you're all right." His breath smelled like cinnamon.

She nodded and he helped her stand. Police still peppered the floor, both in the public area and around her teller station, but only a handful of customers remained. Her brain felt fogged, worse than any head cold she'd ever had. But her gait steadied once she gathered her purse and sweater and walked toward the entrance.

A young man stood behind her and they waited for the police officer to unlock the front door. The man stepped beside her and swung the glass door open. "Allow me."

She nodded. "Thank you."

He strode to a copper-colored motorcycle parked in the front row of the bank lot and worked to loosen the strap on the helmet dangling from the seat. Apparently he was in a hurry to drive home, unlike Mackenna. She couldn't go home, at least not yet.

Today was supposed to be a ten-hour shift at the bank, scheduled from nine to seven because of a community event. An extra-long day at work that allowed Arthur plenty of time to move out. It had been a long time coming and her ultimatum that brought them to this point. In her head, she knew it was the right decision and she was ready to let go. Her heart weighed heavier. She didn't want to witness his final moments in the apartments she'd considered "their" home.

The roar of the Harley jolted her from her reverie. She watched the helmeted young man walk his bike backward, rev the throttle one more time, lift both feet and smoothly ride past her. He waved, and she automatically nodded.

With no real destination in mind, she exited the parking lot out the same driveway as the motorcycle and drove to the mall. At least it would be easy to kill a couple hours there, although she wasn't in the mood to shop. How pathetic that she had nowhere else to go and no one to call. She'd devoted a full year to Arthur, at the expense of the few friendships she'd had. He hadn't liked her friends and, after a while, they grew tired of her excuses not to meet up and stopped calling. Did they sense that Arthur wasn't what he portrayed himself to be? Did they know he was a cheater? She'd known long before she actually acknowledged it, saw the signs, felt her heart growing dark. Knowing and acting are two entirely different challenges.

Thinking that a caffeine fix might settle her nerves, Mackenna walked to the coffee shop, barely noticing the window displays that she passed. Usually she'd linger, admire, maybe even wander inside to try on a pair of shoes or feel the fabric of a new dress. But today was hardly usual.

An extra-large mocha coffee should help. The china cup rattled in its saucer as she carried the drink to the far corner of the deserted shop and took a seat. The morning crowd likely was at their desks by now and lunch was an hour away. Mackenna planted both elbows on the table and dropped her head into her hands. Her fingers trembled against her forehead and tears filled her eyes, surprising her. She wasn't one to cry but this might have some therapeutic benefit.

"Hey, Kenna. You okay?"

Her head jerked up and she focused her blurred eyes on Motorcycle Man. He balanced his helmet on the back of the chair opposite her and leaned on it. "Sorry, didn't mean to scare you. Guess you've had enough of that for one day."

Mackenna wiped the tears from her right cheek with the back of her hand, then swiped at the left side of her face with her fingers. He'd startled her and left her wordless.

Motorcycle Man used his free hand to point to his chest. "I was in the bank this morning? We walked out together? I drove by you on the motorcycle?" His voice inflected with each statement, turning them into questions. "Remember?"

She nodded. "I-I'm sorry. Yes, I remember. I, you . . . I apologize. This whole day has me rattled."

A smile, slow and easy, creased his face. "Don't apologize, ma'am. You have every right to cry after what you've been through." He waited, expecting a response.

Her mind registered his words as if it operated in first gear. He'd called her by name, yet he was a stranger. She didn't like the chills that crawled along her spine. "How do you know my name?"

His eyebrows shot up and lowered in one quick movement.

He slanted his head slightly to the right and dropped his gaze to her left breast.

She followed his eye movement and discovered she still wore her bank identification tag, displaying her name in bold black print. Normally, she clocked out and stuck the magnetized nameplate to the board in the employee lounge. But there was nothing normal about today. In her rush to leave the building, she'd forgotten to punch her time card. Her cheeks grew warm and she lowered her gaze to her hands nested in her lap.

"You waiting for someone?"

Motorcycle Man asked too many questions for her comfort.

"Yes," she lied.

He slid the chair out from under the table. "Me too. How about if I wait with you?"

Yes, she was shaken and her personal and professional worlds were falling apart in tandem but that didn't render her stupid. If he was hitting on her, she wasn't interested and if he was a serial killer, the can of pepper spray in her purse would be a rude surprise.

"If you don't mind, no, I'd rather you not wait with me. Thanks, but I prefer to be alone."

He'd already dropped into the chair and plopped the helmet on the seat to his right. He folded his hands and planted his elbows on the table top. "Really? Because it sure looks to me like you could use a friend."

Tears filled her eyes once more. Now, she had to contend with a stalker.

"You're not a friend. I don't even know your name. Please leave me alone or I'll call security."

His right hand shot toward her. "Jake's the name. Meeting you is my pleasure."

Mackenna's hands remained fisted together in her lap. She eyed his big, calloused paw, and mentally awarded him grooming points for his clean, neatly trimmed fingernails.

Finally, it registered that she didn't intend to shake his hand. He withdrew the bear claw and winked. "No harm. What do you say I simply sit here with you until my friend arrives? We don't even have to talk. But you've had a traumatic experience, the full impact of which probably hasn't hit you yet. You're not going to like being alone when it does. Sometimes it's just good to have another human being close by. I'm a body on the other side of the table and so, you're not alone."

He swiveled in his seat, rested his left arm on the back of the chair, casually propped his right ankle on his left knee and centered his attention on three customers waiting for their orders. Faded blue jeans topped brown leather boots polished to a high sheen.

With both hands wrapped around her mug seeking the familiarity of the hot cup, Mackenna sipped her chocolate coffee. Its warmth caressed her throat and the sweet taste soothed her nerves. She studied her unwanted tablemate. Nicely shaped sideburns stopped just at the top of his earlobe and contrasted with his dark hair, which spilled haphazardly over the top of his ear and lapped his collar in disarray. A little too long for her tastes but, on him, it worked. Just the shadow of a beard. In profile, long, dark eyelashes curled upward. Why did men always inherit the lush eyelash gene?

Today was a warm, spring day, yet he wore a heavy black leather jacket. It looked worn enough to be comfortable. Tight thigh muscles stretched the denim on the leg he'd casually crossed. As more customers filed through the front door, Mackenna hated to admit it but she was glad she didn't occupy the table alone. At least no one else would bother her. But why had he?

"Are you really waiting for a friend?"

"Yes ma'am. She's habitually late but I'm used to it." Royal blue eyes gleamed at her. Dark hair and blue eyes were a rare combination. Which parent had he inherited them from?

"You don't have to call me ma'am. It makes me feel old."

That smile reappeared and the heaviness across her shoulders lightened. Under other circumstances, this guy might be charming, if he wasn't so pushy. "Yes, ma'am. It's how I was raised."

"Texas?"

"Damn, I've tried hard to hide the accent. Alabama."

"You shouldn't. It's appealing. Women like a Southern gentleman."

Now he threw back his head and laughed. "I've never been called that. But thanks."

His laughter shot a small thrill into her stomach and she averted her eyes to her cup.

"You feeling a little better?" His question was soft, like warm honey.

"Yes, thank you."

"I can give you a ride home, if you like. Or follow you to make sure you get there safely."

Alarm bells sounded in her head and she lifted her purse from the floor and rested it in her lap. This didn't feel right.

"I think you should leave me alone. Now."

"Ah, we're back to that, are we?" He winked again and returned his focus to the front of the coffee shop. His chin titled upward as a tall, blonde approached. Jake rose and lightly grasped her elbow.

"This is my friend, Courtney. Court, this is Kenna. Someone robbed the Good Neighbor bank on Mound Avenue this morning and she was the teller at the other end of the robber's gun."

Courtney's mouth formed an oval and she reached out and placed her hand on Mackenna's shoulder, squeezing it lightly. "Oh, I'm so sorry. Are you all right? Is there anything we can do to help?"

Her skin was smooth and her eyes, several shades lighter than her boyfriend's, shined with concern. Mackenna liked her immediately and loosened the grip on her purse.

"No, thank you."

She used a hitchhiker's thumb to point at Motorcycle Man. "Is he making you feel better or worse?"

A nervous laugh escaped Mackenna. "I'm not sure yet."

Jake canted his head and grinned, keeping his lips tight and denying her another bright flash of white teeth.

"I debate that dilemma every day." Courtney laughed when Jake aimed a contrived glare her way and frowned. "He's harmless, I assure you. But seriously, you've probably had a hell of a day. You should go home and relax. Do you need a ride?"

"No, I have my car. And thanks. But, for reasons I'd rather not go into, I can't go home yet. I'm going to sit here and finish my coffee and maybe do a little shopping. I'll be fine."

Courtney offered a warm smile. "Want me to ditch him and hang with you? Girl time is always a good thing."

For the first time today, Mackenna laughed. She didn't know either one of these people yet they seemed inclined to comfort her. It unnerved her but was oddly reassuring.

"I appreciate it but I'd rather be alone."

Courtney and Jake then wished her well and strolled away, granting her wish. She was alone. And lonely.

Off the Grid for Love is available on Amazon and through other eRetailers.

Learn more about Rena Koontz — www.renakoontz.com

www.ingramcontent.com/pod-product-compliance
Lightning Source LLC
Chambersburg PA
CBHW070335260626
47160CB00003B/1054